Bad Apple II: Relative Justice

iBooks
Habent Sua Fata Libelli

iBooks
Manhanset House
Dering Harbor, New York 11965

bricktower@aol.com • www.ibooksinc.com

All rights reserved under the International and
Pan-American Copyright Conventions.

No part of this publication may be reproduced, stored in a retrieval system, or transmitted in any form or by any means, electronic, or otherwise, without the prior written permission of the copyright holder. The iBooks colophon is a registered trademark of J. Boylston & Company, Publishers.

Library of Congress Cataloging-in-Publication Data

Ozeroff, Barry W.
Bad Apple II: Relative Justice
p. cm.
1. FICTION / Mystery & Detective — Hard-Boiled.
2. FICTION / Mystery & Detective — Police Procedural.
3. FICTION / Thrillers / Crime.
Fiction, I. Title.

978-1-59687-864-8, Hardcover

Copyright © 2024 by Barry W. Ozeroff

June 2024

---

iBooks are published by iBooks, an imprint of J. Boylston & Company, Publishers
Manhanset House, Dering Harbor, New York 11965 •www.ibooksinc.com•

Bad Apple II: Relative Justice

Barry W. Ozeroff

Also by Barry W. Ozeroff

Sniper Shot

Return Fire

The Dying of Mortimer Post

Bad Apple I

Available at fine booksellers

Table of Contents

Chapter	1	Banff National Park, Alberta, Canada, July 12th, 2018	7
Chapter	2		14
Chapter	3	Grace Appleby, July 14th, 2018	22
Chapter	4	DJ Appleby, Saskatoon, Alberta	34
Chapter	5	Grace Appleby, Portland, OR	40
Chapter	6		59
Chapter	7	DJ Appleby, Vancouver, BC	75
Chapter	8	Grace Appleby, Gresham, OR	92
Chapter	9		102
Chapter	10		111
Chapter	11		116
Chapter	12	DJ Appleby, Vancouver, BC Canada	121
Chapter	13	Grace Appleby, Clackamas, OR	126
Chapter	14	DJ Appleby, Vancouver, BC	134
Chapter	15	Grace Appleby, Clackamas, OR	142
Chapter	16	DJ Appleby, Vancouver, BC	149
Chapter	17		163
Chapter	18		179
Chapter	19		187
Chapter	20		198
Chapter	21		207
Chapter	22		211
Epilogue		February, 2020	215
About the Author			217

Chapter 1

Banff National Park, Alberta, Canada, July 12th, 2018

In the last two months, I've gone from number nine to number seven on the FBI's Ten Most Wanted list. I guess that makes me upwardly mobile.

Because I am an ex-police officer, I was known in prison as Bad Apple, which is a take on my name, D.J. Appleby. Nobody at the Snake River Correctional Institution in eastern Oregon, which was my last official address, ever called me that; they just called me Bad. It was an honorific I earned the hard way.

I was housed there on a life sentence until ten months ago, when I was severely burned in a fire and had to be airlifted to the burn unit at Emanuel Hospital in Portland, OR. As I was recovering, the European Kindred, a white supremacist prison gang with whom I'd had a recent disagreement, tried to assassinate me. Two EK hitmen and a state correctional officer were killed in the ensuing gunfight, and I managed to escape in the confusion.

I've come a very long way since then. With the help of my uncle, I recovered from my burns and made it out of the country, and I've been living a good life in Canada ever since. I can't honestly say I've been reformed, because I never really was the terrible man I became. I've just gone back to being the man I was before everything went so horribly wrong.

I've done surprisingly well as a fugitive from justice. Life on the run is tenuous at best, and I know it won't last forever, but so far, I've done well. I live in a nice apartment in Saskatoon, and have everything I need and want, with only one glaring exception—my daughter Grace. But I've taken steps to change that, and I'm hoping for the very best.

Grace hasn't had anything to do with me since my arrest over four years ago, but earlier today, I called her and we had a great conversation. I've actually been planning for this for over a month, and just in case she agreed to see me, I rented an isolated cabin in a remote hunting camp in Banff National Park for our reunion, which is where I currently am.

I understood that there were risks involved in calling her, but the conversation couldn't have gone any better. We spoke for an hour, and she not only agreed to come to Canada to see me, but she sounded as excited as I am about it. I gave her all the necessary information how to get here, and I've got money to reimburse her when she arrives tomorrow morning.

I just got back from the store after stocking up on supplies for her visit, and now, as I'm unloading them, I notice a problem. It's a dust trail rising above the trees along the driveway from the paved road over half a mile away.

The cabin I've rented is the only occupied one in the whole hunting camp, and the half-mile gravel driveway doesn't go anywhere else. Grace isn't supposed to arrive until tomorrow, and there's no reason for anyone else to be here. Nobody even knows I'm out here but the guy at the main lodge, and he has my cell phone number if he needs me. Being a fugitive makes you paranoid, so needless to say, I'm starting to freak out right about now. I have maybe thirty or forty seconds before whoever is raising that cloud comes into view.

I've spent almost a year on the Ten Most Wanted list, and I haven't made it that long by not listening to my instincts. Without even thinking about it, I drop everything and make a mad dash into the woods. Then, realizing I've left my gun in the car, I turn and run back. This eats up valuable seconds and the dust cloud gets closer.

I grab the stolen Glock from under the seat and bound into the woods like a frightened rabbit, leaping fallen trees and heading toward the darkest part. My vision is focused down to a narrow field and my breath comes in shallow gasps. My limbs are tingling and shaky. I don't think this is just some benign visitor. The timing with my call to Grace is just too coordinated.

I stop at the base of a double birch tree a hundred yards uphill from the cabin, puffing like a steam locomotive. From here I can see both the last quarter of the driveway and the back of the cabin. My car is in the driveway with the door open and cold groceries on the front seat. The door to the cabin is standing wide open. It would be clear to an eight-year-old that I couldn't have gone far, and the spot in which I am hiding is the first place I'd look if I were them. Obviously, I can't stay here, but I need to see this with my own eyes.

Please God, let it be the UPS guy. But I know it's not.

The car becomes visible for the first time through the trees. It's a Royal Canadian Mounted Police SUV, and there are three more following directly behind it.

I gawk for a moment in utter disbelief. How did this happen? Have they bugged my phone? Impossible, it's a new burner. Have they bugged Grace's? Doubtful, it's been four years, and we've had no contact at all.

No matter how I try to excuse it, there's only one explanation. Grace betrayed me.

The impact of it washes over me like a slow-moving mudslide, suffocating me just as effectively.

My heart says Grace could not have done such a thing; however, the police coming down the driveway say she did. They didn't just randomly show up three hours after I gave her the address.

I can see them quite clearly now. The first three cars are full of officers; at least four each. The last has two guys up front and a canine in the back. They come to a quick stop just before the last curve in the driveway, and drop off four officers, who strike off into the woods in my general direction. Obviously, they are going to circle the cabin and approach it from the rear, giving them a solid perimeter around it.

I'm glad I spotted them, but my situation is still basically hopeless. I want to eat my gun, and it doesn't have anything to do with going back to prison. It's Grace's betrayal. Why did she do this? For a reward? Because of misguided principles? Yes, I'm a convicted murderer who's on the run after escaping from prison, but I'm her *father*. Before I went bad, I was a good guy, and we were close. Intellectually, I understand, but emotionally, I just don't get it.

I watch the cops stage at the jump-off point. I've done the same thing dozens of times in my career. As a former Portland police officer and member of the SERT team, I understand all too well the concept of containing the perimeter in preparation for a tactical assault. I want to disappear, but with a tracking dog in play, there simply isn't anywhere to go. Surrounding me are hundreds of square miles of pine forest and mountains.

I'm no outdoorsman. I have no survival training and no gear—not even a pack of matches. I don't even have a good sense of direction. Just a .40 caliber Glock and two magazines, which I appropriated from a dying prison guard during my escape. Once these cops realize I'm not in the cabin, they'll come after me with the dog, and I won't have a chance. They're trained to follow the fear scent left behind by frightened prey. A blind Chihuahua could probably track me right now.

The four that are cutting through the woods come within thirty yards of me on their way to the cabin, but don't see me. I'm wearing a pair of jeans and a brown plaid flannel shirt; typical mid-summer wear for me here, and good, natural camouflage for these surroundings. Central Canada can get hot in the summer, but not so far this year. Highs have been reaching the lower seventies, but that's only for a couple hours in the afternoon. The rest of the time it's pretty cool, and nights can get downright cold.

Once they're past me, it's time for me to go. There's no right or wrong direction, the forest goes on, unbroken, for a hundred miles in every direction. Any point on the compass is just as good—or just as bad—as the others.

I have two things going for me, and they're both big. First, I've got my wits. I've relied on them many times to get me out of seemingly hopeless situations in the past, and if I ever needed them, I need them now. Second, I have my background. Having been a cop for eighteen years, and a SERT operator for twelve of them, I have a pretty good idea what they will do next, and staying a step ahead of them is the key to not getting caught.

The police are shouting for me to come out with my hands up. That means they're ready to enter. They'll probably give it ten minutes or so, then do an entry and a careful search of the place. I have maybe twenty minutes before they realize I'm gone and the dog starts tracking me. What I do in those minutes will decide my fate.

I'm glad I went back for the gun. If I'm lucky, I can use it to procure a ride from a passing motorist, but there aren't many people around here and it's unlikely I'll run into any roads, let alone any people driving on them.

I don't even know what direction I'm heading, but it's away from the cabin, and that's all that matters. The going is tough, and much slower than I would like. There are no immediate sounds of pursuit, which means they are still probably trying to talk me out of the cabin.

After about twenty minutes of moving at high speed I am exhausted, and the rough terrain forces me to slow down. Soon, I crest a ridge and begin working my way downhill, the sweat pouring off me in rivulets. A short time after that, I come upon a stream.

This, I realize, is very good for me, since not even a tracking dog can locate a human scent in water. I jump in, relishing the cold. The water is thigh deep, and I begin making my way downstream. After the first few steps, however, it occurs to me that downhill is the logical direction for me to go, so I turn around and head upstream.

Now my brain starts kicking in, and I develop a plan. Knowing how canines and their handlers work, I can assume they'll follow my trail to the stream, then run the dog up and down both sides of it, trying to pick up my trail where I came out. So, about a hundred yards upstream, I get out and run toward a clump of trees fifteen or twenty yards away. When I get there, I quickly run around in widening circles and around trees, then carefully backtrack my original steps until I am in the water again.

Now I keep making my way upstream. The idea, of course, is that the dog will pick up my trail, then lose it at the clump of trees, where it, too, will run in circles, and hopefully, the handler will think he lost the trail.

Soon, the stream widens and I enter a pool that's about five feet deep. I haven't gone far enough yet to feel safe, so I remain in the water and get soaked to the chest, holding the gun high above my head as I slowly make my way upstream.

After about thirty minutes of slogging, I decide I'm probably far enough from my entry point to safely step out. Since I originally entered from the left side, the logical choice would be to exit the right side. For that reason, I exit to the left.

After five minutes of easy trekking I come to a tree that has some very low-hanging boughs. I jump up, grab a low branch, and half-climb, half-swing myself onto a limb. My plan is to climb high into the tree and wait it out, but then it occurs to me that this might not be such a good idea after all. If the dog tracks me to the tree, then loses my scent, the cops will see the low boughs and figure it out, and there will be no escape for me then.

Instead, I climb back down and drop to the same spot from which I'd jumped. I walk a wide circle around the tree and then carefully backtrack all the way back to the stream, sticking to my exact trail the entire way. As much as I hate to do it, I re-enter the cold water, and continue trekking upstream until it begins to get dark. It's a miracle I've made it this far.

The shadows are getting long and I can feel the temperature dropping. I slog on, moving much slower now. I'm close to exhaustion, but they still haven't caught me. As the sun goes down behind a ridge, I hear barking far off in the distance. They must be heading toward the tree with the low-hanging boughs. Hoping my ploy worked, I can do nothing more than trudge onward, and eventually the barking fades off into silence.

The woods darken surprisingly fast. Having no choice, I climb out of the water on the right bank, simply because the going looks easier there. I'm freezing cold, and I can't even feel my feet. I don't have the dead reckoning skills to navigate my way out of a broom closet, so I have no idea where I am or what direction I am going.

The hunting cabin where this began is maybe five hundred miles from my apartment in Saskatoon, so even if I knew what direction to head, I'm not about to walk there. I'm soaking wet, I have no phone, I'm completely lost in an endless forest, and even if I find my way out, I can no longer use my credit cards. I only have about $70.00 in my pocket.

I'm in a jam, but I've been in jams before and made it out. The way to do it is to take things one step at a time. And be very lucky.

My first priority is surviving the coming night. The temperature drops quickly at this latitude, even in mid-summer. I use the dying light to look for a suitable place to make a camp.

A hundred yards away from the stream is a downed tree which has left a sizable crater at its base. It hasn't rained in at least a week, and the crater is dry. The roots at the base form a natural wall, and it seems like a good spot. I strip off my wet clothes and wring them out as best I can, then hang them over the roots of the tree in the hopes they might dry out overnight. Then, using a stick and a flat rock, I dig what resembles a shallow grave, just big enough for me to lie in. I gather a large pile of old leaves and moss, using them to both line my sleeping hole and cover myself in the hopes that it might insulate me from the cold and mosquitoes. Finally, exhausted, I crawl into my little nest and work my way into the pile.

I get very little sleep that first night. The temperature drops to what must be the upper forties. Bugs aren't as much of a problem as I thought they would be, but it sure feels like the cold will to do me in. During the long night, I have nothing to do but shiver, try not to despair, and plan my next move.

Obviously, if I am somehow fortunate enough to make it back to Saskatoon, I can't go back to my apartment. Someone will certainly be watching the place. That's too bad, because not only is it a great place, but there's a lot of stuff I want and can use there.

Even more important than my apartment, though, is a nearby storage facility, where I have a five-by-five locker. When I rented it, I was smart enough to put it in the name of Leonard Scott, the alias to my alias of Julian McNab, which is the name I've been using since I first got to Canada.

In this storage unit are two suitcases, each of which holds close to fifty thousand dollars in cash, one in Canadian currency, the other in US. It's what's left of the money given to me by my Uncle Phil, the man who saved my life and helped me after I escaped. Without it, I am as good as captured. With it, I stand a decent chance.

Twice in the first few hours after dark, I hear the distant barking of a dog. But the sound is always far in the distance, and when the impenetrable blackness finally dissolves into milky gray, I am still free.

Chapter 2

My clothes are still damp and clammy from the stream, and I have several itchy welts from insect bites, but I get dressed and move out anyway. It promises to be a beautiful July day, and there isn't a cloud in the sky. When the sun hits my skin, the warmth is utterly rejuvenating. Around mid-morning, I come to a clear patch of soft, springy grass, and decide to let my clothes dry in the sunlight a little longer.

I strip naked and lay my clothes out. Not far from the stream I find a small mountain of blackberry bushes, and gorge myself on the energy-giving fruit. Side note: Don't pick blackberries in the nude unless you absolutely have to.

I am covered with dirt and mud, and after my breakfast, I decide to bathe in the nearby stream. Getting back into the icy water is very difficult, but I force myself to do it, and come out relatively clean. I go back to my sunny spot and lie down to dry off. Again, the sun feels wonderful. I am still free, my thirst is quenched, I am clean, I'm getting warm, and I have a belly full of sweet blackberries. I actually feel quite good, despite my circumstances.

I nap for several hours in the warm sunshine, and awake feeling completely refreshed. My clothes are now dry, and I dress quickly. It suddenly occurs to me that I need to get rid of my Julian McNab ID. Too bad, because it's very high quality and cost a small fortune. I scour my wallet, removing my driver's license, Canadian Citizenship card, Canada Pension Plan card, Saskatchewan Health ID card, two credit cards, and some receipts bearing my name, and bury it all deep in the ground. At home in my apartment is my Julian McNab passport and birth certificate.

It turns out all I have is $52.00 in Canadian money, which I tuck back into my wallet. Less than I thought. In the suitcase containing the Canadian currency back at the storage facility is another wallet with all my Leonard Scott ID. Keeping this storage locker separate from Julian

McNab was probably the smartest thing I've done on the run so far. Both IDs are very well made, and were provided by a forger in Calgary, but I have less of it in the name of Leonard Scott. In fact, all I have is a driver's license, a Canadian Citizenship card, and a passport. I'm told the documents are good enough to pass a visual inspection, but won't stand up to a law enforcement computer check.

Finally, it's time to head out again. My only plan is to try to find a car to steal, and thanks to my Uncle Phil, I know how to do that. But this is a pretty remote area, and there aren't any cars. Hell, there aren't any roads. I need to find my way back to someplace that's at least inhabited. Around here, such places are few and far between.

I wander the entire day, always trying to stick to a somewhat easterly course, which I plot by navigating using the sun as a reference. This area is so sparsely populated I could walk these woods for days without seeing another soul. After what Grace has done, lying down after a few days without food and never getting up again sounds pretty inviting.

But I am still within a two-day walk of the hunting camp, and there are a couple other such camps in the general the area, so there have to be *some* people around. Even if I have nothing but berries to eat, I should be able to survive long enough to find one of them. If I have to steal a car at gunpoint, I'll do it, but I sincerely hope it doesn't come down to that. Witnesses, living or not, will only increase my chances of getting caught. Solitude is the key to making it on the run.

When the sun hits the treetops it's time to make a proper camp. I stop in a place that looks good, and forge a halfway-decent lean-to. I've seen enough survivor shows to have an idea of how to do that. I wish I had the skills to make a fire, but even without one, my clothes are still dry, so I don't have to get naked when I cover myself with dead leaves and dirt, which is good enough.

By the time night falls, I am safely ensconced in a cozy little cocoon about twice the size of a coffin, which may or may not protect me from the elements. My bed consists of dead leaves covered with moss I scraped off the surrounding trees. I have enough room to move, yet the space is still small enough to retain at least some body heat.

I manage to sleep several hours that night, which feels like a real luxury. In the morning, I have no desire to leave the relative warmth of my cocoon until the sun is well up, and by then it is another warm and beautiful day.

I strike the camp and head out again to the east. I dine on more berries around noon, but by then, the sky is starting to cloud up. Off and on throughout the afternoon I hear a helicopter in the distance, but it is never close enough to see. By mid-afternoon, I can tell it is going to rain. Still, there is no sight of humanity, and my spirits are starting to fall. I have no rain gear, and know I am incapable of building a shelter that can stand up to any moisture heavier than fog. I figure my best bet is to keep moving, so that's exactly what I do, even when cold, fat raindrops begin falling.

In five minutes I am thoroughly soaked. My only option is to keep trudging through the woods. It keeps me going and the work helps ward off the cold. The rainfall increases, and pretty soon a ground fog rises, and I completely lose track of what direction I'm going. Still, I figure it is better to move and be miserable than to just sit on a log and be miserable, so I trudge on.

There is no fancy shelter that third night. There is also no sleep. I spend the worst night I can remember in abject misery, just sitting under a tree getting rained on in what has to be mid- to lower forty-degree weather. Thoughts of turning myself in are pointless. Even if I wanted to, which I don't, there's nobody to turn myself in *to*. I spend the night fighting a losing battle with demons of desperation and hopelessness.

As the inky blackness of night once again dissolves to fuzzy shades of gray, the steady rain continues to fall and shows no sign of slackening. When it's light enough to see, I start moving again. Like yesterday, I am simply wandering aimlessly around, hoping I'm not going in circles. Finally, after several hours of miserable schlepping, when I am about ready to just sit down and wait to die, I detect a twinge of woodsmoke in the air, and I'm flooded with renewed hope.

I take a moment to figure out which way the wind is blowing, then strike out in that direction. After another forty minutes of trudging and several additional direction changes, I find myself crouching at the base of a tree looking at a small hunting cabin. I can't take my eyes off a beautiful white Chevy Suburban sitting in the driveway, just asking to be stolen. If I were to take it, I could be in Saskatoon by nightfall.

But there's smoke coming from the chimney, which means someone is inside; someone who would no doubt report their car stolen minutes after I took it.

Briefly, I consider ensuring that the owners of the car can't report it stolen, but I quickly discard that idea. There could be a family in there. The truth is, I'm no longer the tough, hardened criminal I'm reputed to be. I know how to get back to the black place from which to draw on that dark side of me, but I don't want to access that part of myself anymore. I'd rather just check out.

I am freezing. My hands are trembling and my teeth are chattering. My fingers and toes are numb and I have no way of getting warm. Still, I am determined not to risk contact with anyone, because that will just give the police a place to start looking for me.

Dejected, I force myself to turn away. I fade back into the wood line, and follow the cabin's long driveway to a gravel road. Once there, I choose to follow the road to the right, hoping to find other cabins nearby.

As it turns out, I don't have to travel far. Several hundred yards down the road I come upon another driveway, which I follow to another cabin. This one, unlike the last, is dark, with no car in the driveway and no signs of occupation. I sit shivering in the woods watching it for a good fifteen minutes, just to make sure. When I am convinced nobody is home, I make my approach.

Through the windows I can see it's a nice place. It's small, but everything you'd expect to see in a cabin is there. I study the entryways on both the front and back sides but see no alarm panel or contacts. Finally, using a small rock from a nearby creek bed, I break out a pane of glass in the back door, reach through, and unlock it.

No alarms sound and no dogs bark. Satisfied, I go in.

What a refuge the cabin turns out to be! It has a well-stocked pantry, an ample supply of both men's and women's clothing, and best of all, a beater 90's Ford F-150 in the garage with the keys in the ignition. This isn't some hunting cabin for rent. This is someone's second home.

There's no way to tell when the owner might return, but there's also no indication that anyone has been here recently. Dust and cobwebs tell me the door hasn't been opened for a while, and the electricity has been shut off for all areas of the house except the kitchen. The fridge holds a lot of beer and a package of unopened lunch meat which is a month past its expiration date.

I'm convinced I'll be safe here for a day or two while I recover. If my luck holds, I can take the truck and nobody will notice it missing for a long time. Of course, the owners could show up this afternoon, but that's a risk I'm willing to take.

The first thing I do is turn on the electricity to the rest of the house. While the hot water tank heats up, I eat as much as I can hold, including the expired lunch meat, which doesn't smell bad yet, and two frozen dinners. Then I take an exquisitely long, hot shower. Finally, I lie down in the warm, comfortable bed, but despite the fact that I'm exhausted, sleep doesn't come. All I can think about is Grace.

I trusted her implicitly. Naively, I gave her everything she needed to turn me in. I was to pick her up at the airport, but gave her directions to the hunting camp, just in case I couldn't make it. During our conversation, we talked about why I did the things I did; why a cop would commit armed robberies, how I didn't mean to kill the deputy. It was a long conversation; more than long enough for the authorities to trace the call and record my detailed confession for later use against me. I spoke so freely because at no time did I ever suspect she would turn me in. Not once.

But I forgive her. Grace is all I have left. She is everything. She only did what she thought was right, and I can't blame her.

Still, I must have meant *something* to her. I hope it was at least hard for her to betray me; that maybe she felt a *little* bad about what she was doing. I can't picture her breezing her way through our conversation, concerned only with keeping me on the line long enough for some federal marshal to trace the call.

I'd been brutally honest with her about my past. I told her about the death of my sister, the bottled up anger which resulted in me trying to burn the house down as a child, how the child psychologist my mother made me see molested me, and how I later killed him. I wanted her to be able to at least understand *why* I had been compelled to pull armed robberies. I wanted her to fully understand that the shooting of the off-duty deputy had been a tragic mistake for which I could never forgive myself.

I have no doubt that everything I said to Grace will be legally admissible in court as evidence against me. There are no more life sentences for me; a conviction for Dr. McNab's murder will mean the needle. I wonder if Grace thought of that when she called the authorities. It is to these troubling thoughts that I finally fall asleep.

When I get up eight hours later, it's almost 10:00 PM. Physically, I feel great, but inwardly I am miserable and depressed. I don't mind being on the run, and though I don't want to go back to prison, I at least know how to do prison. I just don't think I can do it without Grace in my corner. I don't think I can be Bad again without her.

The weight of the Glock in my waistband is my only comfort now. I have what it takes to put the pistol in my mouth if I have to. Knowing that I have that option gives me the strength to continue, at least for now.

It has now been four days since the RCMP came for me. I can't decide if I should leave now or hole up here for a while. They must be looking for me within a certain radius of how far a man can travel on foot over this type of terrain within the given amount of time. My dichotomy is this: have they already searched this place and marked it off their list, or might they still be searching, and just haven't come this far yet?

The sooner I'm out of the search radius, the better, and that's the deciding factor. Plus, I don't want to give them any longer to connect my Julian McNab identity with my Leonard Scott identity, assuming they haven't already. The sooner I get get my hands on those suitcases the better. If I leave now, I can drive through the night when there won't be many cops out, and be there by morning.

I have no maps, and the truck doesn't have GPS, but finding my way out of here is something I can deal with. The truck has slightly under half a tank of gas, so I should be good for a while.

I'm already thinking ahead to my first public appearance, which will probably be at a gas station. I'm not a guy who blends easily into a crowd. During my years in prison, especially after I joined the European Kindred, I willingly adopted the look of a hardened con. I worked out daily and got buff, grew my hair and beard long, and covered my arms and torso with a colorful array of prison tats. Fortunately, I never got around to covering my neck or face, but I look exactly like what I am.

After the escape, I cut my hair and cleaned myself up a bit, but there was nothing I could do about the tats, or the burn scars I got in the prison fire, all of which are neon signs proclaiming exactly who I am. Fortunately, almost all of my identifying marks can be covered with long sleeves and pants.

By now I'm sure the authorities have updated photos of me. The area where I live in Saskatoon is blanketed with ATMs and surveillance cameras, and I'm equally sure those photos have been plastered all over the news so a wary public can call in sightings of me. Needless to say, I am in need of a disguise. With no other resources than that which I can find in the cabin, I have a rather limited palette from which to paint a new picture of myself.

The cabin closet has both men's and women's clothes. The women's clothes are far too small for me though, so that option is out. Too bad; I once got away from the SERT team posing as a female, and though I made one hideous transvestite, it worked.

Using a backpack conveniently provided by the owners of the cabin, I pack a couple changes of the man's clothes, as much food as I can carry, as well as some shaving gear from the bathroom.

The moment of my escape is anticlimactic. I start the truck, open the garage door, and I simply drive off into the night. I pass no other vehicles, and by just following what appears to be the biggest, most well-maintained roads, I eventually find my way to Alberta Highway 93, which is a nice, paved highway bisecting Banff National Park from the northwest to the southeast. I think I'm north of the hunting cabin, and I don't want to go back the way I came, so I continue heading northwest. After a while, I come to the intersection of Alberta 11, which branches off to the east, the direction I ultimately want to go.

By now I have less than a quarter of a tank of gas. In Canada, you pump your own fuel, and if you have a credit card, you don't need to go into the store. But all I have is cash, so I need to show my face to the attendant. This will be my most vulnerable moment. If the attendant shows any signs of recognition, I'll be in trouble. They'll get my license plate, vehicle description, and have a good fix on me. They'll know roughly where I am and where I'm likely headed, and from that moment on the truck will be next to useless.

But there is no cause for alarm. The station attendant is a bored teenager who doesn't even glance at me. I give him the money, he turns on the pump, and that's it. I'm back on my way in no time.

Four hours later, after following signs to Edmonton, I pull into the parking lot of a twenty-four hour Walmart Superstore. There, I use the remainder of my money to refill the tank and buy a woman's wig, a large flower-print cotton dress, and a bottle of water. By now it's after two in the morning. Saskatoon is a five-hour drive from here, and I know the way.

This time of night there is virtually no traffic. After a while, I pull over, have a light meal of snacks filched from the cabin, and shave as closely as I can. I then change into the flower dress and don the wig. I know I can't actually pass for a woman, but as seen from a surveillance camera, I might. It's better than nothing.

I can't go near my apartment, but I don't believe anyone has connected the name Julian McNab to my alter-alias of Leonard Scott yet, so hopefully the storage unit is still safe.

I arrive at the facility a little after six-thirty in the morning, and circle the place a couple of times, but I see no sign that it's being watched. There are still very few people out and about, so I gather my wits and go in. I'm wearing a pair of shorts under the dress and I've got the Glock in my waistband. I'm prepared to get caught, but I have't decided whether or not I'm willing to go back to prison. What I do not want to do is hurt anyone else. The Glock is still just for me.

Nobody is waiting for me inside. Getting the rest of Uncle Phil's money is anticlimactic. I simply drive up to the gate, enter the code from memory, go to the locker (which, thankfully, I'd had the foresight to secure by means of a combination lock rather than a key lock), and open the door.

Both suitcases, each the size of an airplane carry-on, are still there. I take a couple hundred dollars of Canadian money and put it into the wallet with the Leonard Scott ID, and I'm ready to go. Five minutes after I arrive at the storage place, the suitcases are in the back of the cab and I'm on my way. I haven't even seen another person.

My chances of actually making it have just gone up exponentially. From this point, the locker will go unpaid, and in a month or two, someone will cut the lock off, discover it's empty, and that will be that. If the authorities haven't already connected the two names by now, perhaps they never will.

Chapter 3

Grace Appleby, July 14th, 2018

I hated my parents when I was growing up. They divorced when I was just a little girl. My mom was too busy trying to stay with whatever boyfriend was abusing her at the time to mother me, and my dad was a tough guy loner who never had time for a kid. I hated my mom's boyfriend Todd. On my tenth birthday, my dad and Todd got into a fight about visiting me. My dad ended up beating him up, and in so doing, he became my hero. I started being nice to him, and he responded in kind. As it turned out, all he needed was a little encouragement to turn into a real dad, and he did. I began spending more and more time at his place, and we developed a very good relationship.

By the time I was in high school, Dad made his spare room into a bedroom just for me. He tried so hard to be a good dad. He bought a frilly little girl's bed, and everything he bought me was comically age-inappropriate, like My Little Pony sheets and Barbie blankets and boy-band posters. As embarrassing as it was having a room like that, it was really cute and charming at the same time.

After I got my license, he gave me a key to the apartment, and told me I could go there whenever I wanted. Whenever my mom and I had a fight, or if she and her new boyfriend were fighting, I would go there. He never looked at it as an intrusion. He never had women spend the night, but still, I'd park in a place where he would be sure to see my car, just in case. He was never disappointed that I was there, and actually seemed disappointed when I had to leave.

By my senior year I was more comfortable with him than I'd ever been at my mom's, and was there most every weekend, and sometimes during the week, too. My life was better than ever.

Right up until the day it wasn't.

That day, my mom and I had a really nasty fight. She'd caught me wearing a piece of her jewelry, and accused me of stealing it. I didn't *steal* it steal it; I just wanted to borrow it. She said she wouldn't stand for me snooping around through her stuff like that. I had a smart mouth on me during those years, and I told her if she was afraid I'd find her dildo, she could relax; I already knew where she kept it. That really pissed her off and she hit the roof. She kicked me out, and naturally, I went straight to my dad's apartment.

He wasn't there. This was on a Saturday night, so I just planned to spend the night there. I thought maybe we could do something together the next day. I knew he wouldn't be home too late; my dad never went out drinking or playing poker or anything like that.

My father was a Portland police officer, and at the time, he was the lead negotiator for the SERT team, which is what they call SWAT in Portland. I loved to listen to the stories he'd tell. He could always out-smart the bad guys, and was one of the best hostage negotiators Portland ever had. He said the guys on the tactical team didn't like that about him, because they never got the chance to kick in doors and do their SERT thing when my dad was on the phone. He always talked the bad guy out instead.

Anyway, that night he never came home. I figured he must have had to stay and work overtime, which happened pretty often, and I spent the evening watching TV. My show ended at ten and the news came on. There had been a murder at a restaurant, and the bad guy was holed up inside with hostages. SERT was there, so I knew that my dad wouldn't be home for hours, so after the story was over, I just went to bed. I remember looking forward to hearing how he talked the guy out and saved the day.

An explosion woke me up several hours later. I screamed as the door to my bedroom burst open and several people came running in. They were all yelling and shining bright lights in my face, and all I could see were gun barrels pointed at me. I was terrified, certain I was going to be raped, which, naturally, is my biggest fear. Then I was grabbed and thrown facedown onto the floor. I wasn't wearing anything but my bra and panties, not even a nightgown, because I hadn't planned on spending the night and hadn't brought pajamas with me. My arms were pinned behind my back and I was handcuffed.

Men were now moving through the little apartment, yelling, "Bedroom, clear! Kitchen, clear," and that's when I realized they were the police. It was SERT, raiding my dad's apartment! One of their own!

When they were done, they turned on all the lights and threw a blanket around me. Then they walked me out to this gray steel-plated vehicle that's a cross between a tank and a truck. I'd been in it before, when my dad took me on a ride-along and showed me all the SERT equipment. It's called the Bearcat, though I can't imagine why.

Inside was a detective, and he started asking me all kinds of questions about my dad. Where was he, where would he go in an emergency, has he called me, when did I last talk to him—on and on he went. At first they thought I was his girlfriend, but when they found out he was my dad, they began treating me with a little more respect. They took off the handcuffs and someone went into my room and brought out my clothes. They let me dress in the Bearcat, but they didn't let me go.

They said the reason they were here was because my father was the one who had robbed the restaurant and had shot and killed a deputy sheriff. Worse, my father had escaped after SERT had him cornered, and now the whole police department was searching for him.

This made no sense at all, and I refused to believe a word of it. My father, the hero of the hostage negotiation team? It was ridiculous. My dad *worked* with these people. He was a police officer, for God's sake. The detective might as well have told me my father stole a flying saucer and flew to Jupiter.

Crying, I yelled at him to stop saying horrible things about my dad, but he just kept right on asking me questions about where he might have gone, and did he have another vehicle, and who were his best friends, etc. During this whole time, I wasn't allowed back into the apartment.

They stayed and searched the place for hours and hours, but of course they didn't find anything. They took the computer and a bunch of other stuff with them and fixed the door before they left, and suddenly, they were gone, and I was alone.

My mom showed up, our fight now long forgotten. All we could do was cry and watch TV. Of course, everything they said was true. Reporters interviewed a girl who had been in the restaurant when it was robbed, and she had identified my dad as the suspect. Then there was footage of them towing his car from the scene. Grave-faced officers, many of whom

I had met, talked about the loss of an off-duty sheriff's deputy, but nobody ever mentioned who had done the crime. Not yet. That would all come the next day.

When that part of the story broke, things really got crazy. The story dominated the news for days. Another cop had gone bad, only this one wasn't just racist or corrupt. This one had killed another cop while committing an armed robbery. Someone from the DA's office said they were considering seeking the death penalty.

The manhunt for my father was the biggest thing that had happened in the Pacific Northwest since that guy hijacked an airliner and parachuted out of it with a bunch of money way back when. It was on the Today show in the morning, and the national news that night. There were pictures of my father everywhere, and people were cautioned that he was armed and dangerous. I got into two fights the first day I went back to school, so I just stayed away for a week. It was without a doubt the worst time of my life.

Three days later they caught him. They tracked him to an empty house where he was hiding, and the Portland SERT team went in to get him. There was live coverage from the scene, and when my father came out, they zoomed in on his face with a telephoto lens, and he was crying. They freeze-framed that shot and held it on the screen while the reporter went on and on about what a shock it was, and in light of all the recent stories of cops going bad, this was maybe the worst one. Blah blah blah.

Everything became just noise to me. All I could see was my dad's face, wet with tears and snot, and contorted into an expression of anguish. If you could feel a color, I felt black. I had never seen him cry before.

My dad was a murderer. That realization made me turn on him. I wanted to hate him, but deep down in my heart, I wasn't sure I could. I still wasn't sure I believed it all. I needed to hear it from him first.

They charged him with capital murder, and the headlines the next morning confirmed that the District Attorney had decided seek the death penalty.

A few days after his arrest, I was at home alone in my room when the phone rang. It was a machine asking if I would accept the charges for a collect phone call from the Multnomah County jail. I said yes, and my father came on the line.

As soon as he started talking, I interrupted him, and asked if he really robbed that restaurant and killed the sheriff's deputy. "Tell me you didn't do it, and I'll believe you," I said, and I meant it. I would have come back to life if he just said no, but he didn't.

Instead, he said, "Yes, honey, I did, but there's an expla—"

I didn't give him any more time, I just hung up on him. Then I crawled into bed and didn't get up for two days.

I was in mourning, only worse than had my father actually died. I wanted nothing more to do with him. Every good memory of him was now stained. Were the times we shared really good? He was a criminal, capable of murder, and now he was in jail. He had betrayed my trust every day simply by being a good dad, when in reality, he was one of the bad guys. I wished he'd been a bad father so this wouldn't hurt as much.

I stayed depressed for weeks, but life went on, and I still had to live. The day I began healing was the day I met Gladys Knight.

I was coming out of Fred Meyers, and there on the sidewalk was a boy with a box of puppies, trying to give them away. A small crowd had gathered, and were reaching inside, petting and touching five little 8-week-old mixed-breeds puppies. Each one was cuter than the next.

The dogs were all going crazy, standing up on their hind legs, licking hands, and trying to jump up on everyone. I felt my mood lighten just looking at them and touching their warm softness.

I'd never had a pet before, and there was no way I was going to go home alone that day. I didn't even bother to call my mom. I wanted to take them all, but I could only take one. But how to choose?

One wasn't as exuberant as the rest. She was small and mostly black with a few white spots on her chest and paws. She licked my fingers and just stood there looking at me, wagging her tail, while the rest of them jumped, barked, and vied for attention. I felt that of all the people gazing and reaching into the box, this puppy had chosen me. She looked like she trusted me, and I picked her up. She stared at me with deep, liquid eyes, and I knew right then we belonged to each other. We were two lonely souls who had found our forever partners.

I put her in a shopping cart and went back in the store to get food bowls, a collar and leash, and puppy chow. By the time I got her home, my depression was already lifting. She was no real replacement for my dad, but she was buoyant, full of life and love, and the only positive thing I had going. We fell in love instantly.

My dad had taught me how good music used to be back in the day, and I had learned to love R&B, especially from the 70s. After losing him, this little puppy was the best thing that could happen to me. Gladys Knight has a song called *You're the Best Thing That Ever Happened to Me*, so from the first moment, Gladys Knight became her name.

I don't know how I would have made it through those first few months without Gladys Knight. She brightened every day, and whenever things were at their worst, she was always right there to bring me back up again.

I still can't say I've fully recovered from what my father did. In many ways, it's worse than if he'd died. He became a symbol of why people hate the police. That picture of him crying became a meme with all kinds of horrible sayings, and the butt of jokes. That image still haunts and triggers me to this day.

He called several times over the next few months, but I never accepted the call. After a month, the story became less prominent. And then, just when things were starting to get back to normal, came his trial. Suddenly, he was big news again, and I had to re-live the nightmare for a second time. This time, though, I had Gladys Knight to see me though the hardest times.

Before the trial actually got started, they made a deal with my dad. He pled guilty, and rather than death, they gave him life without the possibility of parole. Once that deal was struck, the story died back down and eventually went away.

Fast-forward to last year. By then, I'd moved into an apartment in Clackamas, and had taken a job as assistant manager of the complex. My mother and I, who never saw eye-to-eye on anything, had very little contact. She went through several abusive relationships, and I just couldn't handle the drama.

Gladys Knight and I had become inseparable. She accompanied me everywhere, including work, where she would lay around the office and everyone who came in would adore her. Without her, I don't know what I would have done.

It had been over two years since my father had tried to call me. I had finally closed that chapter of my life, and was learning how to go on despite what he'd done. I hadn't written any letters to him, and I certainly hadn't gone to see him. My life was simply plodding along from one day to the next, with Gladys Knight filling the void left by the "loss" of both my parents.

And then came a day when everything resurfaced in a way that was even worse than the first time.

It happened on one of the rare days I saw my mom. She had talked me into coming to visit and have dinner. She and her then-boyfriend were in the living room and I was in the kitchen when I heard her scream, "Oh my God!"

I went running in and found her staring at the TV. On it was a wanted poster of a scary-looking criminal with long hair and tattoos; the kind of guy you'd cross a busy street to avoid. After a moment, I realized it was him. My father.

He looked at least ten years older. His face had lines in it that weren't there before. And if I thought the picture was bad, the story was positively horrible. He was a member of one of the most feared white-supremacist prison gangs in Oregon, and had a violent prison record. Once, he had crippled a man for life with nothing more than his bare hands and a dinner tray. This time, though, he had killed another prisoner by lighting him on fire and *burning* him to death. In doing this terrible thing, he'd been badly burned himself, and had been transported to a hospital here in Portland. But as bad as all that was, it was just background for the real story, which was that he had escaped and was now on the loose. Members of his prison gang who had completed their sentences and were now out had broken him out of the hospital, killing one of the officers who was guarding him.

I was horrified and repulsed by both his picture and the story. Now, there was *another* giant manhunt for him, and his new prison mug shot was plastered everywhere, just like the last time. Only now it was worse. The picture of him crying was bad, but it at least evoked a little pity. Now, with this new picture, everyone could see who he really was. They even put up side-by-side photos of him all clean-cut in his police uniform receiving the Officer of the Year award next to this hardcore biker-looking prisoner with long hair and tattoos. It was hard to tell they were the same man. In prison, they said, he is known as "Bad," which is short for Bad Apple.

I was immediately filled with dread, because I knew that sooner or later, he'd reach out to me. I couldn't eat, and I couldn't sleep, and I could barely function at work. There was a fifty-thousand dollar reward for information leading to his capture. There's no way he would last out there with a payoff like that, and I couldn't wait for him to be caught. This was worse than the first time. It was like I woke from a nightmare only to discover it was still going on.

The police came around and asked for our computer and cell phones again, and said if we didn't give them up they would get a warrant and take them. They wanted to search them to see if there was any record of him contacting us since he broke out of prison. Of course there wasn't.

Weeks passed, then months, and they never did find him. This story, too, eventually died down, and my life slowly started getting back on track. After nearly a year, things finally began to be normal again, but always, in the back of my mind, I knew he was out there, and someday, somehow, he would reach out to me.

Two days ago my phone rang. My father was the last thing on my mind. My friend Gloria was with me in my room when I took the call. She'd brought a little weed and we'd just gotten high, so I was totally mellowed out, which was a good thing.

The call came from "Unknown Number," but I answered it anyway. I freaked out when I realized it was him, but Gloria told me to keep him on the phone and at least listen to what he had to say. She told me to put on speakerphone, which I did.

He begged me not to hang up and to just give him a few minutes. His voice sounded like a ship that was sinking, and so I agreed. Five minutes is what I would give him. I didn't tell him anyone was with me, and he just started talking. He said I was old enough to know some truths about him that he had never shared with anyone. He said I was the only person he had ever loved, and I believed him, because he was always different when he was around me than he was when he was around my mom. When he spoke to her, he was flat; like a rock you'd choose to skip in a pond. There was no dimension to him. But with me, he was fuller, and had substance and weight.

He told me there were times he had been so suicidal that he'd had a gun to his head, and it was only the thought of me that kept him from pulling the trigger. He said the choices he had made had brought out a rough side of him. In prison, that's the only side that he could show, and it had made him a hard man, but that's not who he really was, and he was tired of not being himself. All he wanted was for things to be the way they'd been before, with me being his daughter and him being my dad, but he knew it was too late for that.

He didn't sound like his picture. Not at all like someone who could burn a man to death. He sounded like my dad. He was fighting tears, but was clearly trying to cover them up. He didn't want me to know he was being emotional, and this moved me. He'd been weakened.

I had pictured my father many ways, but never like this. Never weak or vulnerable. He'd been a hero, a cop, a criminal, and even someone cruel enough to burn another man to death, but never weak. That's how he sounded now. Like a child.

He said he was sorry for forcing me into this position. He wanted to tell me what went wrong; the *why* of the things he'd done. He said if I were ever to understand, I would first have know a little of his history, and that it wouldn't be easy to hear.

The way he talked moved me, and I decided to give him a chance. Gloria kept nodding her head and encouraging me to let him talk. I was afraid of what he had to say, and wasn't sure she should hear it, but having her there made me feel better, so I let her stay. She was my best friend. We took another hit, and I told him I was ready to listen.

His story was terrible. But gradually I began to see him less of an evil man, and more of an abused and damaged soul. A victim. He had a ruined childhood, and it was a wonder he had been successful at all. Every day was a fight to overcome his trauma. The terrible things he'd done were not intentionally directed at people out of a bad heart, but were a response to the damage done to him as a child and the circumstances he'd found himself in. He'd had a crippled older sister, the only person he'd ever been close to, and she had died in his arms. Nobody had ever told me about her before, not even my grandparents.

The worst things he'd done were a direct result of childhood trauma. The man he'd killed in prison had been his principal abuser when he was just a small boy. And to his credit, the media had it wrong; he hadn't burned him alive. He'd smothered him first, and burned his body. It was only slightly less horrifying, but in context, the difference became vast.

The hate I'd felt for him since his arrest began to be edged out by the love I used to feel. He was still my father, only now he was broken and vulnerable. I discovered I wasn't really scared of him now that I was starting to understand him, and found myself wishing I could hug him through the phone. He wasn't trying to justify the things he'd done; only explain them, and I was starting to get it.

The tables turned during this conversation, and I came to side with him. I would never accept what he had done, but it he wasn't asking for acceptance; he just wanted me to know that it wasn't simply what it appeared to be. The rest could come later. Five minutes into the conversation, both Gloria and I were in tears. It would have been impossible, even for a stranger, to hear and not empathize.

I felt ashamed of my behavior toward him over the past four years, and told him so. I asked him to forgive me for ghosting him. He'd never heard the word, but understood instinctively what it meant. We both realized it wasn't too late for us. We could still be father and daughter. It was frightening, because he was one of the most wanted people in the country, and we would have to be very careful, but to be honest, that also injected our relationship with a certain sense of excitement. I wanted to see him, but didn't know how to do it.

Fortunately, my father had thought of this likelihood and prepared a way in advance. He's always been such a resourceful man. He said he was currently in Canada, and had made arrangements for me to travel there. He had money, and would reimburse me, including lost wages, since I don't have vacation time at work. He gave me all the arrangements, including directions how to get to his place in the event he didn't show up at the airport. Naturally, he was very skittish about appearing in public places.

When he thanked me for wanting to see him, he could no longer hide the fact that he was crying, and the quaver in his voice made me terribly sad. A father should never have to beg his daughter to be a part of his life, then thank her for for doing it. I apologized again for how I treated him, and thanked him for trusting in me. By the end of our conversation, we were both excited to reunite. In a way, it would be like meeting for the first time.

To the world, Dean J. Appleby was a violent and dangerous fugitive, capable of murder and torture. To me, he was just my dad, despite his record and his appearance, and I knew I would be safe with him. I'm ashamed to say that I found the illegality of it all to be exciting, but my story wouldn't be complete and I wouldn't be honest if I didn't admit it. Even Gloria, who had known him since we were ten, said she was envious of me. By the end of our conversation, I was ecstatic over the prospect of meeting him again. I wasn't about to abandon him twice.

I was to leave the following day, and Gloria would watch Gladys Knight while I was gone. I would spend a week in Canada with him, and if my boss didn't approve the time off, I'd simply quit.

My mind filled with things I wanted to tell him. Much of it was apologizing for the way I'd treated him, but a good deal of it was anger, that he had done the things he'd done and put me in this position. It was a strange mixture; one even I had trouble sorting. I even thought about writing everything down, but in the end, I would just trust that my mouth would express the way my heart felt.

I flew to Calgary and waited, but he wasn't at the airport. I was a little concerned about it, but it wasn't entirely unexpected, which is why he gave me directions to the camp. After an hour, I went to plan B, and rented a car. This took up most of my money, but he had also assured me that wouldn't be a problem.

Little did I know my nightmare hadn't yet begun.

Finding the hunting lodge wasn't easy, but when I finally arrived, the place was crawling with police. I was confronted before I even got there. When I showed them my driver's license they arrested me and put me in the back of a police car. They said if I didn't cooperate, I would be charged with complicity in his flight from justice.

They took me to a police station and questioned me for hours before ultimately deciding not to charge me.

I was enraged by the way they treated me. They were like rabid dogs; prey-driven and carnivorous. They hammered me about where he actually lived. I told them truthfully that I didn't know. Equally truthfully, I told them I wound't tell them if I knew.

I can be a smartass when I want to be, and an utter bitch when I'm pissed, and I was getting pissed. Finally, I told them he'd mentioned staying in someone's basement just outside Toronto. It was the only Canadian city I could think of on the other side of the country. I could feel the undercurrent of excitement that this little flake of a lie generated, and I liked the way it made me feel.

The only upside to any of this is the fact that he'd clearly gotten away from them. Again. DJ Appleby was smarter than they were, and I told them so. If he could get away from his own SERT team, I said, then getting away from them was child's play.

Being an assistant manager gets me a break on the rent, but it doesn't pay much. I needed my dad to pay me back for this trip, and now I was just about out of money. Fortunately, my return flight was prepaid. I had enough to get a cheap motel room to Calgary after they released me, but lunch would be McDonald's and I had no idea where the rest of my meals would come from until payday.

My hardships were nothing in comparison to where my dad might be, or what his situation must be. He'd eluded them for a year, but now they were again hot on his trail. They must have bugged my phone. If they knew he was here, then they knew where his place was in Saskatoon. He couldn't go back there. Did he have resources? Cash with him? Some way of getting his stuff? Did they know what he was driving?

It wasn't until the day after I got back to Portland that I discovered the truth about what had happened. It was Gloria. She turned him in for the reward money. She had listened to him with fake sympathy, encouraging me to keep him talking. In her black heart, neither of us meant a thing to her. Not compared to the reward money, anyway. She Judased me, not for thirty pieces of silver, but for fifty thousand dollars. When I found out what she did, I walloped her in the face and broke her nose. It was the first time I ever hit anyone, and it felt good.

I believe that God knows the hearts of men. His judgement will probably not be too severe on my father, despite his many and grievous sins. But if He exists, He can see that of the two, Gloria is the one with the black heart, not my dad, and for this, her punishment will be severe.

In the meantime, the joke's on her. My father is still not in custody. The reward was for information leading to his capture, and he is still free. Fuck you, Gloria.

Chapter 4

DJ Appleby, Saskatoon, Alberta

I have no idea how long this truck will be safe. The sooner I can get rid of it the better. I have enough money to buy myself a reliable car using the Leonard Scott ID, but I have to figure out how to permanently disappear this truck. It's a loose end, and any loose end at this point could spell my downfall. Canadian cities are no different than their cousins in the US. There will be some kind of doorbell camera, security footage, or traffic video of me if I were to merely dump it. Same when I buy another car.

Realistically, it's only a matter of time before they catch me. But I want to use my time wisely. I want to see Grace. I want to tell her I understand why she did what she did. I raised her right, and she did what she thought was right. She's a good person, and I don't blame her for not being able to understand. It's just that she sounded so sincere, so convincing. I have to give her credit. She's a hell of a good liar.

I wish I could get in touch with my father's brother, Uncle Phil. He's as shrewd a character as you can find. But calling him is out of the question. He's a felon and an ex-con, and would be my obvious first choice for help. After a close call such as this, the first thing they'll do is bug his phones and keep him under surveillance.

I'm going to have to retool my brain, and get back to the state of mind I was in when Uncle Phil first started training me to operate outside the law. He forced me to think of every potential contingency ahead of time. He aways said when you're on the dark side, you have to keep at least two steps ahead of the cops. That the prisons are full of guys who didn't. Now I've seen that for myself.

Something he did just after I made my escape from the hospital comes to mind. I had stolen a car, and hidden it in a parking structure while waiting for Uncle Phil to come and get me. There was a purse in the car, which I left when he arrived and picked me up. The car went unrecovered for nearly a week.

Several days later, Uncle Phil went back and got the purse. He took it all the way down to Roseburg and left it in a bathroom stall at Roseburg Community College, which is 150 miles south of Portland. It was turned in to campus security before my uncle got home, and the following day, the police released a statement to the press that said they had reason to believe I was headed to south to California when, in reality, I was on my way north to Canada. That's the mindset I need to be in right now.

Now that I have money and ID, I'm in a much better position than last night. But Saskatoon is hot, and so is my apartment, so it's time to beat feet. But where to go? Even though I have resources, I have no plan.

All I can think of is Grace. I want to see her. I want to look her in the eye and tell her I understand. I want to let her know that what she did is okay. Really, I just want to say goodbye, because it's clear she won't have anything to do with me any more. I can't try the phone because obviously her line will be tapped, and, though I hate to say it, I can't trust her any more.

I don't know exactly how I'm going to do it, but in a month or so, when things are a little more settled, she'll come home one day and find me in her apartment. I won't stay long, just long enough to tell her what she did is okay and to say goodbye. Maybe even get a hug.

I want her to see in my eyes that I am not someone she should be afraid of. Then, who knows. Maybe I'll just wait there for the police to come arrest me. I can leave her with Uncle Phil's money, plus, we can arrange it so she gets the bounty that's on my head. Or, perhaps I'll just keep running. Either way, seeing her will bring about the closure I need after what happened yesterday.

In the meantime, I will do what Uncle Phil taught me to do. I fill the tank and hit the road, this time heading east on the Trans-Canadian Highway. Four hours later, hungry and tired, I pull over in a little town called Regina. I stop at a Burger King and get some drive-through food. Then, using my Leonard Scott ID for the first time, I rent a room in a dingy motel and fall into bed in the early afternoon.

I wake up after about six hours of deep sleep feeling refreshed. I take a shower, buy another meal, then head back out on the road. A couple hours later, I take an exit for Winnipeg, in Manitoba. By now it's going on 1:00

AM. I drive around for a while until I find a suitable spot, then leave the truck with a corner of the bumper blocking a handicapped parking spot at a store. There's even a security camera nearby, which is perfect for what I have in mind. After looking furtively around, I wheel the two suitcases away until I'm sure I'm out of camera range.

Now they'll concentrate their search for me here in Winnipeg, when in fact I'll be heading somewhere else. The loose plan is to dress in drag, buy a car, then head back to the States to see Grace.

Then, Uncle Phil mode kicks in again. Why have my trail just stop here in Winnipeg? Why not give them something more to follow?

There are several other cars nearby, and I chose one that appears to be road-worthy. I'm inside and have it hot-wired in less three minutes. On the spur of the moment, I decide to just continue heading east, and jump back on the TCH. At my first gas stop, I pick up a map and look for a likely destination. After studying it, I come to a plan, and strike out for a small border town about six hours east of here called Fort Frances, Ontario.

Fort Frances is on the US/Canadian border, and is separated from International Falls, Minnesota by a short bridge over the Rainy river. I drive all night long, pausing only for a half-hour rest break, and arrive in Fort Frances about around 6:00 AM. I leave the car illegally parked on a street with no visible security cameras about two blocks from the bridge. It should be easy to find a way to cross the river from here if I were so inclined, which I'm not. Instead, I drag my suitcases less than a mile in the opposite direction toward the Greyhound station. Along the way, I don the wig and women's clothing, and try my hand at makeup, which I bought at a gas stop.

I'm not about to win any beauty contests, but the important thing is, on a fuzzy video I will appear to be female. Three hours later, I'm sleeping on a Greyhound bus, heading west toward Regina. My hope is that they will follow my trail to where I dumped the second stolen car and come to the only logical conclusion—that I crossed back into the United States at International Falls. Then maybe they'll suspend the search in Canada and start looking for me back in the States—on the wrong side of the country. Even if the ruse doesn't work, it might throw the mounties off my trail, or at minimum, divert them thousands of miles in the wrong direction.

My actual plan now is to make my way west, all the way to Vancouver, British Columbia, which is the largest city on Canada's west coast and is only maybe five hours by car from Portland. I have no definitive plan from there, but I do know that it will be easier to lose myself in a large metropolitan area rather than out in the boonies.

I've been on the run for six straight days with a ton of stress and not nearly enough sleep. I've only had a few meals and am utterly exhausted, so I spend most of the time on the daylong bus ride to Regina sleeping. Once there, I spend a few days in a motel room just relaxing and looking online for the right vehicle, using a burner phone. Finally, I find a nice, windowless cargo van on Craigslist. I buy it, letting the seller rip me off a little, but it looks mechanically sound. I outfit the van with a thick foam pad, a good sleeping bag, a twelve-volt portable fridge, and a hotplate. I also pick up some rugged clothing, and a decent supply of non-perishable food and water. Finally, I consider myself ready to travel.

Slowly, being careful to avoid the main highway wherever possible, I make my way west toward Vancouver. Rather than take the direct route along the Trans-Canadian Highway, which is about a thousand miles, I take a more northerly, circuitous route that skirts Banff National Forest, where this nightmare began. This adds a couple hundred miles to the trip, but keeps me well off the main roads, which I assume to be more heavily patrolled than the smaller provincial routes.

I get emotional as I pass north of Saskatoon and the life I walked away from. There are so many things in my apartment I'd like, and life had been really good there. I had a nice place with decent furniture, nice clothes, friends, and routines. After a year, the place was really starting to become home. Every morning, even during the winter, I walked a half-mile to Starbucks, and chatted with the morning regulars for an hour or so over coffee. The employees all knew my name and what I like to drink. I struck up a nice friendship with the Mexican barista who works the early shift. We got to know one another pretty well. She came to view me as sort of an eccentric uncle, and strangely, I really miss that. I liked being Julian McNab. He was a hell of a guy, and I miss him.

With Saskatoon and Julian McNab behind me, I am able to concentrate on the future. I begin formulating a plan to re-establish myself in Vancouver. It will be easier to hide in plain sight in a big city than in a small town where everyone knows each other and I would be the outsider. Maybe I could get a job; the type where they pay you under the table. I'm too restless to be retired, and that way I could keep my cash reserves intact to pass along to Grace.

I'm not in a hurry to get there, so I decide to take my time and enjoy the trip. Canada has short, but very pleasant summers, and it's the height of the summer season. The area through which I am traveling is thickly forested and heavily dotted with lakes, rivers, and streams. It's beautiful country.

I like the nights best. I keep clean by bathing in the streams and lakes, and do my laundry there, too. I jury rig a clothesline inside the van, and find that air drying the clothes as I drive with the windows down keeps them from getting stiff. I stop wherever I find a spot that piques my interest; pretty vistas, waterfalls, and glass-smooth lakes reflecting breathtaking vistas of snow-covered mountains. I start looking for a suitable place to stop every afternoon, and the latest I've ever stopped is 6 PM.

I've acquired a fishing pole, a frying pan, and a spice rack, and start catching some of my meals. I go to sleep and rise with the sun. At night, I love to just lie out next to the van in the darkness, watching fireflies and the night sky. Soon, I am making side trips down unused logging roads, and wasting entire days doing nothing but hiking and enjoying what I now view as a well-deserved vacation. I stretch the three-day drive into two weeks, but finally, I decide it's time to end my leisurely ways and get down to the business of finding a new life in the city.

Three weeks after fleeing the hunting camp, I pull into Vancouver to begin yet another life. Two hours later, while driving aimlessly around, I see a man hanging a 'For Rent' sign at a nice-looking apartment complex at the intersection of 13th and Quebec, which is in a trendy nook of the city not far from downtown.

I go in and have a look. It's small, but it's very nice, and I decide to rent it, using my Leonard Scott ID. I make up a fake history of previous addresses on the application, and as I suspected, nobody bothers to check them out. I spend the night in the van outside of town, and the building manager calls me the next day with the good news that I got the place.

I don't like renting a storage unit in the same name as I rented the apartment (had I done that in Saskatoon I would have lost all my money and God only knows where I would be now), but I'm all out of a fake IDs, and I have no other choice. I pay two months in advance at a place called Guardian Storage, which is only about a mile from the apartment, and soon, my money is safely locked away, yet still within easy reach.

The following day, I turn to my old friend Craigslist, and find and land a temp job on a construction crew that does siding, gutters, and downspouts for an outfit called Powell Construction Services. They pay twelve dollars an hour under the table, just the way I like it. The work isn't hard; in fact, I'd spent two summers doing siding when I was a kid, and if you know how to use a measuring tape and run a saw, you pretty much knew how to do it. I'm the oldest and whitest guy on the crew. These other guys are young and strong Hispanics, and keeping up with them isn't easy, but I pull my share of the weight. I speak a little pidgin Spanish from my days as a cop, and the others accept me with no questions.

I like working with my hands and doing an honest day's work for an honest day's pay. Things are finally starting to settle into place, and I feel better now than I have since the betrayal. I'm more worried than ever about getting spotted, though, now that the authorities are aware that I've been living in Canada. Despite the beautiful summer weather, I still wear nothing but long sleeve shirts to hide my tattoos and burn scars. I keep a couple days' growth of a beard and wear my hair a little on the shaggy side. That way, I can easily and quickly alter my appearance with a mustache or shaved head if I have to. I keep a go-bag with a wig, spare clothes, toiletries, some freeze-dried food, and five thousand dollars, half in US dollars and half in Canadian, hidden in the van in case I have to make a hasty getaway. There is a similar go-bag in one of the suitcases back at the storage unit.

Eventually, the business of living begins to overshadow my fear of getting caught, and despite my nerves, I begin to settle into yet another life. There's a trendy little coffee shop called The 49th Parallel at 13th and Main only a few blocks from my apartment. It looks great, and deciding to shake things up a bit, I choose it instead of Starbucks.

Early one morning, I walk in, join the regulars, and start making conversation.

Chapter 5

Grace Appleby. Portland, OR

I return to Portland a wreck. I'm miserable, penniless, and consumed with worry about my father. I used all my money on the trip and I need food, but I refuse to lower myself to ask my mom for a loan.

But these troubles are nothing compared to my dad's. The police are searching for him relentlessly. I am following it all online, and that's how I know they still haven't caught him. I've learned that he did not get away in his car, so he is on foot in a vast wilderness. They are using dogs and helicopters and the Royal Canadian Mounted Police Search and Rescue Unit as well as multiple SWAT teams to track him.

My father has no survivalist skills that I know of. He's not a hunter and was never a boy scout. He was in the military, but not the kind who go behind enemy lines and live off the land or anything. The woods surrounding that hunting camp go on forever in all directions, so his chances are not great. I've also checked the weather forecasts, and it gets down to the mid-40s at night. A cold front bringing rain is moving in, and he is out there in it with nothing but the clothes on his back.

I believe he is still alive. If not, the dogs would find his body. The police have advised everyone for a fifty mile radius to keep their doors and windows locked. I know my father; at least I *think* I do. I know what he is capable of doing, but I do not believe he would hurt an innocent person, even in desperation. I need him not to. If he does, then I've been wrong about him, and I will be as devastated as I was when all this began.

The police were relentless in their questioning of me. I didn't lie when I told them I had no idea where he was. But I did when I said I didn't know who might be helping him. If he's getting any help at all, I know *exactly* where it's coming from.

His father's brother. Uncle Phil. I've heard a great deal about him, but I've never met him. My father refers to Uncle Phil as the black sheep of the family. He's a career criminal. At least, according to my dad, he was until he retired. Apparently he made a lot of money in the 1970's and 80's, mostly in the manufacture and distribution of drugs. I know he did a lot of prison time, but he was out and retired by the time my dad was in high school. His girlfriend was an investment counselor or something, and she somehow legitimized the money, which he then used to help my father out when he escaped from the hospital after being burned. He is the only one who can help.

The first thing I do when I get back to Portland is ask my grandpa for his number. At first, he refuses to give it to me. Nobody in the family will even say my dad's name—they've written him off entirely and try to live in a world where he never existed. But deep inside, I think Grandpa *wants* me to help him. I've always been his little princess, and after only a few minutes of begging he caves in and gives me Uncle Phil's number.

I'm apprehensive about contacting him, because, according to family lore, he's the one who taught my dad how to be a bad guy. I gather my wits and make the call. It's like jumping into into ice cold water. You just have to take the leap, knowing that at first it will hurt and be terrible, but in just a few minutes, you'll get used to it.

It rings a few times, and then he answers with a simple word that's more of a statement than a question: "What."

I don't know why I'm so scared, but I am. "H-hello? Is this Uncle Phil? My name is Grace. My father is your, um, nephew I guess? Dean Appleby? I—"

He cuts me off. "Don't say another word. Are you old enough to drive?"

"Yes."

"Where do you live?"

"In Clackamas. Look, I was just hoping you might help me find—"

"Jesus, kid, what part of shut up don't you understand? If I say that, it's for a reason. Now listen to me. You're a girl, so I know you'll know exactly where the mall is. Go there and meet me in the parking lot by Penny's. I'm driving a old blue pickup. You'll know it. It's seen better days. Be there in thirty minutes. Can you do that without saying anything more?"

"Well, yeah, but I don't know if I should just—"

"You're talking again. Thirty minutes. Don't be late, and don't talk to *anyone* 'til I see you."

The line goes dead.

I almost don't go. I've never been around criminals before, and frankly, I'm scared. This mean old jailbird—who sounds like an asshole, by the way—wants to meet me in a parking lot. It doesn't sound like a good decision on my part. I know I can decide not to go and end it right here, but I think of my father, and how he's spoken of Uncle Phil, and I decide I should at least take the chance. If I don't get a sense that this is good, I can always just drive away. Gladys Knight follows me out to the car, happy to be going somewhere, and we take off.

Thirty minutes later, I'm waiting in the parking lot when he drives in. He was right about the truck. It's old, it's rusty, and it's loud. In fact, it's a lot like him. I always divide people into two categories in my mind—our kind of people, and not our kind of people. Uncle Phil is not our kind of people.

He's at least seventy or older; unshaven, and looks more like an old rancher than anything else. If someone told me he was living in the truck, I'd be inclined to believe him. He does not look like a nice man. If the meeting had been at my place, I wouldn't have let him in.

He pulls up next to me and stares at me for a moment, then rolls down his window. I screw up my courage and return his stare. I won't take any shit from him. If he's a dick to me, I'll just leave.

When I roll my window down, he says, "You look just like him. Get in the truck."

Like hell. I don't even need to screw up my courage to refuse this invitation. My refusal is reactionary, without thinking. "I'm not getting in that truck with you. We can just talk here, or I'm leaving."

He glances around and drops it into gear. "Fine." The truck drives fifty or so feet away, then the brake lights come on and it stops. I can see him shake his head, then the reverse lights come, on and we're face to face again. "Goddamn it," he grumbles. "You obviously want to help him, and so do I. You got brains or you wouldn't have called me. Well, it's time to shit or get off the pot, little girl. Get in the truck or we're done. And so will he be, if he ain't already."

Maybe I'm crazy, but there's something about him that tells me to do this. With every fiber of me saying it's a mistake, I find myself trusting him. Again, I'm leaping into cold water, trusting that I'll get used to it. I pick up Gladys Knight, who is very protective of me, and get into the truck.

"What the hell is that thing," he asks, referring to Gladys Knight.

"This is Gladys Knight, my dog." Let him say one bad word about her. I'll get out of the truck before he can even put it into drive.

"Gladys Knight? Damn, girl, you sure got good taste in music. "I'm not partial to your darker types, mind you, but I do love their music."

Before I can make a comment about racism, he address Gladys Knight in baby-talk, which sounds ridiculous, given his gravelly voice. "Hi there, Gladys Knight! You look like a good dog, don't you? You sure as hell can't be bad with a name like that."

To my amazement, Gladys Knight struggles to break free of my grasp and hops across the seat, wagging her tail to a stranger at whom she would normally be growling. He ruffles her fur and sets her in his lap, turning his face up so she can't lick anything but his chin. Gladys Knight has an innate sense of people. As an example, she never really took to Gloria.

"Cutest goddamn dog I've seen in a long time," he says, pulling out of the lot. "Sorry about the cloak and dagger stuff, but it's a safe bet that someone—cops, FBI, US Marshals—got our phones bugged by now. Don't ever say nothin' about your pa on the phone. If they have been listening, they're probably following us right now, which is why we're doing this in a moving vehicle. They can follow us all they want, but they damn sure can't hear what we're saying."

I don't know if it's Gladys Knight's reaction to him, or the words that are coming out of his mouth, but I do an immediate 180, and decide I like this man. I get an innate feeling that I've done the right thing by seeking him out. "Dad said you were smart. I wasn't sure about calling you, but I'm glad I did."

Uncle Phil croaks out a laugh and says, "So am I, little girl, so am I. I used to be the black sheep of the family, but your old man took that mantle from me. My side of your family's a bunch of characters. We ain't well-schooled, but we're smarter than the rest of them combined."

"Well, you and my dad seem to be pretty similar."

"You speak the truth, young lady. I knew ever since your pa was young that he was more like me than his own daddy. He was just a little squirt you know, small for his age, and got picked on a lot when he was in school.

Bullies always pick on the small and weak. The thing about your pa is, he was smart enough to know where to go for help about it. That right there is where him and me became friends, and I been helping him out off and on ever since. But with this last go-round, he sure outdid me in the black sheep department. Don't mistake that that's something to be proud of, 'cuz it ain't, but if you're gonna do something, then by God, go all the way and don't hold back. Your pa's done some stupid stuff. I know he got his reasons, but look where he ended up—first prison, where he was running the joint, and now he's free and on the lam. That's some bad-assery right there. But deep inside, your pa's a good man, no matter the bad shit he's done. He just got fucked up as a little kid is all, but he done the best he could with what he had. Hell, listen to me, rambling on like a old lady."

"He told me about all the help you've given him," I say. "He said if it wasn't for you, he would have died in prison."

"Well, don't let your old man fool you. Yes indeed I helped him when he needed it, but he's smarter than I am, and mostly, he was able to get his own self out of trouble. I helped him out with money, but I can't really take the credit for that, neither. Back when I was young and stupid, I made some money the wrong way, and went to prison for it myself. But it was my woman who turned it into something big. She died many years ago, and I never used any of it. Don't need it, and don't need nothing it can buy. So I just kept it. I bought a safe and there it sits, just waiting for my old ass to croak so I could give it to your pa. But he needed it before I checked out, and that's what it was there for, so I was happy to help him out some. Now why don't you start talking so I can shut up. I don't socialize much, so when I do, I got a tendency toward diarrhea of the mouth. What's on your mind, little girl?"

"I don't know where to start. I was seventeen when he got arrested. We'd only been close for a few years. I barely even knew him until I was ten. But I've really come to love and respect him in since. When he got arrested, it shattered my whole world. He'd always been one of the good guys. He was my hero. Anyway, after that Killer Burger thing, I didn't want anything more to do with him. Nobody in the family did. I'm ashamed of the way I treated him now."

"Hell, you was just a little girl. Your old man burst your bubble about who he really was. Who could blame you?"

"It was the worst time of my life. I know it hurt him."

At this point, I'm already fighting tears, and I can tell he's aware of it, but doesn't know how to react. His bony hand cups his chin and he stares out the window, then he leans to the right and farts quietly. I can't tell if he hopes I didn't hear it, or just doesn't care, or is maybe trying to cheer me up. Finally, he says, "Well? What turned you around?"

"He called me last week. He begged me just to listen to him, and I did. He told me about a lot of terrible stuff that happened to him as child. His handicapped sister dying in his arms—I didn't even know about her. And he was molested, not once, but twice. The first by a child psychologist when he just a little kid. Sexually molested. Then, as a teenager in high school, by a female teacher. So much trauma, it accumulated over the years. It made him the way he is. I don't remember all the details, but when he explained it all, it made sense of what he was doing by committing armed robbery. And shooting the deputy, well, that was more of a reflex; something that was trained into him as a cop. See a threat, take care of it. He admits that he should be imprisoned for killing the deputy. But when he had the opportunity to escape, he took it. I would have, too."

Uncle Phil says, "I helped him through a lot, but I wasn't even aware of some of that stuff in his background you just mentioned."

"We had a really good conversation. I mean, by the end, we were both sobbing. He didn't ask me to forgive him, but I did. He said he forgave me for turning my back on him when he needed me after his arrest. Suddenly, I wanted to see him more than anything in the world. Well, he'd already made arrangements for me to come up to Canada just in case I'd be willing to. I used all my money to get there, and he was going to reimburse me, but when I got there, he wasn't at the airport. I rented a car and drove to the address. He'd rented a hunting lodge in Banff National Park, but by the time I got there, cops were crawling all over the place. I was taken to the police station, where they questioned me for hours, but of course I had nothing to give them. I wouldn't have told them even if I knew where he was."

Uncle Phil's eyes narrow and he becomes all business. "What exactly did you tell them?"

"Well, to be honest, I lied, and told them he'd mentioned Toronto a couple of times. It's just the biggest city I could think of that's on the opposite side of Canada from where he really is. I said he was living in a basement and working as a janitor somewhere."

The look of approval he gives me makes me blush.

"What?"

"You got good instincts, little girl. That was a good thing to say. Hell, I'm proud of you."

"I just don't want them to find him, that's all."

"I can see a lot of your pa in you, and I ain't saying that in a bad way. So you didn't say nothing about me?"

"Of course not."

"You're a good kid. I'm surprised the cops haven't been around to pay me a visit yet. I was the first place they looked the first time, when he outsmarted his own SWAT team. That's because they know I've been in the joint myself. Ever since he got away I figure my phone's probably been bugged. Yours too, which is probably how they figured out where he was."

"Actually, that's not how they found out. I was with a friend of mine when my dad called me, and she turned him in for the reward money."

"Jesus H. Christ on a crutch! That ain't no kind of friend!"

"I punched her when I found out," I said, rubbing my sore wrist. "I hurt my wrist, but I think I broke her nose. Plus, the joke's on her, because the reward money is only good if it leads to his arrest, which hasn't happened. Yet."

Uncle Phil reaches out and actually pats my knee, which, instead of creeping me out, makes me feel good. Normally, if someone tries to touch me when I'm holding Gladys Knight, she'll growl, but all she did was sit there and wag her tail.

Uncle Phil says, "You hurt your wrist because you didn't lock it when you punched her. Here, make a fist, then lock your wrist so's I can't bend it."

I do, and at a red light, he tries to bend my wrist. He's a skinny old guy, but his hands are surprisingly strong. When my wrist bends, I tighten it up so it's like a steel bar, and this time, he can't bend it.

"That's it, just like that. Next time you punch someone, lock your wrist up like that. And hit 'em with the first two knuckles, these, right here," he says, touching the first and second knuckles. "That's what them big bones are for. You'll do a lot more damage that way."

"Uh, thanks for the lesson. I'll try to keep that in mind from now on. Nobody's ever given me fighting lessons before." I remember my dad telling me that Uncle Phil taught him to fight when he was in high school.

He looks at me with a critical eye. "I bet you'd be a natural fighter. She's lucky she only got a broken nose, considering the blood you got running through your veins. You could'a flat-out killed her, which is what she deserved."

I don't know if he's exaggerating, being honest, or just kidding, but the way he says it stirs something in me. My mind moves closer to something, like when you find an important piece of a puzzle, but it still doesn't quite tell you what the picture is. After a moment, I shake my head and let it go and say, "I'm done with her. If she ever talks to me again I'll break a whole lot more than her nose."

"I bet you will. So what can I do for ya, Gracie?"

"I don't exactly know," I say honestly. "I want to find my father, and I want to help him when I do, but I have no idea how to do that. I have nowhere else to turn."

We pull into a parking lot and stop. "Look, Grace, you may think I don't know you, 'cuz we only just met. But the fact is, I'm pretty good at reading people, and I bet I already know you pretty damn good. Maybe better than you know yourself, and you know why? It's because you're so much like your pa, and I know your pa better than anyone else alive. I suppose that's because he's so much like me. But the moment you got in this truck, I could tell the biggest part of you came from my side of the family, not your ma's, and I don't even know your ma."

"I always felt my dad and I were alike," I say. "I think that's part of why I was so hurt when he got arrested."

"You both got the same constitution. Hell, you even look like him, only a damn sight prettier. Never be ashamed of who you are, little girl. Ours ain't such a bad line to take after. I may be a washed-up old ex-con, but I wasn't always old, I wasn't always washed-up, and I wasn't always a ex-con, neither. You might say I was kind of hot shit back in the day. Not unlike your old man. He's a lot like me, and you, you're a lot like him, which means you're a lot like me too, whether that's for the good or for the bad. Like the old saying goes, the apple didn't fall too far from the tree."

"So you'll help me?"

He smiles for the first time, and I can see that at some point in his past, he'd been a good looking man. "I would have anyway," he says.

"What do we do? Where do we start?"

"A lot of that depends on you. What do you do for a living?"

"I'm the assistant manager at the apartment complex where I live."

"A waste of your talents. Quit your job. I got a better one for you."

"Doing what?"

"Bounty hunter. All expenses paid. You in?"

Dad said this guy changed his life. Maybe Uncle Phil is right; maybe the apple hasn't fallen too far from the tree. I hate my job anyway.

"I'm in," I say with the confidence of knowing instinctively that I've made the right choice. "Where do we start?"

An hour ago I was a normal twenty-one year old girl with a regular job and no real idea of what I wanted to do with my life. With a phone call, I quit both my job and that life, and now I'm the partner of an uncouth old ex-con, about to embark on an international manhunt for a wanted murderer. Not to arrest him, but to save him. How I'll pay the bills or maintain my apartment is beyond me, but Uncle Phil did say 'all expenses paid.' What that means, I don't know, but we're going to find my dad, and that's the only thing that matters.

I've learned that Uncle Phil has only given my dad about half the money he'd saved. He said he will use the rest to finance our journey and keep my dad afloat once we find him.

The first thing we have to do is go to the passport office and get passport cards so we can legally cross the border. The cards come through in four days, and in the meantime, Uncle Phil has his truck tuned up, and gives me a shopping list and money. By the time the truck is ready, so are we. I go home and pack the night before we leave, and go to bed genuinely excited.

I leave my apartment at five in the morning, park my car in Uncle Phil's garage, and we take off. Gladys Knight loves nothing more than car trips, so she's as excited as I am about hitting the road. Uncle Phil seems genuinely glad to have her along. He's already grown fond of her, and she loves him too.

Though I am worried sick about my father, I know from the Internet that he has still not been caught, nor have they found his body. The RCMP admits that the trail has grown cold, but they are still looking for him with all available assets.

For the first time in my life, I feel like I am doing something for my father. I want him to know that I care and want to help him. I have never had an adventure before, and going to Canada with my outlaw uncle in search of my outlaw father is definitely an adventure.

Uncle Phil says he believes the authorities are still keeping their eyes on us, and are probably aware that we've obtained passports and are preparing to leave the country. They may be alerted when we cross the border, but after that they'll lose track of us, since we'll be using only cash and no credit cards.

It's kind of thrilling to be doing something that toes the line of legality with a bona-fide criminal like Uncle Phil. It's fascinating to get a glimpse of things on the other side of the law, but even though helping a fugitive is technically illegal, I don't feel in my heart that we're really doing anything wrong. To me this is more of a righteous cause than a criminal venture, but I have to admit, it kind of feels like I'm a character in book or a movie. If the stakes weren't so high, I'd say it was actually fun.

Uncle Phil knows my dad's last known address in Saskatoon. He says the best way to track him is to follow his original path to Canada, so we drive to where Uncle Phil dropped him off, which is in the middle of nowhere in Washington State. The route we take goes north from Spokane, Washington, across the Columbia River, then on up to Northport, Washington. From there, it only a short drive on I-25 to the US/Canadian border.

At the border station, the Canadian authorities ask us routine questions about where we're headed and what we intend to do while we're in Canada, where we're going to stay, etcetera. Uncle Phil handles them with ease. We're just a grandfather and his granddaughter on vacation, and the ordeal is anything but scary or tense. The border agent offers Gladys Knight a treat, and with barely a glance at the truck, they wave us through. Just like that, we're no longer in the United States.

I try to imagine my father walking across this very spot over a year ago. Uncle Phil says it was a cool, dark night, and my dad had nothing but a backpack full of money, a gun, and his brains. He had to sneak into the woods a mile south of the border, and bypass the border station, then eventually make his way back to the road alone, all in the dark. How bleak his future must have looked at that point! It hurts my heart to imagine him walking along this road at three in the morning, cold, alone, and terrified, with a death sentence hanging over him. How did he even make it? How strong he must be to have done such a thing.

Now, following in those footsteps with Uncle Phil, I feel just a little bit like an outlaw myself. I don't know if we'll even find him or not, but if we do, I'll happily break the law to help him out. I guess that would make me a criminal, too.

We drive through the small towns through which my father must have passed. Everywhere I look, I think to myself, did he see this? Did he drink from that fountain? How far is he from here right now? The process of following him a year behind is somber and saddening.

This would be a long distance to travel on foot. Somewhere along the way, probably in Calgary, Uncle Phil thinks, my father acquired his fake IDs. He has two of them. The first, which is totally blown now, is in the name of Julian McNab. Not even Uncle Phil knows the name on the second ID. How can we possibly find him if we don't even know what name he's using?

We spend the night in Calgary, and leave the following morning. When we get to Saskatoon, the first thing we do is go to his apartment, but it's already been cleaned out and is up for rent. Uncle Phil and I walk through it, pretending to be potential tenants. The sense that we are in the same space he once occupied leaves me feeling wistful and sad. I don't like being behind him. I need to be with him.

It's a nice apartment. Small, but homey. My father must have been comfortable here. At least he hadn't been living in a dump. Thinking about how he must have felt after I'd cut him out of my life increases my sadness, and I want to go. I want to do something proactive to find him. But I don't know what to do or how to do it.

Obviously, there's nothing here that can help us. We spend an hour driving around the area, trying to get a feel for the places and things he saw every day. We go into a nearby grocery store and show his picture around, but nobody recognizes him. I don't know what we were hoping to find, but at least it's a starting point.

We pass a Starbucks, and I remember that my dad is a habitual latte drinker. He used to take me all the time when I stayed at his place. We check at the coffee shop, but nobody recognizes his picture. By now it's getting late, so we head to a motel and get a couple of rooms.

Our plan is to go to Canmore in the morning, to the cabin he rented for our reunion. We'll have a look around and get the lay of the land as best we can, and see if anything stands out. Assuming we find nothing, our next move will be to go to the police station and see if we can find out anything out there.

In the morning we stop by the Starbucks for coffee. Because I'm younger and possibly a little prettier than Uncle Phil, I become the spokesman of our team. I pull out the picture of my father again and show it to the morning barista.

"Have you ever seen this guy in here?" I ask. "He's my dad, and I'm trying to find him."

The barista turns to another young lady at the drive-through window and said, "Seleena, someone's looking for your 6:00 AM extra-hot vanilla."

My heart starts racing. The barista, a pretty Hispanic girl about my own age, drops what she's doing and comes over to us. She takes us to a table and sits down with us, and I wonder if there's a romantic interest between them. Because of this possibility, I take an instant dislike to her.

"Hi, I'm Grace Ap... McNab. I'm Julian's daughter. Do you know my father?"

"I'm Seleena, and yes, Julian's a regular, one of our favorites. He comes in every morning, usually real early. Sometimes, he's the first one in the store when we open at six. What can I do for you?"

"I'm his uncle," says Uncle Phil. " Did my nephew say anything before he disappeared about where he was going, or when he'd be back?"

"Disappeared? What do you mean, disappeared? He told me he was going to meet someone."

"Maybe that's not the right word," I say. "See, he didn't tell the family about his plans, and we haven't heard from him since he left, so naturally we're concerned. You said you guys are friends?"

"Yes, he's been coming in for close to a year. He's really nice, and yeah, we've developed a friendship." She looks at me and can probably read my face, then adds, "It's nothing more. I've never talked to him or even seen him outside the restaurant before. I'm friends with lots of customers."

"What exactly did he say the last time you saw him?" Uncle Phil asks.

"Well, he came in, just like usual, only this time, he was pretty excited. He said he was taking a fishing vacation with someone very dear to him, someone he hadn't seen for a long time. I asked him where he was going, and he said he got an AirB&B for a week. He said he hadn't seen her for several years. He never said who she was, so I just assumed it was, you know, an old girlfriend. I actually thought he'd be back by now."

She doesn't seem to know anything that can help us, but I want to know everything. "Is that it? I mean, did he say anything else? Anything, no matter how small?"

"Well, one other thing." she says. "We talked for quite a while, because there were only a couple people in the restaurant, and he said he'd had a falling out with her. They hadn't seen each other in several years, and he was kind of, I don't know, I guess you'd say nervous, or worried about meeting her. He made it sound like it might not go well. You know, like, apprehensive about it. I thought he was afraid he wouldn't get lai... you know, get back together with her or something. But I could tell he was worried about it. He said something like, 'I hope she doesn't betray me,' which was kind of odd. Like, maybe she had an affair on him before or something. It was just an unusual word for that kind of conversation. I'd kind of forgotten about it, but now I'm worried because you guys are here. You're his family; you should know where he is."

The word goes through me like a knife. "Are you sure that's the word he used?" I ask. "Betray?"

"Yeah, but that's a pretty strong word, and I don't think he meant like, you know, she would do anything to purposefully hurt him. In fact, he was trying to find another word. Anyway, then he switched topics, just like that. It was like he didn't want to discuss his old girlfriend anymore."

"What did he switch topics to?" I asked.

"Nothing," she said. "He just told me that the assistant manager, Taco is into me. Julian—your dad—he's like that. He's like a kind of father-slash-older brother-slash-uncle-slash good friend kind of a guy to me. Anyway, now I'm kind of worried because he hasn't been back since."

"Isn't there anything else?" I ask. "Anything, no matter how small?"

"Not really. Just that, well, he was right about Taco. He asked me out a couple days later, and now we're kind of a thing."

We leave the restaurant in a daze. "My father was afraid I'd betray him?" I say to Uncle Phil. "Why would he think that? Our phone conversation was so real and heartfelt, we literally *cried* together. How could I possibly betray him?"

"Being in prison screws with your mind," he tells me. "It makes you paranoid and distrustful of everyone. It's one of the many bad ways being on the inside screws you up. I'm sorry, Grace."

"But Uncle Phil! When the police showed up at the cabin, he must have thought that's what happened! He must think that *I* did this!"

"Well, yeah, I suppose he might. But you gotta remember, little girl, it wasn't like that. You didn't do it. And like I said, your old man's a smart guy. He'll realize at some point you wouldn't do that."

"Well, now we have to find him now more than ever! We have to let him know I didn't do this!"

"We'll do our best, little girl. Just relax, and think about getting the job done. Next stop's that hunting cabin, and I say we hit the road now."

We do just that. It takes over seven hours to get to the park, and once inside, another ninety minutes to get to the cabin. The roads get progressively smaller until we're basically on just a dirt track, but finally we pull in to the long driveway of the cabin. The last time I saw this place, it was crawling with Royal Canadian Mounted Police officers, and they'd taken me in for questioning. This time, the place is empty. We park by the cabin, but it's locked and we can't get inside.

"He must have seen them coming," Uncle Phil says. "You grow eyes in the back of your head when you're on the inside. I suppose that's one of the more beneficial aspects of being in prison. I don't imagine your pa must have had a lot of time to grab anything. He probably heard them coming and went straight out the back into the woods."

We walk around to the back door, which faces east. There would have been little if any time to get from the door to the cover of the woods before anyone coming down the driveway could see you. In fact, it almost seemed impossible.

"Let's take a walk," he says, and we strike out in the direction that seems likely he would have gone. Gladys Knight runs around sniffing everything, always staying within sight. She's great off-leash. I'm disappointed though; I was kind of hoping she might pick up a trail or something.

There's nothing to be seen but trees in all directions. "He would have gone east," Uncle Phil says. "The exact opposite direction from the cops. But at some point, he'd have changed direction. If he was smart, he'd have gone downhill to the nearest crick, then take to the water to confuse the dogs. Hell, it's all just speculation. Maybe he just climbed a tree or something."

"What are we going to do out here, Uncle Phil? Just wander around?"

"Let's make a giant circle, and if we don't see nothing, we'll go to the sheriff's office or whatever they got here, and see if they got any stolen car reports. He would of had to stole the first car he could find."

"Do you think he could have frozen to death, or starved? I mean, don't you think they'd have found his body by now if he did?"

His eyes narrow, but he isn't looking at anything. "I suppose anything's possible, little girl. But I don't feel like he's dead. I feel like he's alive. I feel like he's out there, waiting for us. I know it sounds silly, but I'd bet my left nut your pa ain't dead."

I try to access my inner criminal psyche, but get nothing. God, I hope Uncle Phil is right.

There is nothing to see out here, no way to predict which direction he might have gone, or how he could have gotten away from the police. I'm not as convinced as my uncle that he's still alive. These woods are daunting and endless. A survivalist with tools could make it out here, but my dad did't even like camping, and I doubt he had anything useful with him. Maybe a gun, but not the hunting kind.

After ten minutes, we realize there is nothing we can achieve out here, so we head for the police station. On the way, we concoct a plan. I will tell them I'm a college student doing research about crime in rural Canada, and try to get information on recent thefts and burglaries in the area.

But when the moment comes, I never get the chance. As soon as I enter the police station, the cop behind the desk recognizes me from the last time I was here. I remember him, too. He's a lieutenant, and he was a real asshole.

"What are *you* doing here?" he asks when he sees me.

I've always been pretty good at thinking on my feet. I actually should have seen this coming, but I didn't. I don't hesitate to answer, and just switch gears, like I just got back to Canada and the police station is my natural first stop.

I say, "Well, like I said the last time I saw you, I really don't know what happened to my father. I came back hoping you might be able to give me an update on the search for him."

"Let me ask you something, young lady. If your father had been at that hunting camp, and we didn't know he was there, would you have turned him in to us?"

"I don't know."

"Don't lie to me. We both know you wouldn't."

"All right, no, I wouldn't. Neither would you if he were your father."

"You see? That's my point. You just don't get it."

"Look, can't you understand that I'm just a girl who wants to see her dad again?"

"Young lady, your father shot and killed a police officer while committing an armed robbery. And he *was* a cop. He's left a trail of warm bodies everywhere he's been since then. Now he's an escaped convict, so I don't want to hear about how you miss your daddy. You're this close to aiding and abetting a known fugitive. Now unless you want to tell me where your father is, I don't want to hear anything else from you."

With that, he heads into an office and slams the door behind him. Tears of anger come to my eyes. Yes, my father did all those things, but if these guys had any idea of *why* he did them, maybe they'd at least realize there's more to the story.

A records clerk looks up as the lieutenant walks out. When he's out of sight, she brings me a box of tissues. "Honey, I'm sorry he's acting like that. His brother was a mountie in the Moose Jaw office. He was killed in the line of duty eight years ago by a wanted man they were trying to arrest. I hope you understand."

"I do, but I just want to know what happened to my father. Thank you for the tissues. You're very nice."

She looks around conspiratorially, then says, "I'm probably not supposed to say anything, but a car was reported stolen from a cabin about fifteen miles from where your father was hiding. It didn't get reported until three days ago. The car was recovered yesterday, all the way over in Winnipeg. It had your father's prints all over it."

"You have a good heart," I tell her. "Thank you so much."

Winnipeg, according to my phone, is nine hundred miles east of here. We make it as far as Regina before stopping for the night. Fortunately,

Canada seems to be a very dog-friendly country. We never have problems finding a room that welcomes Gladys Knight. We eat Burger King drive-through food, which we take back to our rooms, and Gladys Knight gets her own hamburger.

We leave at first light and arrive in Winnipeg in the early afternoon. Since we have nothing to go on, we go right to Winnipeg's Downtown Policing District headquarters. There, I give them the college student story, and they are more than willing to help me.

In sifting through crime reports, I find that a car had been stolen from a medical center parking lot on the morning of July 19th, one week after my dad pulled his disappearing act. This was the day after he would likely have arrived here. I ask the constable if this was a common area for stolen vehicles. She says not really, but coincidentally, another stolen car from a different province had been dumped there the night before. She says it isn't uncommon for a car thief to dump one stolen vehicle and then steal another from the same general location.

"What's the recovery rate for stolen cars?" I ask her, trying hard not to sound interested in *this* particular stolen car.

"About eighty-five percent," she says.

"Like, for example, has this one been recovered?" I asked innocently, pointing to the report of the second car my dad stole.

"Let me check," she says, changing screens on her console. She pages through several different screens, then says, "Yes, the following day. Wow, all the way over in Fort Frances, Ontario, too. That's quite a distance for a stolen."

"Is that unusual?" I ask.

Concentrating on the screen, she frowns, not really listening to me, and taps some more on the keyboard. "Isn't that interesting," she mutters. "It looks like our Fugitive Apprehension Unit is interested in this vehicle. And they're working with the FBI and the US Marshals Service down in the States. It looks like the guy who stole it is wanted down there. Apparently he's crossed the border and has gone back home. Good riddance."

"Wow," I say.

"And to answer your question, yes, I'd say this one is a pretty unusual case."

I continue asking questions about other types of crimes, making a lot of fake notes, then politely thank her and leave. Once I hook back up with Uncle Phil, we use the map on my phone to find Fort Frances.

"Holy shit," he proclaims when he sees where it is. "Old DJ's making a run for the border. There's a dozen ways he could cross that little river, and then he's in International Falls, Minnesota, back in the good old US of A. He's a resourceful one, your pa is."

The following day, we too make the trip to Fort Frances, a distance of nearly three hundred miles. For today's performance at the police station, I'm doing a paper on the recovery rate for stolen vehicles. It doesn't take me long to discover the car that my dad brought here had been dumped in a parking lot that was within sight of the Fort Frances-International Falls Bridge.

"But that still leaves us with the same question," I say. "Where is he going from here? I doubt that International Falls is his final destination. He's back in the United States, but why cross here? Why not just cross where you live? Does he know anyone on this side of the country?"

"Not that I know of, but you never know what kind of contacts you make on the inside. Of course, his buddies in there tried to kill him. Twice."

"How about someone else he met there? Someone who's not a white supremacist?"

"Could be..." Uncle Phil is clearly deep in thought. He almost looks troubled. He's quiet for a full minute, scratching his jaw like he does. Finally, he mumbles. "No, International Falls ain't where he means to end up. I reckon the only way he's gonna get where he's going would be to steal another car, so I guess we need to cross back into the States ourselves and check with the fuzz down there."

"Maybe it's someone he met in Snake River," I suggest. "He wasn't associating with any of those white supremacists there. Wasn't he like, the boss of the child molester ward or whatever? It could have been someone from there. Maybe we could get word to some of the guys on that ward to call us? Do you think that would be worth the effort, or could you even do that?"

"Maybe..." he says. "Then again, maybe not." A determined look comes into his eyes, and he says, "Maybe we don't have to do any of that. Maybe we're just sitting here spinning our wheels."

"What do you mean?"

He looks at me, and a light comes into his eyes. "God damn," he says, shaking his head. "Good God damn with sugar on top! Your old man skunked me, little girl. He did exactly what I taught him to, and I fell for it hook, line, and sinker. Hell, I took the whole goddamn pole!"

"I don't get it."

His smile is so big he looks like a yellow-toothed Jack-O-lantern. "Little girl, your pa didn't cross any river. He ain't in the United States. He ain't even on this side of Canada. How could I be so damned *blind*?"

"Tell me what you mean!"

"You know, it really bugged me when that gal in Winnipeg told you his prints were all over that stolen car. I thought to myself, my nephew is *smarter* than that. And stealing a car from the same parking lot where you just dumped one? Real amateur move, and your pa's no amateur. No Grace, your old man isn't headed east. He's heading west! He just come this way to throw them off, just like he threw us off."

"You're saying he stole two cars and drove what, a thousand miles, just to make them *think* he's headed east?"

"That's *exactly* what I'm saying. Hell, I taught him this trick myself. It's what you yourself did by instinct when you told the cops that your old man kept talking about living in a basement in Toronto."

"So where's he going?"

"Let me see that map of Canada you got on your phone."

I bring up Google Maps, then zoom in on Canada and hand him the phone. "I figure he's heading somewhere west of that hunting camp. Otherwise, he'd at least have been leading them in the right direction by coming east. He wouldn't go too far north because there's nothing there, and I don't figure he'd have gone south, because there ain't really nothing there, either. Now, when me and him first decided that he should go to Canada, we talked a lot about him staying in a big city. Easier to get lost in, better services for the homeless and all that jazz. So, there's only one place."

"Vancouver, BC," I say, looking over his shoulder.

"I'd bet my left nut on it," he says. "Vancouver's where we got to go."

Chapter 6

We drive for three days, staying at cheap roadside motels at night. You can go very long distances in Canada without getting anything on the radio, so we listen to every CD in Uncle Phil's truck. He loves country music, mostly from people who are either old or already dead. I come to like his brand of country, which is called, appropriately, outlaw country. The lyrics are strong and rebellious: *'I fought the law, and the law won.' 'I shot a man in Reno, just to watch him die.' 'When they put those handcuffs on me, Lord how I fought to resist.' 'I turned twenty-one in prison doin' life without parole.'*

As we approach Calgary and the static is just starting to turn to music, he finds an oldies station. "Regular music from back in the day ain't bad either," he says. "This is Helen Reddy. Listen to the lyrics. She's singing about you, little girl."

I concentrate on the music. *'I am woman, hear me roar! In numbers too big to ignore. If I have to, I can do anything! I am strong. I am invincible. I am woman!'*

It's a good, empowering song, and I like that this is how Uncle Phil views me.

When we finally get to Vancouver, we realize how daunting of a task it will be to try to find one man in such a big city. We're not even sure he is here, it's just Uncle Phil's theory. We have no idea what name he's using, what he's driving, or where he might be staying.

Once I see how spread out the city actually is, I begin to doubt we'll ever find him, and this leads to doubts in Uncle Phil's logic. If he is here, there are just too many places he could be. We don't know if he's got money, is living in a car, or is barely making it on the streets as a homeless bum. It's like looking for a single blade of grass in a newly-mown yard. Even if it's the tallest blade, you're never going to find it.

After driving aimlessly around the city for an hour, we find a motel and check in, getting our customary adjoining rooms. Then we head out to get a bite.

"Uncle Phil, how are we ever going to find my dad in a city this size?"

"Well, that's the hundred-dollar question, isn't it? I suppose it's got a lot to do with whether he got any money left. If he does, he might have rented himself a place. If not, he might be living on the streets. We talked about that, you know, living on the streets, hiding among the homeless. If he had enough money, he might have got himself a camper; could be living in that. We talked about that some, too. Whatever it is, he won't be easy to find. Your pa's crafty, and he knows half the damn western hemisphere's looking for him."

"I hurt just thinking about him on the run. I just can't imagine him living like that. "

"I bet you couldn't imagine him pulling a stickup or being thrown in prison, either."

"Well, you're sure right about that."

"You tell *me*, kid. I mean, you guys are cut from the same cloth. What do you think?"

"I don't know, Uncle Phil. I look at the sheer size of this city and it makes me think what if we're just plain wrong? Why would he come here? I mean, if you were hiding from the police, wouldn't it be better to go where there are *fewer* police? Like maybe out in the country, or up in the Northwest Territories or something?"

"I considered that, but the more I thought of it, the more I realized that ain't what he would do."

"Why not? And how can you be so sure?"

"See, ya gotta put yourself in his shoes, Gracie. Let me learn you something. Close your eyes and think of it from your pa's point of view. You're on the run. You get past the cops by no more than an ass hair... pardon my French; I can be a bit crusty and I ain't used to being in the presence of a proper young woman. You just barely slipped past the cops, and you spend a day or two hiding out in the woods. You got nothin' but the clothes on your back. You're cold; probably wet, tired, and hungry, too. Maybe your starving, no strength to go on, but suddenly, you get lucky and find a car to steal. You spend a solid week laying out a bad trail for the cops to follow, going to all that trouble to make 'em think you went fifteen hundred miles east to cross back into the states, when you're really going in the opposite direction. So now, you got the whole of Canada to go hide in. Where are you gonna go?"

"But how can you be so sure he *didn't* slip back into the US?"

"Because his fingerprints are on file there. Because it'd be a hell of a lot more likely for him to get caught down there. But mostly it's 'cause that's what he wanted us to think."

"Okay, that makes sense, even to me. So, I guess, to answer your question, I don't know where I'd go. There are hundreds of little towns in western Canada. Places without a lot of cops. Probably a lot of towns with *no* cops."

"Yeah, I'm sure there are. Okay, now work it out in your mind. You're on the lam, with damn near nothing. You just arrive in some rough-hewn Canadian frontier town. These ain't tourist areas, because they're hard to get to. Isolated, remote places. What do you do when you get there?"

"Start off by getting a motel, I guess, the same as we do now. Then... Look for a job?"

"Keep in mind that anyplace big enough for a motel's gonna have a constable or sheriff or whatever they have in this country for law enforcement. So now walk me through what you do *after* you get settled. Doesn't matter whether you're living in a motel or just in your car. What do you eventually have to do, and keep doing every day?"

"I don't know."

"Yes you do. What do we do every time we stop in a new city. First thing after we get a room?"

"We eat."

"'Exactly. And so does he. So, picture it. Imagine him going into a store or restaurant in this little frontier town, and walk me through it."

"Well, I imagine everyone would stop what they're doing and look at him. I mean, in small town like that, everyone probably knows everyone else, and in walks this stranger. I guess someone's going to ask where he came from, or what he's doing here."

"Now you're thinking."

"Everything they'd ask are questions he wouldn't want to answer, but it would draw more attention if he didn't. So, he'd be vague. He couldn't say he was staying with a relative, because they'd want to know who, and he couldn't answer that. He couldn't really answer anything without sounding suspicious. People would start talking about him, and eventually word would get around to whatever cop works there. I don't suppose it would be long until the cops would talk to him."

"Yep, and that's exactly what your pa *don't* want."

"So he wouldn't go to a small town. And he couldn't just live out in the wilderness. He'd starve to death, and even if he didn't, the winters here would kill him."

"Which leaves us with what choice?"

"A bigger city. But why not one like Edmonton or Calgary, which are probably closer in size to Portland? They're big enough to have resources too, aren't they?"

"Well, yes," he says. Then he taps my temple with his bony index finger. "But think. Those cities are big enough to have good homeless shelters, cheap apartments, decent medical care and all that, but they're still too far from the only person left that matters to him, which may be the only thing that's keeping him going at this point."

"Me? I'm the one that betrayed him in the first place, at least in his mind. He'd want nothing more to do with me."

"Wrong. You ain't stupid, so quit talking stupid. He forgave you when you turned your back on him, not because you deserved it, kiddo, but because he loves you. He'll do it again, even if he thinks you betrayed him. Channel him in your mind. Put yourself in his predicament. He ain't gonna buy that betrayal bullshit for long. Your old man is a very shrewd operator. Even if he thinks you did it, his love for you will win out in the end. My gut tells me *his* guts are gonna tell him you two are still destined to hook up."

"Do you really think so, Uncle Phil?"

"I know your old man better than anyone, and yes, I think so. But I've also gotten to know you now, and even a washed up old fart like me can tell that you aren't the kind of girl that would betray him. And he knows you a hell of a lot better than I ever will."

"But if he didn't think I betrayed him, wouldn't he go back to Saskatoon, which would be the only place I'd be able to think of to look for him?"

"Gracie," he says with infinite patience. "Switch gears in your brain. Channel your inner outlaw. Like it or not, that's what you got to be to help him—an outlaw. Saskatoon is the *last* place he'd go. He couldn't show his face around there because of all the news stories. Hell, them people at the coffeehouse would turn him in for the reward money in a second. His face and that fifty thousand dollar reward was probably on TV every day for the first two weeks. People remember a face for that kind of money. But that still ain't why he didn't go back to Saskatoon. I don't think he's gonna just wait around waiting for you to have an epiphany and come up here to find him. I think it's more likely that he'll go looking for *you*."

Suddenly, Uncle Phil's reasoning makes utterly perfect sense. There are no other options, given the way my dad thinks. "So you think he *is* planning on crossing the border. Not in Minnesota, but back in Vancouver, which is the closest point to Portland."

"Bingo little girl, you win the microwave! *That's* why we're here. But he can't go right away. There's way too much heat on right now. Now's the time a fugitive on the run is gonna lay low, probably for a month or more. And sometimes the best place to hide is in plain sight. If I'm right, he's living here, getting established like he did in Saskatoon. He ain't gonna have long hair, and he'll have to wear jackets to cover his tats, which ain't gonna help us none. In fact, now that we're here, I gotta tell you, I'm about skunked out of any more bright ideas. I ain't got a clue where to start."

Now intentionally trying to access my inner outlaw, as Uncle Phil put it, I think about everything we've talked about so far. Various scenarios run through my mind, and I let them play out. One by one, I dismiss them, and focus on the most likely one.

"I think we should assume he couldn't get to his money. Saskatoon was too hot, and I don't know that he'd risk it. He probably had some kind of suitcase or backpack ready with enough money to at least give him a start, which is probably what he used to pay for the road trip. So let's say he has that with him. He's on foot, the cops are chasing him, but he steals cars, gets away, and leads them all across Canada in the wrong direction, then doubles back and comes here. He can't drive stolen cars forever, and he probably doesn't have enough money to live on for very long, so he'd have to settle somewhere. Since he got here by car, I think we should assume he's living in it. I mean, at least it's a shelter from cold nights, right?"

"I'd say that's a pretty likely scenario. What else?"

"Well, let's drive around the bad parts of town. I mean, maybe there are places where lots of homeless people live out of derelict vehicles. If we can find places like that, maybe we can find him."

"Now you're cookin', Gracie. Your pa and me talked about him living on the streets before he left, while he was still healing from his burns. He knows Canada ain't like the US; they have good health care, homeless shelters, social programs, and such here. He'd seek that kind of stuff out."

"Okay, let's start with downtown and just kind of work our way out from there."

"Agreed. You see what I told you, Gracie? You're a natural at this. If you wanted to turn to the dark side, you could have worse teachers than me and your pa. But no dark side for you. This is just us trying to help out your old man, nothing else. Don't get any ideas of becoming some kind of junior Bad Apple in that pretty little head of yours. You're too good a person for that."

I smile politely at what I perceive to be intentional duplicity in his words. Isn't that what this whole trip has been about, him encouraging me to take after him and my dad? Because that's the message I've been picking up ever since we got started.

Intended or not, I've felt more comfortable around Uncle Phil than anyone since my dad, and I've been more at home learning how to think like a fugitive than training for my job, or learning things in school, or anything else I've ever done. There is something base about it; something instinctual and animalistic that appeals to me. I find it striking and stirring, as if this is what I was built for.

These feelings are so new I can't put them into words yet. I can't tell Uncle Phil that I feel I was born to do this, or even that I love it. I don't want him to stop instructing me, which, if he knew how I actually felt, I think he might. I'm standing on a threshold here; on one hand I could go back to my old life by rejecting what we're doing, and on the other, I have the opportunity to actually save two people; myself and my father, by continuing. Uncle Phil is a kick in the pants, and there's a lot he can teach me. I feel like, despite what he says, he *wants* me to come to the dark side, and if I'm going to be honest about it, I kind of want to go there. At least until we find my father.

Uncle Phil is an enigma, and I'm growing to love him. He's hardcore to the extreme, but inside, he's a kind, loving soul. He's a little rough around the edges, but he really cares and has no trouble showing love his own way. He's eccentric and unique, like an old copy of a good book. The cover's worn out, the print is faded, and there may be a few torn pages, but what's inside is every bit as exciting as when it was new. You'd rather have that old beat-up original than a new, glossy, reprinted edition.

Uncle Phil is shrewd and spry, and smart as a whip. He has more street smarts than anyone I've ever met, except for maybe my dad. I'm becoming his new protégé, and he makes no attempt to hide the fact that he's as excited about that as I am.

Maybe I've given him a new purpose in life too, like my dad once did when he called him for help. I think ever since his girlfriend died, he's been a lonely man. He's told me a lot about his past on our journeys together. He'd learned to make and sell meth back in the late seventies, before it exploded and came to dominate the drug culture in the eighties. He'd made a "fair amount of money" before he got busted, and his girlfriend, who had foreseen the advent of cell phones and other gadgetry, had invested it tech companies like IBM and Motorola, and made quite a killing. But she passed away while he was in prison, and since he got out, Uncle Phil has lived a very lonely life. Then one day his teenage nephew, my dad, asked him to teach him how to fight, and Uncle Phil has been mentoring him in the ways of the dark side ever since. And now it's my turn. It's romantic in a way, like a storybook for ghetto kids.

It's obvious that, in our short time together, he's come to love me, too. Maybe I'm the daughter he never had. What he's been telling me all along actually *is* true; the apple hasn't fallen very far from the tree. I *am* like my dad. I can feel it in my bones. All three of us have have the same basic nature.

Just like that, I make a snap decision—I'm not going home. When we find my dad, I'll join forces with him. Together, we'll stand a much better chance at living under the radar than he ever could on his own. I'm legitimate. I can do things and go places he can't. That will be my purpose in life, to assist the man who brought me into this world when he needs me the most, not to show apartment models to prospective tenants, and schedule the maintenance guy to fix someone's leaky faucet.

I allow fantasy into this vision, and see us robbing banks and getting through police roadblocks with him disguised as an old man and me with short hair, dressed in drag as a boy posing as his grandson. We'd have fishing poles and camping gear in the car. Just a grandpa teaching his grandson how to fish, officer; no bank robbing father/daughter team in *this* car.

I understand that's not even close to what actual life would be like. In reality, I can see us living together, with me renting apartments and doing other legitimate things he can't do. I'd either need a name change or good, fake ID. Maybe we'd just keep moving around Canada, never staying in the same place too long. Whatever it is, we will do it together, and I won't ever have to go back to my old life.

The next day we spend driving around looking through back alleys and skid row areas of the city wherever we see homeless people ambling about. It's also quite possible that he's living on the street, and not in a car. If he didn't have enough money to buy a used car, that's exactly what he'd be doing.

Vancouver isn't like Portland, with homeless beggars on every corner. Here, they are more concentrated into specific areas, and by mid-afternoon we've located several which look promising. The biggest is Hastings Street in the downtown area. There, the homeless line both sides of the street, and people come along in cars once or twice a day with food for them. This is as good a starting point as any. We park a block north of Hastings and strike out on foot, with Gladys Knight leading the way at the end of her leash.

The first thing we notice is we don't fit in. At least, I don't. My clothes, hair, and skin are clean. Uncle Phil, on the other hand, doesn't look too far removed from these people. After a short time, it's clear that I'm more of a hindrance than a help to him.

"Why don't you take off for a while, and let me handle this part, little girl," Uncle Phil says, handing me the keys to the truck. "We'll meet back at that gas station where we parked, say, in two hours. One o'clock. In the meantime, you look around and see if you can find streets with people living in vehicles. Look for lots of old, broken-down RVs. Trust me, you'll know it when you see it."

After getting numerous stares from creepy homeless guys, I am only too happy to comply. I go back to the truck and start driving around aimlessly. I allow myself to get lost, and I find myself constantly scanning faces. My phone will get me back when it's time. I find a few streets with lots of derelict RVs, but there's nobody just sitting around them, and I don't have the patience to wait for someone to come out. I feel limited in the truck, and decide to strike out on foot, where I can actually see their faces rather than just pass by in a blur. Gladys Knight seems happier to be out of the truck, too.

In a short few blocks, I find myself in an obviously bad area of town, worse than where I'd left Uncle Phil. My understanding of Vancouver is that it's a clean city, and Canada has a very low crime rate compared to the States, but that doesn't mean they don't have crappy areas and street gangs, and I've inadvertently found one of the areas where those things exist. Here there are no homeless people, but there are a lot of sketchy people that look like street thugs and gangbangers. I make a quick about-face and head back to the truck.

As I pass a broken-down apartment building, I catch the attention of four thugs hanging out on the stoop. One of them, a mixed-race guy about my own age, stares at me and calls out, "Hey there, hot stuff! You come down here lookin' for some action, or what?"

I ignore him and keep walking. Three of them stand up and intercept me, loosely surrounding me and forcing me to stop. "Don't pretend you can't hear me, honey," the same guy says, walking right up to me. He's only about five-six or so, but he's thick and solid. "I seen your fine ass staring at me. You wanna have my babies, don't you?"

His buddies all laugh.

Terrified, I pick Gladys Knight up and step around them, but he once again blocks my path. Gladys Knight growls low in the back of her throat and he laughs at her. Then he looks at me and says, "I know your ho ass heard me. Didn't your mama teach you any manners?"

I try to channel Uncle Phil. He'd tell me not to show weakness or fear. My voice is surprisingly strong, given that my heart is racing and I'm trembling. "I heard you," I say confidently. "I was just ignoring you."

He turns to his buddies, a look of surprise on his face, then turns to me with a hard expression and says, "Really? Well, you ain't gonna ignore me for long."

Gladys Knight starts barking, sounding as threatening as she can, but again, they just laugh. I'm hoping the threat of getting bitten will give me a chance to get out of this, because despite my pretended bravado, I am now terrified.

Even though this is a public place, it's their turf, and they could probably do anything they want to me without interference from anyone around. All I can think of is to start screaming my head off. If they touch me, I'll fight. I'll kick him in the balls if I can, and I know that for what it's worth, Gladys Knight will be fighting right alongside me, biting ankles and calves at every opportunity.

However, salvation comes from an unexpected source. A police car turns the corner and starts heading toward us. I seriously think he must have been sent by God.

"Not today," I say. "My ride just got here, and I have to go now. But maybe we'll meet again sometime." I wave my arms over my head and step out to the street. My new friends see the cop and disappear into doorways and around corners. Thankfully, the officer pulls over. He's a nice guy, and takes me back to the truck after chiding me for being alone in a bad neighborhood. Thankfully, he doesn't even ask me my name.

The experience leaves me shaken. So far, I'm not a very good outlaw. The moment things got scary, who did I turn to? The police. The enemy, now, I guess. And I'm *grateful* for it. So far, I'm a pretty lousy criminal.

This incident has been an eye-opener. The world of my father and uncle is not as easy—nor as romantic—as I've imagined. All I have is an immature, little-girl storybook idea of life as an outlaw. But this isn't a young adult novel. My father has killed men. He ran a ward in a state prison full of people who molest children. For all I know, he might be dead now. If he's not, and they catch him, he will be executed. In another thirty seconds back on that street, I may have been raped.

This world is a hard place, and unless I change my attitude, I have no business being here. I decide to start taking this a little more seriously. If I'm actually going to embrace this type of outlaw lifestyle—and I am really starting to believe Uncle Phil when he says it's in my DNA—then I will have to learn how to take care of myself.

I pick up Uncle Phil at the gas station shortly after one. His search for my father among the homeless of Hastings Street has proven to be fruitless. We sit in a burger joint and I tell him about what happened to me. It isn't even so much the encounter with the thugs that has me upset. It's more the collision between my own world and that of my dad's and uncle's. Theirs is darker and uglier, yet somehow more appealing than mine, and I can feel it pulling me in with its powerful gravitational field. The problem is, I'm totally unprepared to inhabit it.

After I explain what happened, Uncle Phil says, "You say you turned to the enemy to get you out of trouble. First off, the cops ain't your enemy, and they ain't mine, either. What they do is good. They're the good guys. We are too; we just operate outside the law they try to enforce. Your problem is you put yourself in a bad spot, and I hope you learned a valuable lesson about not doing stupid shit like that."

"I did, but you need to teach me more, Uncle Phil. You need to teach me how to fight, like you did my father. I mean, what am I? I'm just a regular girl. I'm no arch criminal. At least, not yet. I don't even know *what* I am, or what I want to be; I just know there's no way I can ever go back to the lifestyle I left behind before all this got started. I'm no longer that same person. I'm not cut out for that."

"Look, Gracie, I'm not your pa, and it ain't up to me to—"

"Yes it is, Uncle Phil! You're all I have. Like you said, I'm more like you and my dad than anyone else. But right now, I'm nothing more than a girl running around looking in bad places for my escaped convict father. I don't think I'll ever feel right until I've hooked up with him again. And I won't always be able to turn to the police to get me out of the kind of situations I might find myself in, like at that slum back there. I need to be able to rely on myself. I don't want to be helpless. I know I'm not big or strong, but neither are you, and you've been able to take care of yourself your whole life. You were in prison. At least I'm athletic and I'm in good shape. I want to be able to take care of myself, too, just like you. Uncle Phil, I know you can help me. You helped my father; now will you help me? Teach me to fight, like you taught him."

"Look, Grace, yeah, I know I told you you're more like your pa and me than the rest of your family, and it's the gospel truth. But that don't mean you're gonna end up *living* like we do. It don't mean that you're gonna knock over liquor stores and steal old ladies' purses. That's street nigger shit. What it means is what you already figured out for yourself. You ain't cut out to be a clerk or a secretary. I got no idea what your life's gonna be like, Grace. Me, I was what you call an entrepreneur. I found a commodity and a market, and just let supply and demand make me a pile of cash. Your pa, his life took a completely different track. He was a good guy, but life fucked him over as a kid, and it took its toll on him. But he's cut from the same cloth as I was, and now he's where he is, but he's making it out there, despite all the odds stacked up against him.

"You, you ended up with the better parts of both of us. You ain't a criminal, Grace, and you ain't gonna be a criminal. You're a good guy, like your pa, only you're just now realizing you're better than what you been doing with your life so far. I don't know where you're gonna end up either, but I'll be damned if it's going to be living a life of crime."

"I don't want to be a *criminal* criminal. I want to be independent and strong, like you two. I *am* independent and strong. I just need you to teach me to be more street. I don't know what I'm going to end up doing either, but right now, I know what I am doing. Right now, I am inhabiting *your* world, only it's foreign to me. You need to teach me your ways, so that we can do what we came here to do. My father needs us both. I need you to help me find him, and I think you need me to help you. I mean, like it or not, right now, I'm your protégé, and you are my mentor. I'm not looking for you to give me my black belt in street thuggery or whatever this is; I just want you to teach me how to do what we came here to do. That's all I'm asking."

"Goddamn, Gracie, that was a good speech. Okay, you convinced me. I can do what you're asking. For your old man."

"So, what am I supposed to do if I find myself in that situation again?"

"Well Jesus H. Christ on a crutch, little girl. Ain't it obvious? You don't get yourself in that situation in the first place! It's about thinking on your feet, having a sense of street smarts over book smarts. Or, in your case, street smarts on *top* of book smarts, 'cause you got 'em both. Be smart enough to avoid situations like that alley. When it comes to doing that kind of stuff, you're gonna have to let me—"

"No, I'm not gonna have to let *you* do anything. I mean, yeah, I get it that you're better cut out for finding my dad among street people than me, and you're right, I don't want to stick up liquor stores for a living. But damn it, Uncle Phil, this isn't the last time I'm going to find myself in some situation where I'm vulnerable. I want to learn to take care of myself. I'm not interested in learning to fight by the rules. I want to know how to fight quick and dirty, and stop somebody from raping or killing me. Or help someone like you or my dad if you ever need it. I don't want to just sit on the sidelines and scream like a little girl. And God forbid I ever end up in prison, but if I do, I want to know how to take out whoever is targeting me. You know the kind of people I'm talking about, Uncle Phil. Help me out here."

"Damn, Gracie, you should hear yourself. You sure do got your old man's line of bullshit."

I smile at him. "Think of it like this, Uncle Phil. I'm the third generation that's going to run the family restaurant. We've been successful because everyone likes our secret recipe. All I'm saying is, I think it's time you passed it on down the line."

This brings a rare smile to his cracked face. "Arguing with you is like trying to keep a cat off the furniture. You know goddamn well the minute you turn your back, he'll be right up there. Don't matter what you throw at him. Fine. What do you want to know?"

"If you were me, and you were confronted with four thugs like I was this afternoon, what would you do?"

He thinks for a moment, then says, "Well, I would have probably done the same thing as you. I'd be a smartass to the leader, to take his attention away. Then I'd probably step in close, and when I was within range, I'd punch him in the throat with my knuckles, like this." He makes the knuckles of his right hand into a rigid wedge, and jabs it slow-motion into my throat.

"I was going to kick him in the balls, but I didn't know when to do it. I was thinking I should attack him before they could attack me. But the others were crowding in so close it would have been hard to get one good lick in before the others swarmed me. What would you have done about that?"

"First off, a kick in the balls is very effective, but only if you land it right. If you don't, it doesn't do anything but piss him off. I'd start with a throat punch. Anyway, long before we started fighting, as soon as they began messing with me, I would have assessed the whole group and ranked them in the order of toughness. The leader will be easy to pick out. His second-in-command will be close to him. You'll know him because he won't be sitting around waiting for orders; he'll act before being told to, but only after the leader. The others will wait to be told what to do. They'll be the yes men, talking shit and just playing backup. They're the last guys you'll go after.

"Now when you decide you're gonna have to attack, you gotta move like lightning, and have it all planned out first. I'd hit the leader, then, if

I moved fast enough, I might have time get a shot in on his second, too. You'd have to do something really good to him to take him out of the game on such short notice. Maybe gouge an eye or something. Lock your index finger like steel, and jab it into an open eye at least to the middle knuckle. Give him something to think about other than messing you up. Think dirty. Like you said, you ain't there it to fight clean, you're in it to win. Otherwise, you're just spinning your wheels."

"Okay, this is good!" I say. "What next?"

"Well, right about then, I guess, is where the other two would commence to beating my ass to a bloody pulp."

His answer takes the wind right out of my sails. "But…"

"Ain't no buts about it, little girl. Do you think you're gonna throw down with four guys and come out in one piece? Or even come out of it at all? Do you think *anyone* who ain't a Texas Ranger named Walker would? Nope, you find yourself facing those kind of odds, the only thing you can do after you hit the second guy is turn around, bend over, and kiss your ass goodbye. But I'd rather let them know who they was messing with before they took to beating the Jesus outta me. That's just who I am. Sometimes, you got to do that, because it's better than the alternative. Just know that it may be your last fight, because it ain't up to you whether you live or die at that point. It's up to them."

"I wouldn't want to die because I was walking down the wrong street. That's just not right."

"Me neither. Most things ain't worth dying for, Gracie, but at some point, you might find yourself stranded up on top of a hill that *is* worth dying over. If that day ever comes for me, you better be damn sure I'll give them a fight they won't soon forget. It doesn't matter if I'm a old fart or not. And it doesn't matter if you're a girl, neither. If that day ever comes, be relentless. Don't stop. Use every weapon you have available— tree branch, teeth, fingernails, cell phone, car keys—anything. It doesn't matter what. If you can hit him, stab him, or shoot him with it, do it. Twice. And keep on going no matter what. If you're tired, or weak, or you can't move, hell, even if you got a leg cut off, it doesn't matter. When you're on that hill, there will be strength. Just keep going, like a machine. You'll know when it it's time to stop when one of you is dead." He once again taps me on the head with his bony finger. *"That's* the attitude you need to have."

"How will you know if it's a hill worth dying over?"

He thinks about that for a moment, then says, "Well, I figure when that time comes for me, I'll just know. I don't suspect there'll be much doubt about it when I'm actually faced with it. I'll recognize it, and I'll know what I got to do about it. And I swear to God I hope you're never in that situation, but if you are, you'll know it, too. Just remember what I said. Be a machine. Do not let them win. If you die over it, then well, it was worth it. For me, I already made up my mind about that. I don't reckon anything else will matter much. And I'm good with that."

This whole topic is very sobering, but I know from my little experience on that street that if I am really going to do this to help my dad, then it's a necessary conversation. Again, I feel that I'm at a crossroads. I could still abandon what I'm doing now and choose to go back to the only life I've ever known, or I could continue with what I've started and embrace this new, darker life. Uncle Phil seems to know this too, because he stays silent and waits for me, as if he knows I'm contemplating the final choice.

A long moment goes by, and then I say, "Teach me. I don't even feel capable of doing any damage. I hope it won't be four to one, but I know at some point I'm going to have to defend myself one on one. So teach me."

"On our side of the street, it ain't always defending yourself. There may be times when you have to start the fight, like your pa had to do when he first was in prison."

"I never thought of that, but your right. I'll need to know how to do all that, and I want you to teach me."

He gives me a critical stare. It's not the kind of look an old uncle gives to a favorite niece. It's the coldly critical stare of a hard man, piercing and evaluating. It's unnerving. I've never seen him look so serious, and so... scary. Then his expression softens, and he says, "How far away is my nose from your fist?"

"Why? Do you want me to hit you?"

"Just answer the question without making a damn inquisition of it. How far?"

"Oh, I get it. Wax on, wax off. Okay, about two feet."

"No it ain't. It's three. Always add another foot in your mind, and that way, you'll get a good follow-through. See, it's all about the follow-through..."

And thus begin my lessons in street fighting.

Uncle Phil and I spend entire days trying to infiltrate the city's homeless population, spending time in shelters and soup kitchens, showing my dad's picture everywhere we go. Despite all our efforts, after a solid week we aren't any closer than we were the moment we arrived in town. When I see the conditions the homeless live in my heart breaks. I pray we're on the wrong track and that he is better off than the miserable people we encounter. They are destitute and broken, and I can't picture my father living like them. Our searches after dark are especially heartbreaking. There's a surprising number of children living on the streets, some of them very small. I wonder what life will be like for these people once the weather changes. How can they possibly exist outdoors here in the wintertime?

In the evenings, after spending the day looking for my father, Uncle Phil continues training me in street survival and prison-style fighting. His lessons progress from telling me, to showing me, to having me practice and demonstrate on him. It's nothing you'd learn in a dojo, either. Eye gouges, throat punches, foot stomps, shin rakes, elbow breaks… It's all gutter stuff. Uncle Phil may be old, but he's wiry and tough as nails. He's also fast, and, at my specific request, he doesn't hold back in teaching me. It drives poor Gladys Knight crazy. When we first started contact training, she barked and growled, and the first time he knocked me down, she bit him, drawing blood. Now, we have to lock her in the bathroom when we train, but it doesn't slow us down.

There's only one way to actually train to fight, and it's neither painless nor easy. By the end of the first week of training, I'm covered in bruises. By the end of the second, so is he.

All of our attempts at locating my father prove fruitless. Nobody we show his picture to has ever seen him. After more than two weeks in Vancouver, we figure the effort is hopeless and isn't going to pay off. Uncle Phil's finances start running low. He has more money at home, but we need to go back to Oregon to access it. Neither one of us wants to give up, but I'm pretty much convinced that finding my father in this city, if he's actually even here, isn't going to happen.

A month after we left Oregon, we admit defeat and decide it's time to go home. We go to bed early, anticipating an early start in the morning.

Chapter 7

DJ Appleby, Vancouver, BC

My initial fear of getting caught again begins to wane as the summer wears on. The authorities must not have linked Julian McNab to Leonard Scott, but eventually they might, and that's my biggest fear. I'm fresh out of aliases. At some point, I'll have to search for a new way to get fake ID, because the guy in Calgary told me I was just too hot to work with any more.

So far, I've only had to show my ID to the apartment complex manager when I rented my place, and to Dave Powell, my boss, just to prove that I could drive his truck. The guy in Calgary had said that my passports would be good enough to get me over the border on a routine crossing, but only if they just looked at them. They wouldn't hold up to a computer scan because the numbers weren't in the system.

Dave takes me aside one day in late August and tells me he's been watching me and is very pleased with my performance. He says he landed a new contract which includes siding a rectory and dormitory at a convent just outside of town. He has to add a crew to take on the job, and he asks me to be the supervisor. I'll have to hire the crew, and I'll be responsible for ordering the materials, acquiring the tools, and managing the labor—the whole enchilada. He says if it works out as he hopes, we'll become his main crew, and I'll get the best of his contracts. For this, he offers to double my salary, and I take it without question.

By now I'm a familiar face to the people at the grocery store and my coffee shop, where I'm known simply as Len. I'm settling into my new life in Vancouver, and I'm starting to breathe a little easier. I have a nice little apartment, a reliable van, and a job with responsibilities. I've been living off my salary since I got hired, and my money is safely ensconced in a storage unit less than a mile from my apartment. I never forget who

I really am though. I know I can't let my guard down for a minute. Every investigative agency in two countries is looking for me.

I realize that I can't keep this up forever. Every night, I go to bed knowing that a SWAT team could burst into my home before I get up. If I'm going to permanently avoid capture, I'm going to have to do something drastic, and the only thing I can think of is to go to a place where the authorities can't touch me.

There are countries that have non-extradition treaties with the United States. Morocco, for one. There, as I understand it, foreign criminals can live aboveboard without the fear of extradition as long as they stay out of local trouble. This becomes my long-term plan, and I begin to take small steps toward it. Obvious obstacles to this plan are how to get there, and mastering Arabic, a difficult language for Americans to learn, and most of all, Grace. To address the easiest, I purchase a Rosetta Stone course, which keeps me busy in the long hours between work and bedtime.

The most important thing I have to do before making a permanent move like that is to see Grace one last time. I know it looks bad, what happened at the hunting camp, but in my bones I just don't believe she had it in her to coldly set me up like that after our phone call. There has to be another explanation.

The moves I've made since then to throw the police off my trail have also ensured that Grace couldn't find me either, if she were inclined to look. There's no way I can call her or otherwise contact her, because the police would have to be incompetent idiots to not bug her phones and keep her under digital and physical surveillance. The only way left for me to talk to her before making such a permanent move is to go to Oregon and confront her face to face.

Going back to the States will be both bold and stupid of me. There, I'm one injury, one speeding ticket, or one alert citizen away from arrest. I will be at risk every moment of every day, especially in Portland. But nobody ever accused me of being cautious or smart.

The siding job has taken two weeks, and will be complete in a few days. That's when I'll go down to confront Grace. I want to be able to stay in Canada as long as I need to, so I don't want to leave Dave hanging. He's already told me we're his best crew, and that he's landed new contracts that will keep us busy until the weather shuts us down for the winter.

I tell him I'd like a few days off after the convent job is finished, and he is more than happy to let me go, as long as I promise to come back. I'll feel bad for him when I actually make the move to Morocco. But one step at a time, and the first is seeing Grace. Getting safely across the border will be the toughest part.

There are three border crossing stations in the immediate Vancouver area, all just south and east of the city. The biggest and busiest is Peace Arch, which connects British Columbia Highway 99 with I-5 in Washington State. The other two, which are much smaller, are several miles east of I-5. All are staffed 24/7. I think my best chances are at Peace Arch during rush hour, when I will have a lot more traffic to hide in. They will be less likely to do secondary searches, and as long as I have my passport and paperwork in order, I am likely to be moved through as fast as they can with the rest of the traffic.

On a day off I decide to drive down to Peace Arch and check it out for myself. As I suspected, security is quite heavy here. There are long lines, and almost all the cars are just passing through the border station, with very few being directed to the secondary search area for closer inspection. After sitting and watching for a while, I decide to check out the area between Peace Arch and the next one over, the Pacific Highway Crossing. To my surprise, I discover there is virtually no border security between the two.

I work my way east and south through neighborhoods, past a golf course, all the way down to a street called Zero Avenue, which is geographically no more than half a mile or so east of the Peace Arch crossing.

This is as far south as you can get in Canada. The houses on Zero Avenue are all on the north side of street, which is Canada. The south side of the road is all grass, and there's a narrow ditch about three feet wide and three feet deep a few feet south of the roadway. The ditch is the actual border itself. On the other side of the ditch is a well-manicured park, with a mown lawn, playground equipment, bathrooms, and a large parking lot. The park is in the United States. Apart from the ditch, security is nonexistent. No fences, no markers, no border patrol stations. In fact, there are several land bridges crossing the ditch, allowing foot traffic to pass between the countries without scrutiny. Yellow concrete slabs block vehicles from crossing these land bridges, but there's room enough for people to cross on foot. A bicycle or even a motorcycle would easily be able to cross. There are even signs telling Canadians that dogs need to be leashed while in the park.

The ditch is too deep for a four-wheel-drive vehicle to cross, but it is narrow enough for me to jump it. I quickly formulate a plan whereby I cut two 2x6-inch boards to six feet; long and wide enough to span the ditch, yet short enough to still carry in the van. All I'd have to do is come down here in the middle of the night, toss the ramps across the ditch, and drive into the US. Easy peasy. Same to get me back into Canada.

I park and get out, and as I stroll down Zero Avenue, a US Border Patrol vehicle pulls into the park. The driver gets out and leans against his truck, basically checking out the girls and just hanging out. At one point, he looks at me and waves. Incredulous, I return the gesture.

Could crossing illegally from one country to the other really be that easy? Trust and goodwill is all warm and fuzzy, but the lack of physical security is actually scary. I could drive across a homemade bridge just as easily whether my van is empty or carrying a dirty bomb.

The same holds true between the Pacific Highway crossing and Lynden Crossing. Heavy security at the border stations and nothing between them. The problem is, other than the park, there's nowhere else to get a vehicle across. There's either a fence, or woods. The only other places I see to get a vehicle across are the border stations themselves.

I return to my apartment and get online. Using Google Earth, I check other areas of the border, and confirm my suspicions. There are no shared roads between the countries without an official border station. There are shared fields, shared lakes, and shared woods. At one notable point 280 miles east of the Peace Arch crossing, Canadian Route 3 dips down so close to the border the lines almost merge. Zooming in, I measure less than a quarter of a mile between Canadian Route 3 and a dirt road located just south of the border on the US side. The area between them appears to be empty, fairly level no-man's land.

A four-wheel drive truck should easily be able to get off Canadian Route 3, bounce across a couple hundred yards of scrubby, treeless land, and end up on the dirt road. From there, it's about eight hours to Portland.

Crossing at this point is by far the safest method of getting a vehicle into the US without risk of getting caught. Crossing at one of the checkpoints would be the fastest, and my ID is probably good enough to get me out of Canada, but it is an unnecessary risk I decide to take only in an emergency. Crossing at the park has inherent risks, too. It's a safe bet that the US Border Patrol hangs out there a lot. For all I know, there are cameras or motion detectors that would alert them if a vehicle crosses there. However, it's better to be prepared in advance than to be caught with my pants down.

For that reason, my next stop is Home Depot, where, for forty-two dollars and eighty-five cents, I walk out with two ready-made ramps. The store even cut them to my specs for me free gratis. Now *that*, I think, is customer service.

At 5:30 in the morning a few days before the siding job is supposed to wrap up, I walk into the 49th Parallel as usual. I make small talk with the barista, and take my drink to my customary table in the back of the restaurant. I've been sitting with my back to the wall and backing into parking spaces my entire adult life, the mild paranoia and hyperawareness being a side-effect of nearly two decades in law enforcement. Those traits, I have found, serve me well as an escaped prisoner, too.

People are just starting to trickle in, but so far, none of the regulars who like to chat are here, so I wake up my iPad and resume the research I've been doing into commercial shipping routes to Morocco.

I've been tinkering with the idea of shipping myself there. I'd have to buy a commercial shipping container, stock it with plenty of fresh water, non-perishable food, and do some custom modifications to it. I'd have to engineer a concealed entry, some sort of airtight method of storing bodily wastes, and an air circulation system ventilated to the outside. I'd build sleeping quarters inside, install a gravity-fed 500-gallon tank of fresh water, and an empty 500-gallon tank to take the dirty water, with a trough of some sort between them for bathing, cooking, etc. It would probably take me several months to build, but when it was ready, all I'd have to do is weigh it and prepay shipping to Casablanca, then simply get in, have it picked up, and mail myself to freedom.

It is a bold plan, but a good one. Once there, I could use the container as a dwelling until I get myself established. There are tons of logistics to work out, like renting warehouse space to work on it, where in Morocco to have it delivered, how to heat and cool it, etc, and I am deep into the research when I sense something going on at the front of the coffee shop.

Someone has come in, but what catches my attention is they're not ordering or standing in line. Instead, they're scanning the crowd. Probably just looking for a friend, but it's got my spidey sense tingling, and I've learned to trust my instincts.

The 49th Parallel has a side door that opens to the street. I've long ago determined that this would be my escape route in an emergency, and even though this isn't an emergency, I get up and make for door. It's not the first time I've made a quick exit just to be on the safe side, and I know it won't be the last.

As soon as I step outside, I am grabbed by the arm in a powerful grip, and a gravelly voice says, "Hold on now, DJ. Don't be in such a hurry—"

I throw an elbow into the solar plexus of the man holding me, cutting him off in mid-sentence. He goes down and I take off, my legs pumping, wondering if I'll hear the shot or feel the bullet first. I get no farther than twenty feet when I am stopped dead in my tracks by a single word, yelled from the doorway through which I had just exited.

"*Daddy!*"

There's no mistaking that voice, and I practically skid to a stop.

It's Grace.

I spin, and there she is, running toward me. I stare at her in wonder as she stops to help the man I knocked down. Refusing to believe my eyes, I see it's Uncle Phil.

"Damn, boy," he coughs. "That's a fine way to greet your old uncle, especially after all we done to find you."

My first thought is that they are working with the police to ensure I get arrested without hurting anyone. I consider running again, but I can't move. I can't take my eyes off her. Slowly, I realize this is no setup, she's genuinely happy to see me. If it were a trap, I'd already be in custody.

"Daddy, it's just us! Nobody's coming," Grace says, reading the changing expressions on my face. "I can't believe we've finally found you!"

"But, I… I don't understand," I stammer. "You turned me in at the cabin."

She runs into my arms and and, through tears, says,"No I didn't! I went there after you didn't show up at the airport, and *I* got arrested. They held me all day, but I didn't tell those bastards anything, not a damn thing, and they ended up letting me go. I found out that it was a friend of mine who turned you in. She was there when you called me. She wanted the reward money. Oh I'm so glad you were able to get away!"

I snuggle her close. Every bit of pain and loneliness since I fled the cabin vanishes in an instant. Uncle Phil steps in and I grab him, too. We just stand there on the sidewalk in front of the coffee shop in a three-way hug, oblivious to those around us.

"Len, you okay?" shouts Addi, my favorite barista, leaning out the side door.

"I'm good," I say, smiling and waving at her. She nods, and goes back to her duties.

"How the hell did you guys find me?" I ask Uncle Phil as we go back inside. "Jesus, if you can find me, then so can the police."

"The hell they can. They ain't got our secret weapon here," he says, putting his arm around Grace. "Let's sit down and I'll tell you all about it."

We sit down at the table I'd just vacated, and Uncle Phil says, "Turns out Gracie here's a natural at this. We followed your trail of stolen cars all the way down to Fort Frances, and it wasn't 'til we got there that I realized you skunked us the same damn way I fooled the cops with that stolen purse trick after you got away from the hospital. You did it so good you even fooled me."

"But... How'd did you know I came to Vancouver?"

"Well, after you led us all the way across the damn wilderness to Ontario, we put our heads together and decided you must be here. We knew you wouldn't go to some small town where you'd stick out like a sore thumb, and this was the biggest town west of Saskatoon. Plus, we figured you'd think Grace dropped a dime on you at the cabin, and that you'd eventually go back to Portland to find her, and Vancouver is only a few hours from Portland. We've spent the last two weeks here lookin' for you on the streets and in homeless shelters. We figured you probably never got the chance to get your hands on the money after you almost got busted. Figured you might be living with the rest of the street bums, or maybe in a tent or a car somewhere."

I'm the one who's impressed. "Wow, Uncle Phil. I mean... really fuckin' *wow!* You guys are amazing! I hope my little trail of stolen cars fooled the police better than it fooled you two. But your assumption about the money is wrong. I *did* get my hands on it after I made it out of those woods. I had it in a storage unit under a different name. I used it to get here, and then I got a place and a job, and even a promotion at work. But what I want to know is, how the hell did you find me *here*, in this coffee shop?"

"That was me, Daddy," Grace says proudly. "We had no idea where you'd be living, or what name you'd be using, and now that we spent all the money Uncle Phil brought, we have to go back to Portland to regroup. We got up at five this morning, and I needed a coffee to get going. We'd already checked every Starbucks in town, but nobody'd seen you. We did that in Saskatoon, too, and met your friend Seleena. But this morning, as we were heading to the freeway, we passed this place, and I thought, 'what if he's still getting coffee, just not going to Starbucks?' So, we turned around and came back. I just walked in, and there you were!"

All I can do is shake my head. "You'd make a hell of a good detective, honey. I'm so proud of you!" Unable to resist, I stand and gather her into my arms again, relishing the fact that she's holding me just as tightly.

When we let go, she winks at me and says, "I like to think I'd make a pretty good fugitive, too. Anyway, I can't believe we found you!" We sit, and she takes my hands in hers across the table.

"You're too pretty to be a fugitive," I say, laughing. " But if you ever do follow in my footsteps, be smarter than me. Being predictable is what led you to me. I can't keep doing that. That's one of the first things I always taught rookies as soon as they'd get in the car back when I was field training officer. Don't become a creature of habit. Damn, I'm glad to see you guys, and Grace…" Tears come to my eyes, and I squeeze her hands tight. "I'm just glad you didn't betray me."

We talk until eight, which is when I have to leave for work. Grace and Uncle Phil are just about out of money, but at least now they don't have to leave today. The last thing I want to do is go to work, but I have established myself, and I don't want to jeopardize that. I want to live as regular a life as I can, which means working and living in an established place under an established identity, and in order to do that, I have to be at work on time every day, including today.

I walk out with them to Uncle Phil's truck, where I meet Grace's little dog, Gladys Knight. It's a friendly little dog, and she seems to like me. I'm ambivalent about animals, but if I was going to have a dog in my life,

I suppose I could do worse. Grace tells me she's housebroken, and that makes her just fine in my book.

I give Uncle Phil the key to my place, and tell them I'll be home as early as possible. At work I can barely concentrate on the job, but the time goes by quickly. I get back just after five and find them as at home in my place as if we'd planned this reunion all along. Uncle Phil is talking about his days in prison, back when he'd been a member of the Aryan Brotherhood.

"Yep, they were badasses, no doubt about that," he says. "Still are. Your old man could speak to that, I reckon. The Brotherhood is responsible for damn near a third of all the murders in prison, but make up less than one percent of the population there. They kind of expect you to stay active after you get out, but most, like me, don't. I never hung out with them boys after I was paroled. Hell, just being in their clubhouse was a violation. They expect you to go to work for them, even when you're still on paper. You need guys like that when you're on the inside, but I never wanted anything to do with them on the outside."

"Me neither," I say, pulling my Glock out from under my flannel and putting it in a drawer. "I hated joining them, but I'd probably be dead today if I hadn't. Of course, *they're* the ones who want me dead now, and trust me, I'm more scared of them than I am of the cops. They've both got reason to come after me, so I guess I'm double-screwed. But if I get caught, I just hope it's by the police, not the Kindred."

Uncle Phil says, "You're right to be more scared of them than the fuzz. What are you carrying there, boy?"

"Glock .40," I say, taking the gun back out. I remove the mag and pull the slide back, ejecting the round, which I catch nimbly. I lock the slide open, then turn the gun around and hand it to him.

"I see you keep it hot," he said, taking it.

"It won't do me any good unless I pull trigger and it goes bang."

Uncle Phil examines the gun for a moment, then thumbs the slide release. He points it at the door and pulls the trigger, eliciting a sharp, metallic *click*. "I ain't shot a gun in a coon's age," he says. "Where's the safety on this thing?"

I hold up my right index finger and flex it. "Right here. Keep your booger hook off the bang button; that's your safety."

"That's the cop in you," he says. "Me, my training's more from the street. I like a thumb latch safety, otherwise I'm afraid I'll shoot my balls off."

"This thing actually has three safeties, but they're all internal and automatic."

"The more fancy-shmancy stuff you got built into it, the more that can go wrong. That's why I don't trust them semi-autos. They ain't as reliable as a good wheel gun."

Grace asks quietly, "Can I see it?"

"Sure. I take the gun from Uncle Phil, lock the slide open again, and hand it to her butt first.

"It's heavy," she says.

"Actually, it ain't," says Uncle Phil. "It's a lot lighter than most. Of course, most guns ain't made out of plastic, either."

"How do I close the top part?" she asks, turning it over and examining it.

I point to the slide release and explain how to thumb it down. She struggles with it for a moment, then the slide slams home and she utters a little squeak. "Cool," she says. "So, do I just pull the trigger to shoot it?"

"Yeah," I say. "Go ahead now, but never, *ever* pull the trigger of a gun you haven't personally checked to see if it's empty."

She points it at the door and says, "You screwed with the wrong girl, asshole!" and dry fires it. "Ha! Got him!"

I say, "Do you remember anything I taught you about gun safety when you were young?"

"A little. All I remember is the laser thing. Treat all guns as if they're laser beams that will destroy anything they're pointed at."

"The laser rule, right. Treat all guns as if they're loaded, and never point one at anything you don't intend to kill or destroy."

Gone are her girlish giggles, replaced with a noticeable interest. "I don't really remember that much, so I sure could certainly use a refresher course."

I hold out my hand, and she hands me the gun, pointing it at me as she does.

"Laser rule, Grace. Here's how you hand someone a weapon." I take it from her and turn it around before handing it to back to her butt-first.

She hands it back to me correctly. I say, "Okay. First, you have to learn to pull the slide back," and I show her how. It takes her several attempts before she realizes how hard she has to grip the weapon and pull. After a few minutes, she's racking the slide like a pro.

I pick up a loaded magazine and say, "This is the magazine. It holds all the bullets. This mag holds twelve rounds, and I always keep one in the chamber, so that's a total of thirteen bullets in the gun. You de-cock the gun by pulling the trigger before you load it. Like you just did. After it goes click, it can't fire again until it's cocked, which happens when you pull the slide back.

"To put the magazine in, you have to make sure it's properly oriented, with the bullets pointing down the barrel. Use your index finger as a guide so you don't have to look at it, like this," I say, demonstrating. "That way, you can reload without taking your eyes off the target. Always make sure the magazine is firmly seated, and then the gun is loaded. But if you were to pull the trigger right now, nothing would happen."

"Because you didn't pull the slide thingy back."

"It's just called the slide, and yes, that's correct. Until you do that, there's still no round in the chamber. When the weapon is loaded, pulling the slide back unblocks the chamber and cocks the firing pin. Then, the top round in the magazine is lined up with the empty chamber, and the spring in the magazine forces the rounds up. The top one goes into the chamber, and then, when you let the slide go, it springs forward, peeling the top round off the magazine and pushing it into the chamber. Since the weapon is cocked, now all you have to do is pull the trigger, and the firing pin strikes the primer on the bullet, and the gun will fire. Just remember, don't put your finger anywhere near the trigger when you're racking the slide."

I demonstrate, keeping my finger well away from the trigger as I rack the weapon. "Now the top round is off the magazine and in the chamber, so it's ready to fire. There are still only twelve rounds in the gun though, but now there's room in the magazine for one more round, since the top one is chambered. Now we'll top it off."

I show her how to eject the mag and load another round into it, then slam the back of the fully-loaded magazine against my palm to make sure the rounds are properly seated. Then I insert it firmly back into the magazine well and check to make sure it's all the way in.

"Now your weapon is fully loaded with one in the chamber," I say. "All you have to now is point it at your target and pull the trigger. One pull, one shot. Thirteen pulls, thirteen shots. Got it?"

"Got it."

"Okay, now I'm going to unload it, and you try."

We futz with the gun for an hour, and when we're done, Grace knows how to load it, unload it, check the indicator to see if there is a round chambered, press-check it for visual confirmation, field strip it, and put it back together. We've gone over the laser rule again, along with the all the elements of basic gun safety, and I particularly stress keeping her finger outside the trigger guard at all times until she's actually ready to shoot.

I even give her an assignment. Every time she sees someone with a gun on TV or in a movie, she is to take note where his index finger is. When she sees someone with his finger on the trigger without shooting someone, she's to say, "Bad cop," or "Bad bad guy." Since she won't be handling guns very often, I figure this might be a good way for her to train herself on trigger safety, the single most important aspect of firearms handling. No gun will fire if your finger is off the trigger.

She and Uncle Phil go out to the pick up a pizza while I take a shower, and when they get back, I hand Grace a bag with the Glock in pieces, intermixed with thirteen rounds and an empty magazine. In little more time than it would take a range master, she puts the gun back together, performs a function check, loads the magazine, loads the weapon, chambers a round, and tops off the mag. She then properly hands me the gun.

I am duly impressed, and promise her we'll go shooting on my next day off.

In addition to the magazine in the pistol, I have two fully loaded mags and the extra round in the chamber, all of which I'd taken from the correctional officer as he lay dying during my escape from the hospital. Whereas there are gun stores here, I'm not willing to enter one to buy ammo. The last thing I want is security camera footage of me shopping in a gun store. I stay away from anyplace that might have received a wanted poster with my mug on it. Consequently, the most I am willing to part with for training Grace is one twelve-round magazine. I'll do it, but I don't like the idea of reducing the number of rounds available to me by one, let alone a third.

On Saturday we drive into the mountains north of town, and follow a fire access road several miles back in the woods until we find a suitable clearing. I have Grace go over everything she's learned one last time, and am proud to see she has retained it all.

Next come lessons on firing techniques and shooting stances, all of which are done with an unloaded weapon. Being athletic and an eager learner, Grace has no problem forming and maintaining a solid shooting platform. I show her how to align the front and back sights with the target, and go over how to squeeze—not pull or slap—the trigger. We practice for an hour just dry firing, then another thirty minutes with her drawing the gun from either her purse or a holster at the small of her back and getting into a shooter's crouch. I never once have to remind her to keep her finger off the trigger; it stays lined up parallel with the barrel every time. When I am satisfied that she knows what she's doing and is confident with the weapon, I have her load up.

I prepare her for the recoil, and particularly for how loud the report will be, since we don't have hearing protection. Finally she's ready to shoot. On her first shot, Grace knocks over a Pepsi can from ten yards. She takes her time on each shot and only misses her target once in twelve rounds, even hitting it at twenty-five yards. I want so badly to let her shoot a second magazine, but carrying a weapon without a spare mag goes against my all training, and I won't do it. Further firearms training will have to wait.

"Hot damn! Ain't she a natural," exclaims Uncle Phil after we're done. "I never could shoot very well myself, but then again, I ain't never had a cop teach me, neither. I tell you what, Gracie girl. We're going to smuggle us another gun or two and a whole bunch of rounds for you to play with when we come back. I don't reckon it'll hurt to keep you in practice."

I say, "Slow down, Uncle Phil, you guys don't need to get busted going over the border."

"Don't get your panties in a bunch, DJ. You ain't dealing with an amateur. You're forgetting I know how to do shit like that."

Grace is delighted with herself, and I am delighted with her too. I've never seen her so happy. It's becoming clear to me, however, that she has an unrealistic and romantic notion about what a life on the run is like, so

I reminded myself to bring her down a notch or two. There's no romance in looking over your shoulder all the time, constantly having to plan every step ahead in case something goes wrong, and never being able to get too deeply involved with another human being.

In an attempt to let her know what my life is actually like, I take Grace on a drive with me and point out how hyperaware I have to be at all times. Just like I was when I noticed her come into the 49th Parallel, I have to be aware of what people are doing using only my peripheral vision, so as not to make them aware that I am watching, and take immediate notice when something doesn't seem right. Once again, she tells me how impressed she is that I had her under peripheral surveillance from the moment she came into the coffee shop.

I teach her how to always keep mental notes of the vehicles in her rearview mirrors, particularly when turning, and we practice making last-second turns and quick stops using the emergency brake to avoid flashing brake lights if there's any possibility someone might be following her. Of course, my attempts to turn her away from the fugitive lifestyle have quite the opposite effect; they only served to further romanticize it.

To her credit, Grace takes to it like a hero in an action movie, and despite myself, I can't help but be proud of her. Uncle Phil started this ball rolling before they found me, and I find it to be a fun and harmless way of passing the time. Any skills Grace actually picks up won't hurt her, and I suppose it's possible that somewhere down the road they might even come in handy. To me, her "training" is more of a harmless game than anything else, but she takes it all very seriously.

She is intrigued with the concept of life on the run. And I'm so happy to be with her and Uncle Phil that I find myself forgetting that I'm a fugitive myself. Uncle Phil and I often regale each other with criminal war stories in much the same way as I used to with other cops during choir practice after work, and Grace sits rapt and attentive, absorbing every word.

When I tell the story of how I was accepted into the European Kindred, which was by being assigned to attack and beat a black guy who had dissed the gang, Grace tells me that Uncle Phil has been giving her some pointers on street survival and dirty fighting. This gets me going, and I start showing her the basics of self-defense and ground fighting, training her as I was trained throughout my police career. I was never the best at it, but I had eighteen years of defensive tactics and arrest and control training to draw from, not to mention two years of hardcore prison experience. I teach her the carotid neck restraint I'd used to kill Dr. McNab, and make sure she understands that if she ever needs to use it, to release it once her opponent stops moving, or she could easily kill him.

We take to watching mixed martial arts competitions on TV, and rather than just cheering on the action, Grace studies the techniques and uses the DVR to stop and rewind in order to dissect the moves the fighters make. She often asks to use Uncle Phil and me as subjects to try out the moves she learns.

One morning, she's gone when I get up. She comes in after a few minutes, drenched in sweat, having just run three miles. She used to be on track team in high school, and now she's taken to physical training again. I tease her about this, calling her GI Jane, and she just smiles condescendingly at me.

Eventually, though, the time comes for them to leave. Things have changed a great deal since they first found me. Grace now plans to ditch her entire life, and move in with me. Uncle Phil says he isn't about to let us go off playing fugitive while he sits around drinking himself to death at home in Gresham, so he announces that he, too, will move up here to be with me.

Uncle Phil has used most of the money that's he's brought with him, and Grace is already late on her rent and utilities. The plan is for them to go back to Oregon to tie up loose ends, grab the rest of Uncle Phil's money and anything else they need, then come back up here for the long haul. They estimate maybe three or five days for them to shut down their lives in the States and rejoin me on at least a semi-permanent basis.

Eventually, they will get their names changed in the US, and then apply for permanent Canadian visas under their new names. They might even apply for Canadian citizenship. Once they have everything in order, they'll be able to purchase a home and do all kinds of stuff to legitimize our situation. Concurrently, I'll keep working on ways to get all three of us over to Morocco where we can live aboveboard and without fear of extradition or arrest. Wherever we go or whatever we do, I couldn't be happier at the thought of us all living together.

While they are gone, I will begin the search for a larger, more suitable place. Until we can find one, they'll stay here with me. Grace will get a job, and we'll all build a new life together. I make sure they each have a key to my place, and finally, with hugs all around, I kiss my daughter goodbye, and they are on their way.

I have to say, when I ran off into the woods at the hunting camp with the police hot on my trail, I would have never dreamed that my life could once again turn around and be so satisfying. For the first time in many years, I feel truly complete. I am eager to dive into this new phase of my life—*our* lives. Wryly, I recall hoping that I might achieve some degree of understanding from Grace; maybe some pity, and an occasional visit or phone call. What I actually ended up with is way beyond my wildest fantasies. Grace and Uncle Phil are giving up everything for me, and I will once again have a family.

Right after they leave, I begin the search for a bigger place. I want a house or condo with two master bedrooms and an extra bedroom and bathroom. Rent won't be a problem. I have more than enough of Uncle Phil's money left over to cover any unexpected costs, and with what I make in construction, I won't have to draw much from my cash supply to make ends meet. Once Grace gets a job, we'll be financially independent, and we can put Uncle Phil's cash away to save for her after we're gone.

The day after they leave, I make an appointment to look at a house for rent on the city's northeast side. The place looks just fine. I tell the owner I can prepay the first three months plus all the deposits, in cash. I'm hoping this might avoid some (or all) of the paperwork, but there's no such luck. He has me fill out an application, which asks for ten years' previous rental history, three references, and ten years' worth of employment history.

This is clearly going to be a problem, since the only rental history I have is the place I'm in right now, plus the made-up history I'd created to get into it. And I have an employment gap of nearly three years while I was in prison. I end up taking the application home, telling him I'll return it in a day or two. Housing could well prove to be more of a problem than I anticipated.

Between Uncle Phil and I, we probably have between $250,000 and $275,000 in cash. But even if we were going to buy a house, we can't just pile banded-together hundred-dollar bills onto a table. We'll have to figure out some way to legitimize it.

Where there's a will, there's a way. To me, it doesn't matter. We can stay in this tiny apartment, or we can buy the nicest house in British Columbia; it isn't about where you are, it's about about who you're with.

Chapter 8

Grace Appleby, Gresham, OR

It's amazing how much simply following a daily routine can camouflage the things we've come to dislike. I never realized how much I hated my life until I left it. My job, my apartment, my so-called friends, dating, social networking, and every other aspect of my life that had been routine got disrupted with the one phone call I made to Uncle Phil, and now I have no desire to go back to any of it. The only thing from my past I want to keep is Gladys Knight. The weeks I spent in Canada have opened my eyes to a world I had no idea existed. I feel awakened. I have purpose now, as if living with my dad and helping him stay ahead of the authorities is what I was born to do. As strange as it sounds, Canada feels more like home than Oregon ever did.

Uncle Phil and I are heading back to Oregon to put our lives there on hold. We'll take whatever we need, including his money, and go back to Canada in a day or so. Then we'll work on finding a way for us to all go to Morocco. With their money and ingenuity, I'm sure it won't take long to figure it out.

We're just north of Seattle when Uncle Phil's truck starts making a terrible noise and running very rough. We pull off to the side of the freeway, but when we get going again, the truck won't shift out of second gear. He thinks the transmission is shot. If so, it will cost more to repair it than the truck is worth. It's almost ten at night, and there isn't anywhere to stop, so we limp down I-5 and take the first exit we come to.

We're in a suburb of Seattle, and there isn't much open at this hour. Our only choice is to walk around looking for a motel, but I have a better idea.

"Uncle Phil, why don't we just steal a car? We could take it to Portland, then dump it when we get there."

"Little girl, did you not listen to a thing your pa and I taught you? You don't go risking getting busted just so you can have fun stealing a car. I told you, street crime is nigger bullshit. Dumbass kids do that. We got enough money for a motel, then we can see about the truck in the morning. You have to be sensible and fly under the radar when you don't want attention."

"What do we have, like a hundred bucks? Seriously, that's a Motel Six and not enough for a tow truck. Or even for breakfast! Screw the truck, let the cops tow it. We can steal a car and dump it somewhere in Portland before the owner even wakes up. It's not street crime, it's a necessity. Plus, it'll be good experience for me."

Uncle Phil just shakes his head and smiles. I can tell he sees the logic in my plan and is considering it. "You're plain determined to be an outlaw, aren't you? I swear, when you got your mind set on something, you don't stop 'til you get your way. But stealing a car ain't as easy as you might think."

"I wouldn't know because you never taught me how. My dad said you taught him. So, teach *me*."

"It just so happens that I know a thing or two about it," he says. We walk back to the truck and Uncle Phil looks around until he finds a small pebble and a bigger rock.

"The easiest way to get into a locked car is to just bust a window. But you gotta be smart about it. Stupid car thieves break out a back window so they don't have to sit on broken glass. Break out the driver's window."

"I've got to buy a vowel on this one, Uncle Phil. Why's that so stupid?"

He sighs and shakes his head. "I ain't even gonna answer that. Think about it, and you tell me."

Then I picture it. "Because, who drives around with their back window down?"

"Bingo! Nobody. You get in a car and you want some air, you put your driver's window down. So, sit on the goddamn broken glass; it ain't gonna cut your ass. But again, be smart. You don't drive a car around in the rain with your window down. Same if it's freezing cold out; cops will hone right in on that. But on a night like this, it's okay. Folks always drive with windows down on nights like this. The best way to do it is to use two rocks, one big, the other small. Use the bigger rock like a hammer. Put the little pebble against the corner of the window, like this. Then, give 'er a whack with the big rock, and the window will shatter. Just remember two things. One, it's gonna be loud, like a gunshot, and two, don't worry about the noise. Most folks won't hear it, and even if someone does, they're not about to get their lazy ass up out of bed at this hour to go have a look. What's loud to you isn't loud to anyone not close to you, especially if they're indoors."

Then, he proceeds to give me the same lesson in auto theft that he gave my dad, using his truck as an example. It doesn't take long before I can rip open the underside of the steering column, locate the ignition wires and strip them with my teeth, then twist them together like a pro to start the truck.

"You got to choose your car careful," Uncle Phil says as we walk around looking for a good vehicle. "Folks'll call the cops if they see you wandering around lookin' inside of cars. So be nonchalant. Just walk down the street, taking quick glances at the ones you want. And you don't want a Cadillac, or some jacked up four wheel drive, neither. You want a crappy looking old beater nobody'll notice, especially the cops. Plus, they're a lot easier to steal. And always remember, these days everybody's got a camera, so you got to check for them before you make your move. See, look at that." He pointed to a medical office across the street. "You see 'em?"

I look where he's pointing, and after a few moments I spot them. "Yes! The little globes made out of dark glass. One, two… three! See that last one? The one on the far corner?"

"Yep, that's what I'm talkin' about. You gotta scout around, find a place that don't have none. These days, folks even got cameras on their front porch, so try to keep away from residential streets. You can't see them cameras as good as you can the commercial ones."

"Good point. I'd have never thought of that."

"You gotta learn to think of everything. And another thing. Once you steal a car, you have to drive it like a little old lady going to church. In fact, when you're on the run, you *always* drive like a old lady goin' to church. Dumbest thing you can do is get pulled over by the cops for speeding or not signaling a turn."

We walk a little farther, and finally come to a street that has no buildings on it. There are several cars parked along on one side, but no streetlights for half a block in either direction.

"This looks good," I whisper. "There aren't any cameras, and I don't even see any buildings with windows facing this way. How about one of these?"

Uncle Phil nods and says, "I'll keep a eye out. You pick one and break in like I showed you. Get the damn thing hotwired, and we'll be on our happy little way."

I choose a mid-nineties Honda Civic, and start hammering away at the window, but it won't break. "Give it a *hard* shot, dammit," grunts Uncle Phil. I haul back and wallop the little stone, and the window shatters with a loud pop, showering my hand with fragments. They land half-in and half-out of the car. I don't let the noise scare me into slowing down, and in a flash, I'm inside, sitting on the broken glass.

I chop away at the underside of the steering column using Uncle Phil's Buck knife. It takes three or four minutes, but then I rip the pieces away and pull the wires out. It takes almost five minutes of frustrating work for me to sort out and strip the wires, but then I have the car started. The whole affair takes about ten minutes, but I persevere, and get the job done.

I've stolen my first car.

Uncle Phil gets in the passenger seat and claps me on the back. "Not too bad for your first one," he says with pride. "We're turning you into a class-A bad guy."

The car has three-quarters of a tank, and I drive like an old lady all the way back to Gresham. Just after 2:00 AM, I get off I-84 at 181st, only a mile or so from Uncle Phil's place, and pass a Gresham patrol car headed in the opposite direction. I play it cool and keep my eyes on the road, but I watch him in my peripheral vision as we pass each other.

Once past me, the cop hooks a U-turn, then falls in behind us. My heart leaps to my throat. "Uncle Phil, he's following us!"

"I see him," he says calmly, eyeing the side mirror. "Just don't panic. Keep your cool and don't do a damn thing different. Keep on going in this direction, only we ain't going home as long as he's back there. That's the thing about older cars, 'specially these foreign jobbers. They're took so much, they're like a sign at this hour advertising that this is a stolen car. Just keep lookin' straight ahead and don't do nothin' different."

"But Uncle Phil, won't he run the plate and find out it's stolen?"

"Relax, darlin', we just stole the damn thing a few hours ago. Chances are the owner won't report it missing 'til at least seven or eight in the morning. It ain't in the system 'til it's reported."

The police car, a Chevy Tahoe driven by a young, bearded officer, moves into the lane to our right, then pulls adjacent to us. I look down and see that we're doing thirty-eight in a forty zone.

"Shit," Uncle Phil says, not sounding so relaxed now as the car pulls up next to us. "Watch for side streets on your left. When I say go, make a hard left onto the side street and punch it. Kill the lights at the same time, and turn onto the first street you come to. Don't touch the brake pedal. We'll make a couple of fast turns and hopefully lose him in the blocks. Then pull into the nearest driveway, and remember to stay off the goddamn brakes. Remember what you learned about using the emergency brake? It don't light up the taillights. Once we're in the driveway, kill it and take off. Dive into the bushes next to a house, and just sit tight and lay low. By then I'll be in the driver's seat with my hands up. But don't do a damn thing until I say. You got it?"

"Got it," I say, tight-lipped. My heart is racing, and I can feel the sweat coursing down my chest. I'm trembling with a mixture of fear, adrenaline, and excitement.

The cop is keeping pace with us. I can see he's on the radio. Uncle Phil says, "Grace, this ain't good. Goddamn it, I should have known better than to take a fucking Honda. These little rice-burners are the most goddamn stole car there ever was. I'm sorry, honey. None of us needs this kind of shit right now, least of all your pa. When this goes down, remember, emergency brake *only*. And as soon as we come to a stop, you get out and run like hell. Stay hid for at least an hour, then make your way to my place, bust in, and wait for me to call with instructions from jail. You got it?"

"I'm not leaving you, Uncle—"

"God damn it Grace, you'll do as you're fucking told!"

I've never heard him sound like this before. I'm no longer excited. The shit just got very real, and now I'm scared.

The officer is still abreast of us, and I instinctively know it'll be more suspicious for me to look straight ahead and pretend he's not there rather than to acknowledge him. In either case, he clearly isn't going away.

"Easy, girl," says Uncle Phil without moving his lips. "Don't even look at him."

I turn my head toward the officer.

"Grace... God damn it, don't do *nothin'*," warns Uncle Phil, his voice as taut as a guitar string. "This next left turn, coming up right here... Okay, *go now!*"

I pass the street without changing my course or speed.

"Grace, goddamn it; this ain't the time to freeze up. Shit, I shoulda been driving. Take that next left—this one, Grace!"

I turn on the interior light and wave cheerily at the officer. I even pick up Gladys Knight's paw and wave at him with it. Then I mouth the words 'thank you' and give him a thumbs-up.

"God damn it, Grace!" snarls Uncle Phil through a fake smile and a half-hearted wave at the cop.

The officer looks confused, then he smiles and waves back. He drops back, falls in behind us, then makes another U-turn and drives off in the opposite direction.

"Yeah!" I yell, pumping my fist in the air. "I knew it! No way he'd figure we were up to no good. Just a kindly old grandfather and his granddaughter getting home late. It just seemed like the right thing to do. I'm sorry I didn't listen to you, Uncle Phil."

He sucks in a tremendous lungful of air. "Jesus H. Christ little girl! I don't know whether to kick your ass for not listening to me, or kiss it for showing me up so bad. I guess it doesn't matter now, because obviously you done good. If it'd been me driving, he'd be chasing us now, and we'd no doubt get our asses busted. That was as fine a demonstration of staying cool and thinking on your feet as I ever seen. Gracie, my dear, I believe you just passed your final exam! You're a bona-fide criminal now, and giving *me* lessons on how to do it! I have to tell you, I am duly impressed!"

I feel myself getting flushed with excitement. Heartfelt praise coming from a man like Uncle Phil is the best positive feedback I can imagine. "I'm just doing what you've already taught me, Uncle Phil. Remember what you said? The police aren't the enemy. They're the good guys."

"Yeah, but... Well shit. You're a hell of a good learner, little girl."

We dump the car in a manufactured home park, wipe it clean of fingerprints, then cut through a field back to 181st Avenue. From there, it's a three-minute walk to Uncle Phil's place on a dead-end street off

Burnside in the middle of Rockwood, the "other side of the tracks" part of Gresham.

Nothing has been disturbed at his place, despite that we've been gone for over a month. My car is still in the garage where I'd left it. "You ought to just stay here and crash on the couch," Uncle Phil says. "There isn't much I got to do to close up shop. It won't take me but a couple of hours. In the morning, we'll take your car, and I'll drop you off at your place in Clackamas so's you can do what you need to do. While you're doing that, I'll go take care of my business, which is down in Woodburn. I'll pick you up when I'm done, which should be right around noon. If you can wrap up your business quick-like, we could hit the road by midafternoon tomorrow and be back in Canada by the next morning. How's that sound?"

"Uncle Phil, the last thing I want to do is hold us up, but there's no way I can do everything by then. I have an apartment full of stuff. I've got to make arrangements to store it all somewhere, then find people to help me move. I have to pack up the things I'll need in Canada, then box everything else up for storage. God, I don't even have any boxes! I have to give them a move-out notice, schedule an inspection, cancel the utilities… Shit, they're gonna keep my security deposit, and the broken lease will go on my rental history. I guess that's a small price to pay for getting my dad back, but still. Uncle Phil, it's all so overwhelming, I don't know what to do! Why can't I just leave it all and walk away? Let them deal with it."

"Quit panicking, Grace. If you just walked away from it, what will that tell the authorities?"

"That I've found my father. You're right. But how am I supposed to do everything I need to?"

Uncle Phil shakes his head and says, "And here I thought you were a hardened criminal! Je-zooey little girl, if you're gonna get your panties up in a bunch about something small like this, how are you going to make it on the dark side, where the problems are actually real? Your pa and me have been trying to teach you to think through this kind of crap one step at a time; you don't try to solve every goddamn thing all at once. Now take a breath and think about it. What do you gotta do first?"

"Um, the biggest thing is taking care of my stuff. I'll need to find a place to store it all. But any storage place will require a down payment, which I don't have, but I suppose I could put it on my credit card."

"Okay, now at least you're thinking rational. What next?"

"Well, moving it all, I guess. Actually, one of my co-worker's boyfriend has a truck, and I know they'd be willing to help me move, so I could ask them. As for the notice, I can call Cyndi, the rental manager, and tell them I have a family emergency and have to break the lease. I won't say anything about Canada. In fact, I can pull that trick you taught my dad. I'll tell them that I have to move to Phoenix on super-short notice. That way, if the police every come asking, they'll be pointed in the wrong direction. Cyndi's cool; she'll write me a lease exception, and I won't have to pay the fine. As for the utility companies, I have a list them all on my desk, and I can just email them to cancel services... I guess there really isn't all that much to worry about when I consider everything individually."

"That's my little criminal! Work the problem. Find the solution. When you feel yourself panicking, you have to stop, slow things down, and think. Break big problems up into individual segments and work through each one."

"But there's no way I can do this all in a day, Uncle Phil. Maybe three if everyone can help."

"You're right, but at least you see it ain't insurmountable. Just remember to take things one step at a time."

"Sorry about acting like a little girl, Uncle Phil. But the fact is, I can't do it all without your help. I don't have enough money. Would you be willing to help me?"

"Glad you finally worked your way down to the real solution to your problem. Asking me for help is the conclusion I was hoping you'd come to, because money is something I happen to have plenty of. So, let's just do this. Instead of worrying your pretty little head off about getting out of your lease and moving, just set everything up so's you can pay it online. Rent, phone bill, gas, electric—all of it. That way, we'll just keep paying it, and nobody will even notice you ain't here. Next month, you'll give proper notice that you're moving, say at the end of October, and we'll come back and have movers put it all in storage. That way, we're not in a hurry, and you can get everything tied up nice and legal. All you gotta do now is go home, make those arrangements, which I bet you know how to do on the computer, and grab the shit you need for Canada, and we'll be on the road tomorrow afternoon. No loose ends and no worries. How's that sound?"

For the first time, I jump up and wrap my arms around my uncle. "Oh Uncle Phil, you're a lifesaver! I already pay everything online! What a generous thing! But are you sure you can afford it? It'll take me a long time to pay you back. I mean, I'll definitely get a job in Vancouver, and I can make payments."

Uncomfortable with the contact, he pats me hesitantly on the back, then peels my arms from around his neck. "Jesus, little girl, quit your yapping, will ya? You're driving me crazy. I wouldn't have suggested it if I couldn't afford it, and you don't have to pay me back. My money's *family* money. Besides, you found us your pa, so I'd say you've earned it."

"I don't know what to say."

"Don't say nothing; it's already done. Now come with me, I got something important to show you." He leads me to the spare room. In the closet, there is a full-size gun safe.

"I don't need one this big, but I got it because it weighs way too much for anyone to even try to get it outta here. I had to pour a concrete pad and have the wall partially dismantled just to get it in. Now listen up, and write this down in that sharp little mind of yours, but not on paper. The combination is 14-17-30-2. Right, left, right, left. Got it? 14-17-30-2. Memorize it."

I commit it to memory, associating the first two numbers to significant events I can easily remember in my life at those ages, and the last two numbers to the age I want to be when I have my first child and the number of children I want.

Uncle Phil dials the combination and swings the door open. Inside is a red pull-along hard-shell suitcase. There is also a pistol and an assault rifle. Both guns have several magazines full of bullets. The rounds for the rifle are thin, and seem ridiculously long compared to the ones in my dad's gun.

"You can probably guess what's in the suitcase, and no, we're not bringing the damn rifle. Next time we come down here, I'll teach you how to shoot it, but I'm not about to try to cross an international border with an AR-15. I'm an ex-con, and as such, I'm not allowed to have firearms of any kind. My ass'll be back the joint the moment they ever catch me with one. The pistol's a lot easier to hide, and we can smuggle that across no problem. It's a Sig Sauer by the way, which is different from your Pa's Glock, mostly because it's got a safety. I have a silencer for it too, but don't be fooled by the name. A silencer sure as hell don't make it silent, but it does make it quieter."

"They're beautiful guns, Uncle Phil. I'd really love to learn to shoot that rifle."

"Not now, little girl. We got no use for a rifle like that. We're trying to stay out of view of the authorities, not go to war with them. Hell, I got no use for the pistol either, but carrying this kind of money, I think it's prudent to keep the damn thing."

I open the suitcase. It's filled to the brim with cash. "Oh my God!"

"I don't even know how much there is, but it's well north of a hundred grand," he says. "No more than one-fifty, but probably not quite that much. It's all I got left. I don't use it though. I just live off of my social security. Everything I got's paid for. I keep this in reserve for your old man. It's coming with us."

"How are we going to get it across the border?"

"The Sig will go in the suitcase with the money. Sometimes it's easier to just hide in plain sight. I figure we'll just stick it with the rest of the luggage in the trunk of the car, and cross with the morning commuters. They'll be a lot less likely to do searches then, and like you just proved, we don't fit the profile for criminals."

Uncle Phil is like a magician. He swoops in when things get so difficult it's hard to see my way through, makes me work it all out so I'm capable of doing what I need to. Then he provides a way out so I don't have to do anything at all. He's a shrewd and capable teacher. He and my father are the most well-equipped men I can think of to school me in the ways of the real world. There's nobody I'd rather have as mentors in my life, regardless of which side I'm on, than them.

I sleep for a few hours on his couch. When we get up, we walk to a nearby Shari's for breakfast. Because of Uncle Phil's generosity, all I have to do now is pack the stuff I'll need for the next couple of months. It should only take an hour, and I'm excited to get back on the road.

Another lesson I've learned: Having a little money makes things a hell of a lot easier.

Chapter 9

Driving my car, Uncle Phil drops Gladys Knight and me off at the apartment at 8:30 in the morning. Gladys Knight is clearly happy to be home, but for me, coming here is like going back into your elementary school for the first time as an adult. Everything is much smaller and more insignificant than the way you remember it. Even though I've only been gone a month, this has now become a place from my past. It's my apartment and it's full of my things, but it's like visiting a memory. The place hasn't changed, I have.

I turn my attention to packing my things. As a girl, I'm relatively disappointing. It's not that I'm not feminine; I just wear my femininity in a more practical way than most girls. I know how to apply makeup, but I rarely use anything other than lipstick. I don't shower every day; instead, I have a keen nose, and when anything begins to smell, then I bathe. It's usually every other day, but I stay clean. I can't remember the last time I used perfume. I think I smell good naturally. So girly stuff is one less thing I have to worry about.

I have the usual feminine knickknacks, and a ton of old stuffed animals from my childhood, but I can walk away from all of that and never see it again, and I would never know the difference. I am a bit of a clothes horse though, and sorting what to bring and what to leave will occupy most of the time until Uncle Phil gets here.

I'm not a clean freak, and some of what I want to bring is dirty, so I start a load of laundry. I'm in the process of throwing away perishables from the fridge when Uncle Phil knocks on the door, sending Gladys Knight into a frenzy. I can't believe how fast the time has passed. I look at the clock and see he's almost half an hour early. I'm simply not ready to go yet.

A man like Uncle Phil isn't going to be happy about having to wait for a woman to do her laundry. This bothers me more than it should, because it isn't my fault, and I want him to be impressed with everything about me.

Sheepishly, I open the door, wiping my hands on my pants. Instead of Uncle Phil, however, there are two guys who look like bikers standing there. The taller of the two is over six feet and heavyset. He's probably a little older than my dad, has long hair that's half-brown and half-gray and a long, thick, graying beard. The other guy is maybe two inches shorter; thin and wiry, and has a heavy mustache crawling down past the corners of his mouth to the bottom of his chin, and a soul patch under the middle of his lower lip.

It doesn't take a criminal genius to see these guys are trouble. I try to slam the door on them, but the big guy hits it with his shoulder like a football player. As it explodes in on me, I see a fist coming my way, getting bigger. I never even get the chance to put my hands up.

My head explodes in a bright stab of pain. The blow jerks my vision around like special effects in a bad movie, and I fall backwards into my living room, seeing black. I hear Gladys Knight growling and snarling, and I know she's latched onto a leg, but she then gives a hideous cry of pain, and I hear her claws retreating down the hallway.

By the time the picture clears, they are standing over me and the door is closed. The guy with the soul patch places a heavy motorcycle boot on my abdomen, pinning me to the floor, while the hairy one peers toward the back of my apartment. He now has a pistol in his hand.

My thoughts and perceptions take several moments to unscramble. I've never been punched before, not even by a girl, let alone a biker, and the pain is blinding. My jaw feels out of place and doesn't seem to line up right when I close it. Running my tongue along the inside of my mouth, I can feel that my lips are torn and bleeding on the inside where they were mashed against my teeth by his fist. I can also feel them swelling. But my biggest concern is Gladys Knight. They better not have hurt my dog.

It takes a good five seconds for my mind and my vision to align, and when they do, I see a third guy stepping into the living room from the kitchen. This one is short, stocky, and bald, and is covered from the crown of his head to the backs of his hands with tattoos. He must have come in through the patio door at the same time these two entered the front.

"He ain't here," says Baldy. "I checked the whole place."

Hairy gives me a contemptible look and says, "Well, shit. I bet *she* knows where he is." He bends down, grabs me by the hair, and roughly yanks me to my feet. He then pushes me down into a kitchen chair and pulls another one up facing it. He sits down opposite me, staring me down with eyes as flat and lifeless as a shark's.

"Where's your old man at?"

I still don't get it. All I can think of is that these guys are some kind of skip tracers trying to arrest my father for the reward money. Clearly, they aren't cops.

When I don't answer him, Hairy slaps me across the face, causing my head to ring like a bell. The pain, sharp and stinging, brings tears to my eyes.

He speaks patiently and slowly. "I said, where's your old man at?"

"Who are you?" I mumble, trying to buy time to think.

He doesn't answer me. Instead, he punches me directly in the nose. My chair falls over backwards.

I wake up on the floor. I've only been out a a few seconds, but I can see in my peripheral vision that my nose is swelling and split at the top. I'm certain that it's broken. The pain is blinding. There is no sign of Gladys Knight, and I hope she remains hidden, wherever she is.

Baldy is smoking a cigarette. Obviously I'm not thinking straight, because my first thought is is how strict the apartment complex is about smoking. I could get kicked out if someone complains.

Slowly, my mind begins working right, and then it hits me. These guys aren't bounty hunters. They're from the European Kindred, the white supremacist prison gang my dad joined in the penitentiary. I recall quite vividly the story about how he betrayed them, exposing their plot to kill a prison guard, and how they in turn tried to assassinate him at the hospital. They killed the guard watching him, and in the confusion, my dad was able to escape. Obviously, they've come to finish the job.

I resolve not to tell them a thing, regardless of what they do to me. Then I think of all they *can* do to me. My dad said he fears this gang far more than he fears the police. They have no boundaries, and are accountable to no one. I have to strain to hold my bladder as I feel my resolve weaken. I don't know if I could hold up to rape or torture.

Suddenly, all the "training" from Uncle Phil and my father seems like storybook adventure time. What good can Uncle Phil's advice do me now?

Take out the two toughest guys? I can't even move now. How am I supposed to...

Uncle Phil! He's supposed to pick me up at noon! How long until he gets here? Carefully, I open my eyes and try to look at the clock on the stove.

"Well, look who's awake," says Hairy. Baldy and Soul Patch are next to him, and all are looking at me. I feel blood dripping from my nose onto the front of my blouse. I can't see it because the swelling under my left eye is forcing it shut.

Hairy, who is clearly the one in charge, very calmly states, "We need to find your father, and you're going to tell us where he is. If you don't, then we're going to have to really hurt you. Understand?"

I pretend to zone out from the pain.

Hairy and Baldy are looking at me like I'm a specimen on display, but Soul Patch has a different expression on his face. It is both hungry and lascivious, and from his eyes I know exactly what is on his mind. He can barely wait. Hairy sees me reading his face and says, "Looks like you and Kickstart are making eyes at each other. Is that what you want? I bet he'd like the opportunity to make you feel appreciated."

How I wish I were half the girl Uncle Phil thinks I am. I want to say something brave and defiant, like *in your dreams, asshole*, or even a simple *fuck you*, but the truth is, I'm way too frightened to say anything, and these men can do anything they want with me. I just pray that nothing they do will force me to tell them anything about my father. The dread is in knowing what they will do. Unconsciously, I clamp my thighs together.

Hairy looks at me patiently and says, "Now one last time. Where's your old man at?"

"I... I don't know. I never visited him. I... I don't want anything to do with him. Not after what he did."

"Really? Well then, why don't you tell me where you've been the past month?"

I close my eyes. Obviously, they've been watching my place. "Helping the Canadian police. Trying to find him... They tracked him to Fort Frances. In Ontario." I say with dramatic resignation. "That's where he crossed. Back... to the States."

Hairy looks at the others and says, "That's good, but you don't look like the type that would give it up that easy. You're lying to me, aren't you, Grace?"

"No. That's all I know, I swear. I can't give you what I don't know!"

He shrugs his shoulders and gets up. "Fine. We'll try it another way."

My heart starts thumping, and suddenly I have to pee so bad I'm not sure I can hold it. But instead of approaching me, he turns and heads down the hall.

I don't know what he's doing, but it's more intimidating than having him here overtly threatening me. I want to scream, to get the attention of someone in the surrounding apartments, but I know that my upstairs neighbors work, and the apartment next to me is rented by three students, all of whom go to school during the day. My garage is below us, so a scream won't do anything but get me more hurt.

Soul Patch moves closer to me until he's sitting right next to me. His arm is touching mine. The miasma radiating from him is nauseating and overpowering. It's a combination of body odor, stale alcohol, and the stench of dead cigarettes.

Hairy comes back in, and to my horror, I see that he is now holding Gladys Knight. Oh God, no. Not my dog! The poor thing is trembling, and her tail is tight against her belly.

"Please don't hurt my dog," I beg, tears now streaming down my face. I haven't cried during this entire episode so far, but I can't take the idea of him hurting Gladys Knight.

He's cradling her gently, trying to soothe her, but she's trembling and is clearly terrified. She turns her pleading eyes on me, but there's nothing I can do. I've never seen her like this before. Her normal reaction to fear is aggression.

Hairy says in a friendly, inquisitive tone, "You got a real cute dog here. What's his name?"

"She's a girl," I respond. "Her name is Gladys Knight."

He looks at me like I've said the wrong thing. "No shit? You name her that 'cause she's black?" he asks with genuine curiosity.

"No. Because she reminds me of one of her songs."

"Yeah? Their music isn't bad. I don't like coon-tune rap though, just the rhythm and blues stuff. Stinger, what'd they call that nigger shit from the 70's?"

Baldy says, "Uh, Motown?"

I make a mental note. Hairy is in charge, and Stinger is his number two. Obviously Soul Patch is the pawn, but he's the one I fear the most. I can feel his hunger for me.

"Yeah, that's it. Some of that shit is okay. Which song?"

I glance quickly at Soul Patch. He's leering at me, and I immediately look away. Hairy's still petting Gladys Knight, waiting for me to answer. "Please," I beg, "*Please* don't hurt her. She's scared. Please give her to me. Please?"

Just then, a knock at the door startles us all into silence. Uncle Phil!

Hairy's hand goes around Gladys Knight's throat, and he whispers, "Not a fucking sound."

I obey, not because he has Gladys Knight, but because I don't want Uncle Phil coming in here. Even together, we have no chance against these men.

Hairy says, "Stinger, who is it?"

Baldy goes to the door and peeks through the peephole. "I don't know. Some crusty old fuck."

Hairy looks from me to Gladys Knight and back, then says, "Who is he?"

"P-probably my neighbor," I stammer.

"If you make a sound, you'll watch your dog will die. It's up to you, Grace."

I will Uncle Phil to just go away.

He knocks again, and we hear a muffled, "Grace? It's me."

I close my eyes. There's a long pause, then we hear him going down the stairs.

A full thirty seconds go by, and then Hairy says, "Which one does she remind you of?"

"What?"

"You named your dog Roberta Flack or whatever because she reminds you of a song. Which song?"

I hate it that he's not brassy and vulgar. His subdued manner is more threatening than cursing and yelling. I say, "It was Gladys Knight. The song is *You're the Best Thing That Ever Happened to Me*."

"Why do you like that song so much?"

"Please, don't hurt her. She's just a little dog." Tears are coming down my face, because I know he's about to do something awful.

"I asked you why. If you're aren't straight with me, I won't just hurt her, I'll kill her."

"Because I got her after my dad got arrested. It was the worst time of my life, and I needed to have someone to love. She literally was the best thing that ever happened to me."

"Now see, I get that. You lost a person you loved, and you got a dog to compensate. That's really moving. Really tender. But now it's time. Tell me where your father is. For real this time, Grace. For *her*," he adds, indicating Gladys Knight.

In the moment of silence that follows, I think of a video I once saw, where a dozen cops were chasing a deer through town. The police could never get too close to it because it was so fast and nimble. Finally, they got it cornered on a basketball court where two brick walls met. The deer stopped, turned in a slow circle as the cordon of men closed around it, then just stood there and let them put ropes over its antlers. As they led it away, its tongue was hanging out. Not because it was tired, but because it was afraid.

In this brief pause, I'm no different than the deer. I'm painted into a corner, utterly powerless to prevent anyone—myself, my father, or Gladys Knight—from getting hurt. Every option I take will end up badly, and there's not a thing I can do about it.

And then, like the deer and its tongue, Gladys Knight's bladder lets go. I know at this moment that she's a goner, and before I can say another word, Hairy forces her right front leg over her head until the bone snaps. Gladys Knight yelps in pain and yips and whines without stopping. It is the most dreadful sound I've ever heard.

"*No!*" I scream, as sobs wrack my body. "Please, no more!"

Hairy grabs her left front leg and says, "Where is he, Grace?"

Through my sobs, I choke out, "Toronto! Don't break her leg, please! He's living in someone's basement and working at a nursing home as a janitor. That's all I know. Oh please, don't hurt her any more!"

"I don't believe you." He snaps the other leg, and I lunge at him, but Soul Patch locks his arms around me so I can't move.

Gladys Knight, her front legs now ruined, has had enough. No longer docile, she sinks her front teeth into the meat of Hairy's hand, shaking her head violently, tearing the skin and opening a painful gash.

Hairy sweeps her to the floor like a mosquito. Pitifully, she tries to get up on useless legs making that awful noise, but her cries are cut short as Hairy punts her like a football with his heavy boot. The hollow thud of the kick and the sound of her striking the wall will stay with me forever. She collapses unmoving to the floor, and I am happy that she is out of her misery.

Hairy's hand has a long, jagged wound where she bit him, and I am proud of Gladys Knight's constitution. She fought him to the bitter end. Hairy covers the wound with a dirty hand and says, "Fine. We'll do it Ratt's way. Grace, we're gonna take a little ride to our place. Once your old man gets wind of this, he'll come to us. In the meantime, I'm sure Kickstart and the rest of the boys will keep you pretty busy. I hope you're good at sucking cock, because they can get a little rough if you're not."

He addresses the other two. "Stinger, go get the van. And Kicky, I know you've been waiting patiently for a month. Well, she's ours now, so you can break her in. Have at it, brother."

Soul Patch, with that disgusting lear, doesn't hesitate. He grabs the lapel of my blouse and rips it open, then literally tears my bra off, breaking the snap in the back.

I knew it would come down to this. That innate sense of vulnerability all women feel when alone in close quarters with a strange man has been smoldering in me since they burst in. But they're not getting it for free. Like Uncle Phil and Gladys Knight taught me, it's going to cost them.

Channeling Uncle Phil, I make my hand into a stiff wedge, and strike for Soul Patch's throat. He sees it coming and easily sidesteps out of range. He then punches me in the face, and I go to the ground. Before I can recover, his knee is in my stomach, and all I can do is hit him futilely on his sides and back. Laughing, he doesn't even try to stop me. He unbuckles my belt and drags both my pants and panties down. I try to scream, but I can't even breathe. The more I fight him, the more excited he gets.

He half tears, half pulls his pants down. His orgasm is already starting as he tries to push his way into me. Even though I can't breathe, I squeeze my thighs together with everything I have left in me. Desperately, he tries to force his weakening erection into me as he finishes early. My only goal at this moment is to deny him full entry, even if it costs me my life, but I fail even at that.

During his first desperate thrusts, the door flies off its hinges with a splintering crack, and one of the vertical sections of the jamb bounces off Soul Patch's back. Suddenly, Uncle Phil is in the room, swinging a garden hoe like a battle axe. A blow to the head knocks Soul Patch off me. Hairy is up and moving toward him, but Uncle Phil has enough time to swing the hoe with everything he has. The blade bites deep into Hairy's stomach like an axe biting into a tree trunk. As Uncle Phil struggles to wiggle it free, Baldy flies at him with a knife, and buries the blade in the back of Uncle Phil's neck, just above the spine. My beloved uncle drops like a stringless marionette, the expression of rage on his face making him look like a demon.

My screams are cut short by something hitting me in the head, and then there is only silent, white light.

Chapter 10

Being thrown roughly onto a hard surface jars me into semi-consciousness. My first coherent thought is that I am hurt. Slowly, my senses begin to unscramble, and pain cuts through the fog. Next is the sensation that I am naked, and with that, everything comes flooding back, from Gladys Knight, to the rape, to Uncle Phil's death.

I have so much to mourn, I don't know where to start. I know I've taken a very hard blow to the head. I know I probably have a concussion. I force my eyes open, but my vision is blurry. I am lying in the back of what looks like a cargo van. There are no seats, only a metal floor covered by a dirty moving pad. I'm not tied up, but I am so weak I can barely move.

Hairy is in here with me. He is still alive, but his stomach has been gored open by the hoe and his guts are hanging out. A section of his intestines has been disinterred and ripped open, and blood-laced shit is pooling in the open cavity of his belly. Flakes of debris are stuck to his intestines, and his dirty hands are clutching the pile, unsuccessfully trying to hold it all in place. His skin is pale and sweaty, and his eyes are locked on mine. They are bright with hatred and pain. The other two are nowhere to be seen.

After a moment, the Baldy gets in the driver's seat and we are speeding away. Hairy and I roll around the floor like loose cargo, which not only hurts, but also gets me covered with his blood.

I curl up into a ball and struggle to get my pants up. My thighs are sticky and smeared, and I gag at the thought of what it is. I've never had unwanted sex, or been hurt during sex before, but I'm hurt now. I get my pants up, but I cannot close my blouse; the buttons are all gone, as is my bra. I pray that the police see us driving recklessly and stop us.

What Hairy said when he ordered Soul Patch to rape me is not lost on me. Somebody named Ratt has ordered them to take me back to their clubhouse to be held as bait for my father. While they wait for him, they will pass me around like a sex doll. The thought of it makes me want to find a way to kill myself.

When I was in high school, word went around that one of the girls on the swim team had been raped at a party. The whole team signed a get well card and sent it to her in the hospital. When I saw her next, I didn't know what to say, so I just acted as though nothing had happened. No matter how hard I tried to think of her as just Jill, all I thought of when I saw her was that she was a rape victim. That became her new identity to me. Even though I knew her before, I didn't know her after.

Now, *I'm* that girl. Rape isn't defined by any particular act that happens to you. It occurs when your choice to participate is removed; when your ability to say no is gone. The effects of it will never leave you, but the fact that you are a victim of rape doesn't mean you have to view yourself as a victim. There's nothing that says you have to *act* like a victim.

As Hairy and I roll around on the floor, my mind goes back Gladys Knight. Her bladder let go because she instinctively knew what was coming when Harry got ahold of her. She was terrified, but once he hurt her, she decided she wasn't going to have any more of it. That's the moment she found herself on top of the hill worth dying over, and that's the moment when she fought back. Despite insurmountable odds, she resisted with everything she had, and it cost her her life, but not before she'd given Hairy a fight he won't soon forget.

Which, I suddenly realized, is exactly what Uncle Phil had done. When I didn't answer the door, he knew something was wrong. He had more street smarts than anyone I've ever met. I'm sure he knew exactly who was there, and why. He went down the stairs, not to leave, but to arm himself with the first thing he could find—the garden hoe—and against all odds, he unleashed hell on the people who were holding me. He did exactly as he taught me to do against multiple aggressors; he went after the two strongest ones. *I* was Uncle Phil's hill worth dying over.

Now I'm on the hill. Can I give them a fight they won't soon forget, or will I just be another victim? Can I do what Uncle Phil, and even Gladys Knight, did?

I can, and I will. I am an Appleby, cut from the same cloth as Uncle Phil and my father. I may be raped, kidnapped, and hurt, but I am not powerless. I am smaller and weaker than my enemies, but I am not nothing. Not by a long shot. And they have underestimated me. They did not bother to bind me. They have mistaken me for insignificant, and that mistake will come back on them.

I will fight them however I can with whatever I can find. I will take vengeance for what they did to Gladys Knight, to Uncle Phil, and to my father. If I die trying, so be it. At least I will have died well. But even if that happens, the fight will not be over. There is still another. Someone who is not weak and small. When my father finds out what these men have done, he will make them wish they had never heard of the Applebys.

Hairy's eyes have never left mine; not even when he broke Gladys Knight's legs. His hands are still clutching his intestines, his eyes still unwaveringly locked on my own. It is hard not to be intimidated by that animalistic stare, but the sights and sounds of his cruelty to Gladys Knight bubble to the surface, and boiling rage begins to overpower his intimidation.

"Hang in there, Skid," Baldy yells. "Kicky's gonna meet us at the mall, and we'll take off in his truck. Just don't fuckin' die on me, man."

Hairy makes no reply. His flat, sharklike eyes remain locked on mine.

I make an effort to control my anger. I can't just react; I have to think through the problem. I allow my rage to infuse my muscles with strength. Uncle Phil and my father haven't been training me to be a criminal; they've been training me to be a survivor. A warrior. To think my way out of situations like this. To fight through the pain, and move in ways that aren't expected.

I take another, more critical look at Hairy. He's lying on his side clutching his eviscerated guts, trying to intimidate me with his stare. I study his body, looking for a way to exploit his weakness and cause him more pain, and that's when I see it. A metal clip in the corner of his pants pocket.

Of course. These are men who favor knives. I remember too clearly the efficiency of Baldy's knife as it slid into Uncle Phil's neck. Well, I can be efficient, too. Their love of knives will be their end. Fueled by hatred and vengefulness, I lash out and snatch the knife from his pocket. It has a thumb latch, and the blade swings neatly open and locks into place when I push it.

Hairy's gaze flickers to the knife, and when he looks back at me, there is fear in his eyes. He lets go of his guts, weakly raising his arms as if to ward me off, but it is too late to change what is already in motion.

I strike like a snake, imagining his neck a foot farther away than it actually is. The blade enters just behind his throat, and I drive it in to the hilt. His eyes open impossibly wide and his hands wrap around my own. I jerk the blade toward me, intending to open his throat, but it's like trying to saw through dried leather, and I can't. Instead, I pull it out, and it is followed by a rhythmic jet of pulsing, hot blood. His last breath is nothing more than a gurgle.

"You shouldn't have killed my dog," I whisper in his ear. It is the last thing he hears. His eyes roll up, showing only the whites, then he shudders and remains still.

One down, and one to go.

I work my way over Hairy's body and crouch just behind the driver's seat. Entirely unaware of what is in store for him, Baldy concentrates on his driving. We are in the back parking lot of the Clackamas Town Center mall. Baldy is no doubt hoping to bury the van in a sea of cars until Soul Patch can get here. He pulls into an empty parking space far away from the buildings.

As he puts it in park, I rise up behind him like the angel of death, and plunge the knife deep into his ear with every ounce of strength I have. He goes instantly rigid.

"That's for Uncle Phil," I whisper as his soul leaves his body.

As fast as it started, the action is over. Hardly believing the turn of events, I survey the carnage of the van. From somewhere deep within me, a primal scream erupts. With it comes a river of pent-up rage and adrenaline.

I am woman. Hear me roar.

As the van returns to sepulchral silence, I, too, deflate. I suddenly become aware of how badly I am hurt. My head is ringing and my senses are dulled. My thoughts are muddled and slow. There is a frighteningly large, swollen lump at the base of my skull. My hair is matted with blood, my nose is broken, and my lips and eyes are swollen. Two teeth are loose. The inside of my mouth feels like so much shredded meat. My blouse, bloodstained and missing all the buttons, hangs open, exposing my breasts, which are streaked with the blood of a man I have just killed. Most horribly, my worst fear has become reality. I've been raped.

But I won. The hill is now mine.

Suddenly, I am desperate to be out of this horror show. As I'm about to get out, a cell phone on the console begins to ring. The screen says it's a call from Kickstart. I let it ring until it stops. He must be close, and is probably calling to find out where we are. I need to be gone before he gets here.

Then I realize what I am holding. A phone! I think of how I felt when the police car turned the corner and rescued me from those hoods in Vancouver. I am three digits away from salvation.

I dial 9 and 1, but before I can dial the second 1, I stop. The police have no doubt already discovered Uncle Phil's body in my apartment. I can still hear the sirens. If I call them, I will be saved, but then I will have to explain what happened, and why Uncle Phil was there, and why these men did what they did. And once I do that, the focus of everything will change. The spotlight will turn back to my father. They will backtrack my movements and see that Uncle Phil and I were in Canada for four weeks. They will know that we found him, and will press me to reveal what I know. They will threaten to charge me with helping him. They will find some way to track where I have been, and then they will catch him.

If my father and Uncle Phil taught me anything, it's to rely on my gut feelings, and do what I inherently know to be right, and I know to stay away from the police right now. I would rather be the sex slave of the European Kindred than be responsible, even remotely, for my father's capture.

If I can't turn to the police, then it is up to me to rescue myself. And the first thing I need to do is get away before Soul Patch gets here.

My mind is once again functioning. I take Baldy's knife, the one he used to kill Uncle Phil. I also take the pistol from the back of Hairy's waistband. It is smaller than my father's Glock. Stamped on the slide is the word Taurus. I examine it quickly and discover a safety switch on the left side. Again, I silently thank Uncle Phil, this time for showing me what that little switch is. I shove the gun into my own waistband.

Feeling like death warmed over, I open the door and step out into bright sunshine.

Chapter 11

I can't be seen in this condition or people will call the police. I have to find a way out of here. I have to get to my father, but before I leave, I have go to Uncle Phil's house and get the suitcase in his gun safe. It's all that's left of him, and my father will need it. But I must hurry. Uncle Phil is lying dead on my living room floor, and once they figure out who he is, they will go to his house to investigate. The suitcase and I need to be gone by then.

Obviously, I cannot take this van. I'm sure the police have a description of it and will be looking for it. As loud as the disturbance was in my apartment was, a dozen people have probably called 911.

Thirty feet away is an early 2000's Toyota Camry. It represents Canada and my father. All I have to do is steal it, and I can be on my way to an outlaw life in Canada with him. To the dark side.

A Clackamas County Sheriff's deputy is slowly cruising the parking lot not too far away. He represents my old life and a clean future, but one without my dad. All I have to do is flag him down to stay on the light side. If I do, I won't go to prison. Eventually, I'll probably marry and have kids. Maybe I'll even be normal. But I'll lose my father.

Once again I'm at a major crossroads in my life. I have a clear choice to make, and I must make it right now. The light side, or the dark side. Everything I have done so far, I've done of necessity, and I'm guilty of no crime other than helping my dad in Canada. But what I do now will impact me for the rest of my life. Where I will be in five years, ten years, forty years, hinges on what I do next. If I choose the dark side, they won't just be looking for my father; they'll be looking for me too, and when they find me, I will go to jail.

With no more hesitation, I try the door of the Toyota, finding it unlocked. I jump in, and begin chopping away at the underside of the steering column with Hairy's knife. Much faster than I did in Seattle, I get the wires out, sorted through, and twisted together, and the engine starts as smoothly as if I'd used a key.

As I pull out of the lot, one of the police cars stops behind the van. Its overhead lights come on, and numerous other police cars converge on it from all directions. I don't envy them for what they are about to see.

Calmly, driving like an old lady on her way to church, I leave the lot, pulling out onto Sunnyside Road. Moments later, I'm safely headed up I-205 on my way to Gresham. Along the way I look in the glove box and find a cheap pair of Dollar Tree sunglasses. They're perfect, considering my swollen, black eyes. I drive directly to Uncle Phil's house.

There's nothing going on when I arrive. No police, no bad guys, nothing. I want to be in and out before they get the around to coming here. I park the stolen Toyota boldly in the driveway, not having time to waste trying to be stealthy. I go to the back door, and with the butt of Hairy's gun, break the glass and go in, relying on what Uncle Phil said about how people don't listen or care about noises.

The police will have already identified me as the tenant of the apartment and the kidnap victim. I am equally certain that if they haven't already associated me and Uncle Phil with my father, they will very shortly, and this whole thing will go off in an entirely new direction. I already know they've found the van, and since I'm not in it, they are probably assuming Soul Patch killed Hairy and Baldy and took me away. Obviously, they won't think that I did it; otherwise, I would have called the police. Any real victim would.

I go directly to the safe in the closet of the spare room where, to my horror, discover I can't remember the combination. Uncle Phil told me to commit it to memory, but my mind is blank. It's four numbers, and starts with a turn to the right. That's all I can remember.

Frantically, I wrack my brain, but I just can't come up with it. Frustration overtakes me, and I begin to panic. Tears spring to my eyes. I instantly quell them, vowing not to go into little girl mode. I can cry all I want later on when there's time. Right now, I have to think. I have to remember the combination. I leave the spare room and go to Uncle Phil's bedroom, hoping that if I take my mind off it, I might remember.

His room is surprisingly neat. I had envisioned the bed being a mess, with dirty clothes strewn everywhere, maybe a rack of porno DVDs by the TV. I'm kind of pleased to see that the bed is made and the dresser is full of clean, folded clothes. I rummage through them, not expecting to find a scrap of paper labeled 'safe combo,' but hoping nonetheless.

I'm desperate to clean myself up, to wash out every last vestige of the disgusting animal who raped me. Uncle Phil isn't too much bigger than me, and his clothes are clean. I select two pairs of his underwear, two pairs of black socks, and a couple of T-shirts from his dresser. I take off my bloody blouse, clean myself up using a wet washcloth, and put on a black T-shirt that says 'CSN&Y.' I think it stands for a railroad.

In the closet I find a pair of dark blue sweat pants, which I also take. In the kitchen, I put the washcloth and my blouse in one trash bag, and the rest of the clean clothes in another.

What I really want is a shower and a gallon of Summer's Eve. I want to scrub myself out with a wire brush and fill myself up with hand sanitizer. The pain would be worth it. I look longingly at the shower, but I know I don't have enough time, so I pass it by. Now, for the first time, a new horror occurs to me. What if Soul Patch made me pregnant? I know he came early, but he still penetrated me and I know at least some of it got in me. I can't imagine having a baby fathered by a monster like him…

A baby! That's it! I memorized the combination using events in my life, and those are the last two numbers—30 for the age I wanted be when I had kids, and 2 for the number of kids I planned to have! From there remembering the other two numbers is easy. The first number is 14, how old I was when I received my first kiss, and the second is 17, how old I was when I got my driver's license. That's it, 14-17-30-2. Right, left, right, left.

I run to the guest room and dial the combination. The bolts release with a solid *clack*, and the door swings slowly open. The red suitcase is still there, as are the weapons and spare magazines. The assault rifle has three magazines—all loaded—and the pistol, which looks a hell of a lot like the one I took from Hairy, has another three, plus a metal tube, which must be the silencer.

I pull the suitcase out. It's heavier than I thought it would be, full of Uncle Phil's cash. I send a silent thank-you to him.

This triggers a wave of initial grief, and I break down in tears. I don't just cry for Uncle Phil. I cry for my father and everything he's been through, and for the dark days he spent thinking his life was over because I failed him.

I weep as much for myself as I do for them. I am hurt, alone, hungry, and scared. I cry because my nightmare isn't over. In fact, it's probably just beginning, and I have no idea how it will end. I cry until the realization comes to me that I have no time for luxuries such as tears. I have to move, and I have to do it now.

Somehow, weeping has given me strength. I am alive because of the things my father and Uncle Phil have taught me. I have chosen this life, and now I must see it through. I must go help my father. I must become the person they've been training me to be.

Quickly, I close and re-lock the safe door, then go through the house looking for anything else I might be able to use. I use the toilet, then wad a quarter of a roll of toilet paper up, wet it, and do a rudimentary job of cleaning myself. I use the remainder of the roll with soap and water to wash my thighs and butt. When I'm done, I am tender and sore down there, but at least I'm no longer sticky.

In the medicine cabinet, I find some Ibuprofen, and down five pills, putting the rest in my pocket. In Uncle Phil's closet I find a green canvas Army duffel bag that has to be left over from the '60s. I pack it with the spare clothes I've already set aside, as well as soap, shampoo, and deodorant from the bathroom.

Fortunately, the bag is deep enough to accommodate the rifle. I dump the spare mags in with it, adding Hairy's pistol and the knives I took from him and Baldy. Uncle Phil has a suede belt clip for his gun, which I stick in my waistband behind my back. I put on a black knit cap, which conceals the bloody mess that is my hair, and a blue windbreaker, which conceals the gun in my belt. Finally, I throw some apples into a grocery sack and take a long drink from the faucet. then it's time to hit the road.

With the duffle slung across my back, I wheel the red suitcase out to the Toyota and load everything into the backseat. I figure by now the car must have been reported stolen, and may even be linked to the ever-expanding crime scene at the mall. There will be two crime scenes now, the mall, and my apartment, and I am central to both. Everyone will be looking for me.

I'll need another unreported stolen car for the actual border crossing itself, but for now, I need to be away from Uncle Phil's house. I pull out, and head up 181st, going toward the freeway.

Suddenly, the adrenaline I've been running on dries up all at once, and I feel exhausted and unable to carry on. I'm so overwhelmed by pain and anguish I can hardly move. Uncle Phil is dead. How am I supposed to go on by myself?

I pull into the lot of a nearby Albertsons, and barely get it parked before dissolving into a mess of anguished tears. I can't stop the pictures of Uncle Phil bursting in to save me, only to get stabbed to death in front of me. Same thing with my baby, Gladys Knight, and being raped by the disgusting Soul Patch. It's all too much.

I wish I was dead.

Only the thought of my father keeps me going. I have to get up to see him, but there's no way I can drive to Canada in a stolen car, especially looking and feeling the way I do. I'm exhausted, and need to rest. I need to clean up, and get my wounds treated. I probably should be in a hospital.

How am I going to get across the border? This car came from the mall. If it's not reported stolen yet, it will be soon. It's a risk just to drive it. I need another car, a safe one, or at least one that won't be reported stolen until after I'm across the border. But I barely have enough energy to drive, let alone steal another car. That's out of the question for now.

I shouldn't even be seen in public, and need to be off the street. To the police, I'm a kidnap victim. They'll be putting my description out. I'm also Dean Appleby's daughter. If I am found, his chances of making it go way down. But where am I to go?

I can't risk a motel. By tonight, my picture will be all over the news. Then another thought hits me. My passport card, which is my only hope for crossing the border, is in the glove box of my car, still parked at my apartment complex where Uncle Phil left it. It's probably now part of the crime scene. There's no way I can sneak a stolen car full of money across the border without a passport.

I've been training to become an outlaw, and I've done pretty well so far, considering. But now, I need to rest. For the moment, there's no more fight left in me. I need somewhere safe to go and lick my wounds, and I can think of only one place. It's the last place they'll look. It's also the hardest to get to.

Wondering if I am actually insane, or just being stupid, I drive directly there.

Chapter 12

DJ Appleby, Vancouver, BC Canada

Uncle Phil, Grace, and I collectively decided against contacting one another other by cell phone. The authorities have almost certainly tapped both of theirs. They've both turned off location services, and actually keep their phones off until they have to use them. Therefore, I have no way of knowing when they'll return, other than their estimate of three to five days. We have emergency burners, but we keep them turned off, and only check them occasionally. It's likely that the FBI or US Marshals know that Uncle Phil and Grace crossed the border, and seeing that I'm on the Ten Most Wanted list, we're not taking any chances. Cell phone communications are a major weakness for criminals, and are relentlessly exploited by law enforcement in their quest to hunt them down.

Since we can't talk by phone, I race home after work every day, hoping to find them there. Realistically, I expect it to take them longer than three days, but I have to admit that by the second day, I am disappointed to find the apartment dark and empty.

I haven't been back to the 49th Parallel since the day they found me there. On the third morning after they left, I go there bright and early. "Morning, Len," Addi says as she starts my latte. She doesn't even bother to ask what I want any more. "I haven't seen you around lately. Where've you been?"

I'm relieved that she doesn't bring up my attempt to run away the last time I was here. "With family," I answer. "I don't know if you saw the other day or not, but I met some relatives here. I've been busy with them."

"Yeah, I wondered what was up with that. An older gentleman and a girl."

"Right. My uncle and my..." I don't want to say daughter. In fact I don't want to talk about them at all. In my mind, I always picture the police taking a statement after the fact, so I need to limit what Addi might tell them. "Grand niece, I guess you'd call her," I finish.

"I get so confused how all that works," she says amiably. "That would be what, your uncle's granddaughter? Your cousin's daughter? Isn't that, like, your second cousin or something?"

"Something like that. It was just good to see them."

"So they've gone home now? Where's that?"

"They, uh, moved to the States some time ago. Washington, actually."

"Uh oh. That's not a good place to be right now," she says. "Isn't that where that bloodbath just happened? With the family of that escaped prisoner? It was either Washington or Oregon, I always get those two confused. Anyway, I'm glad I don't live down there. Did you know that in the states, they have more murders in the average small town than we get in all of Canada? It's crazy down there."

She's rambling on, but I don't hear a word she's saying. I'm just trying to fight to keep control. Bloodbath? Escaped prisoner? What the hell is she talking about? A terrible feeling of dread overcomes me, and I don't trust myself to say anything. Addi, in the meantime, doesn't wait for or expect a reply. She's a talker. She finishes my drink and hands it to me.

"Watch out, Len," she says, nodding to the door. "They've come to get you."

I turn and see two police officers walking in. My heart skips a beat, but it's clear from their demeanor that they're just here to order coffee. I attempt to say something witty, but I've lost my voice. Instead, I just try to smile. If Addi notices my hand shaking, she doesn't show it.

I sit down and immediately wake up my iPad, then go right to the website of the NBC affiliate in Portland. My own mugshot is the first thing that pops up, staring right at me from the top of the page. The headline reads "Three Dead in Two Gruesome Crime Scenes. Fugitive's Daughter Missing."

I am completely lost to everything going on around me. I try to read the story so fast I don't comprehend a thing, and force myself to slow down. My heart is hammering so hard it's giving me nystagmus. As I read, I can feel the color draining from my face. By the second paragraph, I am reading through tears.

Yesterday morning, neighbors had called in sounds of a scuffle at Grace's apartment complex, followed by someone screaming. Moments later, according to the lady who called police, a large man with long hair carried a naked woman out of the apartment and threw her into a white van. The witness said the woman was either dead or badly injured, she couldn't tell which. Another man, who also appeared to be badly injured and was bleeding heavily, was carried to the van, which then took off at a high rate of speed.

Clackamas County sheriff deputies, as well as police from Portland, Gresham, and Happy Valley had responded to the call. They surrounded the place, and two hours later, CCSO SWAT went in and cleared the apartment.

According to the story, they found a man identified as Phillip Appleby dead inside. They weren't saying the manner of death. They had already identified the woman seen carried to the van as "Grace Appleby, the daughter of former PPB officer Dean J. Appleby, currently a fugitive from justice, who is believed to be hiding in Canada." A related link is entitled "Fugitive Cop Back in US?" I don't even glance at the second story.

The story goes on to say that police eventually located the van in the Clackamas Town Center parking lot, less than a mile from the crime scene. Inside, they found two men dead, who they believe to be the same people the witnesses had seen coming out of the apartment with the woman. There was a great deal of blood in the van, and the naked woman was missing. What had happened in the van was not known. A police spokesman refused to speculate, but said police were concerned for the woman's welfare, and wanted to find her. Nobody was speculating on the identity of the two suspects.

Of course, I already know who they are.

EK must have been watching either Grace or Uncle Phil in the hopes they would lead them to me. They must have confronted them at her apartment. Uncle Phil had no doubt died trying to defend Grace. As to Grace's nakedness, well, I don't even want to think about that, but it can only mean one thing.

I try to think of something more positive. Is it possible that Grace was responsible for the carnage in the van? Had she shown them that one doesn't fuck with the Applebys and live to tell the tale? Grace is tough, but is she *that* tough?

Not likely. As much as I want to believe it, the idea of Grace defeating two armed EK badasses while naked and injured isn't exactly realistic. A far more likely scenario is there had been other EK guys in the van, and some kind of infighting took place, perhaps about what to do with her. I shudder to think of her being passed around a group of animals like EK. The thought makes me physically ill.

I have to go to Oregon and find Grace. I have to leave right this minute.

I stand up, leaving my drink untouched, but I'm lightheaded and hyperventilating, and feel like I'm going to pass out.

"Sir, are you okay?"

I look up and try to focus. It's one of the police officers.

"I'm fine. I just got a little lightheaded," I say. A surreptitious glance at my iPad shows that it is still displaying my picture on the screen in full view of the officers.

"You sure? We can always call you an ambulance."

Turning off the screen would only turn their attention to it. "Really, I'm fine. I just stood up too fast, that's all. Thank you." Addi is looking on with a concerned look on her face. I bite the inside of my lower lip until I taste blood, and force myself to focus. How can I help Grace if I get caught?

The cops are scrutinizing me. Forcing a smile, I drew a deep breath and say to the barista, "Addi, these guys' drinks are on me tomorrow, okay?"

"Sure, Len," she says.

"Thanks, hon. Fellas, I mean it. Stop by tomorrow and Addi here will hook you up. I'll square it with her the next time I'm in. My way of saying thanks to Vancouver's finest."

They thank me and go back to their own table. Having been in their shoes many times, I know they won't return tomorrow. But they're no longer interested in me, and the danger has passed. How long can I expect that to last now that my picture's being spread all over the news again?

I turn off the iPad and head out the door, trying as hard as I can to walk slowly and naturally.

On my way home, I call Dave Powell and tell him I won't be able to make it in for a couple of days due to a death in the family. As soon as I get home, I pack a bag with several days' worth of clothes.

I'm going to Oregon, and I have no idea if I will ever return. The world has become an empty place with nothing left for me. Just like before, only it's infinitely worse. They've killed Uncle Phil, and have probably killed

Grace by now, too. In fact, I hope they have. I know what EK will do with her if she's still alive, and she's better off dead.

As for me, my mission has become crystal clear. It's twofold. First, I will rescue Grace if they haven't already killed her. Second, I will slaughter every member of EK I can find.

Chapter 13

Grace Appleby, Clackamas, OR

The only place I can think to go is home. Not to my apartment, but to my apartment complex, where, until recently, I was an assistant manager. Specifically, I will go to the apartment of a woman named Mrs. Goldberg.

Mrs. Goldberg is a single woman in her 70s. She's fairly well off and lives by herself. Three weeks ago, she sent me an email saying that said she was going to be in Malaysia visiting her sister for the entire month of August, and asked me to check up on the place. Nothing more than taking in the mail and such. I've neglected to do it because I've been in Canada. She borrowed a lockbox from me to put on the door for a friend in the event of an emergency. I set the combination, which is the address of the apartment complex.

The problem is, her apartment is very close to mine, and that whole area is probably flooded with police right now. But if I *could* get there, I'd have access to a shower, a fully stocked kitchen, and best of all, a car that won't be reported stolen for another week.

There are two driveways that lead into the complex; one on the north side and the other on the south. Both my apartment and Mrs. Goldberg's are close to the north driveway.

As I approach the complex, I have to weave my way in and out of numerous police cars that are parked haphazardly in the roadway. The north driveway is blocked off with yellow crime scene tape, and two large Clackamas County SWAT trucks are parked there, along with another large van that says COMMAND POST. At least a dozen police cars are clogging the parking lot, and officers are milling about everywhere.

Several news vans are parked illegally, inhibiting traffic along the street for blocks in each direction, and two helicopters clatter overhead. Through all of this, I have to weave a stolen car full of cash, guns, and bloody evidence, and try not to be spotted by the legions of officers, all of whom are looking for me.

I pull into the south driveway, which is still open for tenants. There are no guest spaces available, so I leave the car, which is probably already linked to the scene at the mall, in a fire lane close to the display unit. Mrs. Goldberg's place is in the building just south of mine, so at least I don't have to walk directly past my unit.

I wipe down the inside of the car with my shirt, trying to clean my prints off anything I may have touched, then get out and open the back door. It seems to take forever and my heart is in my throat as I remove everything from the backseat. There are numerous police cars parked less than a hundred feet from me.

With the duffel over my shoulder, I pull the suitcase behind me with one hand, carrying two bags full of clothes in the other, and start making my way toward Mrs. Goldberg's front door. I'm wearing the knit cap with my hair stuffed into it, and the Dollar Tree sunglasses.

Along the way, I pass two police officers walking away from the crime scene, but they are absorbed in conversation and don't notice me. Finally, I make it to Mrs. Goldberg's porch without being stopped. I'm so nervous and shaky that it takes me three tries to get the lockbox open, but finally, I get the key and go in, dragging everything inside with me. I close the door behind me and sag with relief.

Peeking between the blinds like a criminal in a noir film, I see that no one has followed me and nothing has changed. I leave everything in the kitchen and head right to the bathroom, where I strip, turn the water on as hot as I can take it, and step into the shower.

I can't describe how good it feels to have hot water coursing through my hair, despite the how it stings the various open wounds on my head and face. Pink water courses down my body and disappears in the drain, and I just stand there until it is no longer pink. After spending several minutes just soaking luxuriously, I lay down in the tub on my back and open my legs, trying to wash every last vestige of Soul Patch out of me.

Mrs. Goldberg has the best of everything, and I repeatedly lather and rinse myself with the most expensive soap, shampoo, and conditioner I've ever used. Washing my various wounds hurts, but it's a good pain, and I welcome it for the opportunity to be clean.

I finally step out after fifteen luxurious minutes, clean as the day I was born, but still feeling dirty. Drying off with Mrs. Goldberg's expensive towels is like wrapping myself in baby bunnies. Her robe is velvety soft and feels wonderful against my skin. I'm clean and I smell good, and that goes a long way, but nothing can change the fact that Uncle Phil is dead, and no cleansing will ever wash away the stain of what Soul Patch did to to me. And even worse, there's no way to prevent my mind from replaying every horrible image of what has happened since those men first knocked on my door.

Tears course down my face as I think about it, and all the good feelings from being clean become meaningless. I'm in a dark place. If I force the memories of Gladys Knight, Uncle Phil, the rape, and the killing out of my mind, then the close-ups of my dad crying as he was taken into custody and the fact that I turned my back on him are waiting to replace them.

Four long years he had to live knowing that I disowned him. All he wanted was to have a relationship with me, but I spurned him. And now, he's out there, waiting for me and Uncle Phil to get back, but Uncle Phil isn't coming. And I might not be either. I don't have my passport, and even if I did, I don't know if I could make it past the border now. If I'm flagged in their computer, my journey will end right there.

When my sobbing finally subsides, I feel much better. Grief is a weight that holds me down, and though I haven't really yet begun to grieve, I've at least let a little of the pressure off, and I can think a little more clearly. I have things I need to do.

The clothes I put on at Uncle Phil's house are now filthy, and I stuff them in the bag with the bloody clothes I was wearing in the van. Then I dress in the second set of clothes I brought from Uncle Phil's house. As I do, I try to come up with a plan.

The key is the passport. I can't "legally" cross the border without it, and I can't get the guns and money up there without a vehicle. I know Mrs. Goldberg has a car, and finding it shouldn't be a problem. The problem is that my passport is in the glove box of my car, which is parked in the middle of the police crime scene area, marked off with yellow crime scene tape. I don't know what they're going to do with it, but if they tow it away, my passport will be lost forever. I pat my pocket. Thankfully I'd thought to grab my spare keys before those animals showed up.

I'd love to have some of my other things, too. Maybe they will finish up with the crime scene before nightfall, and leave my place locked up. Maybe they won't tow my car away, or won't tow it before tomorrow. Then, I could get what I need out of my apartment, and retrieve my passport under the cover of darkness and make a clean getaway.

This becomes my plan, but it's still a work in progress, and is dependent on the police leaving by nightfall. In the meantime I'm still in a lot of pain, and I'm utterly exhausted. And I've barely even begun to deal with the emotional trauma of what I've been through.

I climb into Mrs. Goldberg's bed, which has satiny linens that might be made of real silk, and smells faintly of perfume. It's 3:45 in the afternoon. I lay there, wanting to sleep, but I am unable to turn off my mind. The horrors of the day play on a continuous loop.

At 4:15, I get out of bed and go to the window. The back door of my apartment is closed, but I can see people inside moving around. I sit and watch for another twenty or so minutes, then have a microwavable turkey dinner. At five, I turn on the TV.

The events that I've been living through for the past five hours are on every channel. They're calling it a home invasion robbery, and are saying they believe that one of the robbers killed the other two in the van and took the female resident of the apartment away in another vehicle, which they believe was stolen from the same area of the parking lot where the van was found.

So far, no names have been released. I know that when the media learns that the last name of the victims is Appleby, the focus of the whole story will change and the spotlight will turn directly onto my father.

Eventually, the news moves on to other stories, but after the weather report they come back to my story with an update. The entire focus of the story has shifted. Now they are reporting that the sole resident of the apartment was the daughter of fugitive Dean Appleby, the escaped former Portland police officer serving a life sentence for murder and armed robbery, who is now believed to be hiding somewhere in the midwest or east coast.

Well, that didn't take long. At least his cross-country ruse worked, and they're no longer looking for him in Canada.

When the news ends, I turn the TV off. Finally, I feel sleepy instead of just tired. I lay down again, and this time, mercifully, I fell into a dreamless sleep.

I pop awake suddenly, feeling like I'm being smothered. I don't know if it was a bad dream, or simple hopelessness that woke me up. I still feel like I've been hit by a truck. It's 3:11 AM, and there's no way I'm going back to sleep.

I look out the window at my apartment. The lights are still on, but I can no longer see any cops around it, and I can't tell if anyone's inside or not. If they're gone, maybe I can break in and get some of my own stuff. The big question is, is my car still there? I really need that passport.

I dress in Uncle Phil's sweatpants and T-shirt and put my shoes on, then quietly open Mrs. Goldberg's front door. Nothing is stirring. The night is, cool, dark, and utterly still.

I creep out and head across the parking lot. The first thing I notice is that the stolen car I'd abandoned in the red zone is gone. No surprise there. Thank God I wiped it down. The next thing of note is there's an empty police car parked on the curb in front of my front door, which tells me there's at least one cop in my apartment.

There goes all my stuff.

Cautiously, I head toward my parking space. Good news and bad on that front. The good news is, my car is still parked in my spot, but the bad news is it's surrounded by crime scene tape, and there's another police car idling right behind it. This one is occupied by a lone officer, who is looking down at his phone.

There goes my passport.

My dad told me the story of how he snuck around the border checkpoint in the woods, dragging a suitcase full of money. I guess if he can do it, so can I. Cut from the same cloth and all that.

I turn around and head back to Mrs. Goldberg's place. Then, I stop and take another look at my car. There are still other cars parked around it. If the cop looks up, he can easily see the driver's door, but probably not the passenger door.

If I sneak up between the cars parked to the right of it, he probably won't be able to see me. All I'd have to do is crack the door open, grab my passport from the glove box, and melt away into the darkness. I pat my right front pocket and confirm the keys are still there.

No, I think to myself. *Grace, this is a monumentally stupid idea.*

Of all the dumb things I've done, trying to break *into* a crime scene to steal something that's under the guard of a police officer would top the list.

But I need that passport.

Even I am not that stupid, and I head back to Mrs. Goldberg's apartment. But before I get there, just to scope things out, I circle around through the lot and approach my car from the right. By staying low and zigzagging my way between cars, I move closer until I am only three cars from my own. I can still keep an eye on the officer, who's head is still buried in his phone. I drop down and move another car closer, then another. Now I'm only one car away.

It's still dark, and nobody is out. Without really thinking about it, I realize I am committed. Somewhere along the way, I've decided to do this stupid thing.

I crawl around the front of the car parked to the right of mine, and hazard a quick glance. I can't even tell if the cop's eyes are open or not. Yes, it's a stupid idea, but luck seems to be with me.

One last peek tells me the officer is not being any more attentive than he was a moment ago. I creep around the front of the car and, keeping as low as I can, move to the passenger door of my car. I slide the key in the lock and unlock it, putting the key back in my pocket. Another glance tells me the officer still isn't looking.

Gently, I ease the door open. The interior light comes on, shining like a beacon. I hadn't considered this, but I go back to Uncle Phil's training about the sound of glass breaking. Nobody is listening. Nobody is interested enough to investigate. Nobody cares. Hoping that the same holds true here, I open the door enough to get my arm in, and open the glove box. It sounds loud, but I know it's not. Hopefully the cop is snoozing or reading instead of watching and listening.

My passport is right on top. I take it, push the glove box closed, ignoring the clicking noise, and close the door. The light still doesn't go off, so I have to shoulder it latched. To me, the sound is deafening, but I don't even check the cop. I immediately crawl around the car parked next to mine, then withdraw the way I came. Before I know it, I'm back in Mrs. Goldberg's apartment.

It's 3:32 AM. Only twenty-one minutes have passed since I woke up, and now I have my passport. I silently than God that my reckless act of monumental stupidity has paid off. I put the passport in the suitcase with the cash, and remove a couple hundred dollars to have at hand, just in case.

I consider loading up and leaving right now, but I'm still tired, and my whole body hurts. The mission to recover my passport has left me exhausted. I'm hungry, it's already starting to get light out. I really need another day to rest and prepare. Uncle Phil said the best time to cross the border would be when it's most congested, which is around 8:00 AM. If I were to leave now, I'd arrive several hours after the morning rush, when they might be more apt to take their time running me or searching the car.

I need to eat and get good rest. In order to time my arrival at the border with the morning rush, I'd have to leave around 2:00 AM. So today will be a rest and recuperation day. I lay down once again in Mrs. Goldberg's bed. Tomorrow, I will head to Canada. Maybe I'll be able to come up with a plan between now and then.

I fall asleep the moment my head hits the pillow.

I wake shortly after 10:00 AM and make myself scrambled eggs and turkey sausages. After breakfast, I put the dirty dishes in the dishwasher, then poke around in Mrs. Goldberg's closet. I am overwhelmed at the amount of nice clothes she has. We're about the same height, although she's heavier than me and has huge boobs compared to mine. Still, most of her stuff should fit me well enough. She has an assortment of outfits from which I can choose. They're all too loose on top, but they'll work, and are infinitely better than Uncle Phils sweats and railroad T-shirts.

I take another long, hot shower. Nothing has felt this good to me in a long time. I use a ton of real shampoo and conditioner made for women. I even shave my legs and armpits, just to feel more feminine. I sterilize her toothbrush with hand sanitizer, then brush my teeth and finish up with mouthwash. Then I dress, choosing a nice, white, pleated knee-length skirt and a gauzy blouse with an alternating beige and brown zigzag pattern. There's even a matching sash to complete the outfit. I use her lotion, and even splash on some expensive perfume. It does wonders for my mental state to look, dress, and, feel like a woman again.

When I'm done, I feel wonderful. It doesn't erase the grief and hurt of losing Uncle Phil or Gladys Knight, or anything else that's happened, but it certainly helps.

I turn on the news at noon. Coverage of the murders is still the biggest story, and now the focus is on my disappearance. Naturally, there's an in-depth side story rehashing my father's fall from grace and his subsequent criminal history and flight from justice.

My elation deflates as I watch. Suddenly, being clean and wearing nice clothes just feels like playing dress-up. I feel tired and damaged again. Is my father aware of what's going on down here? Should I risk leaving a message on his burner?

I can't. It's just too much of a risk. If there's even the slightest chance that such a call would lead the authorities to him, I won't even try. By now, the cops probably have Uncle Phil's burner, and might be able to link it to mine and dad's. I don't want to get rid of it, but I also don't want to risk turning it on.

I need to get to my dad, sooner than later. I have to fight the urge to leave right now. All I have to do is wait fourteen more hours. I can do that. For him, I can do it. Everything will be better when we're together. We'll be two broken-ass fugitives from justice, but we'll have each other, and that's all that matters.

Chapter 14

DJ Appleby, Vancouver, BC

Every second I waste is either another moment of torture for Grace, or another moment that the men who killed her are still stealing air they no longer have the right to breathe. I pack a bag for a week. Next, I head off to Guardian Storage, where I count out five grand in US dollars from my money cache. I make sure I have my passport and relevant paperwork. I haven't yet decided whether I will cross "legally" with the passport, or illegally with my portable bridge over the ditch at the park.

I'm in a veritable quandary over whether or not to take my gun. On one hand, Canada is the last place you want to be caught with a stolen handgun, especially one that's a direct link to my true identity. On the other hand, I'm going to confront the people who raped and kidnapped my daughter, murdered my uncle, and twice tried to kill me. I'm not going there to try to talk some sense into them. I'm going to torture them into telling me where my daughter is, and then I'm going to kill them. All of them. Needless to say, I want a reliable firearm.

Getting a gun on the other side makes for the safest border crossing, but getting a good, reliable firearm on the street will be a problem. If I take my Glock, I will have the right piece for the job. The problem lies in the crossing. Smuggling a gun over the border multiplies my risk of getting caught exponentially. When I bought the van, I created a hiding place for it behind the stereo faceplate, but this is a common dope smuggling spot, and wouldn't stand up to a real search.

In the end, I decide to risk taking the gun with me. The last thing I need is to buy some cheap Saturday night special that had been dropped on its sights, or worse, to be caught trying to acquire one. For this job, I want a weapon I can count on.

I hide the Glock behind the stereo, make sure I have everything I'll need for the trip, and hit the road. From my place to the Peace Arch crossing is a fifty-minute shot down BC 99. From there, it's about five hours to Portland. The EK clubhouse is located near I-205 and Foster Road, pretty much right in the center of Portland. The loose plan is to bust my way in, corral the occupants, find the head honcho, and get to work. If Grace isn't there, I'll give the first guy a chance to talk, and if he refuses, I'll shoot him in the head. Then I'll move on to guy number two, and so on. I figure it won't take more than two before anyone left will be eager to spill the beans.

The drive to the border passes without incident. Now it's time for a little surveillance. I pull into the parking lot of the Peace Arch duty-free shop, which is just north of the crossing itself, and go to the southernmost parking lot. There, I climb to the top of the van and scan the traffic lined up at the port of entry using a small pair of binoculars I keep in the van. The actual border crossing is less than a quarter of a mile south of me.

There are long lines waiting to cross into the US, which isn't surprising. Scanning them, however, I notice that there are two canine teams working the lines. These will either be drug- or bomb-sniffing dogs, or possibly one of each.

I let the binoculars drop around my neck and sit back. Shit! If one of them is a bomb-sniffer, they could find the gun. That's not a chance I'm willing to take.

I'll work my way east to the next crossing and see what the situation is there. If it's a no-go, I'll have to wait until tonight and use the ramps to get over the ditch into Peace Arch Park, and if that's no good, I'll have to take my chances out east where the highway dips close to the border.

The mission to rescue Grace is time-critical, but I can't do anything for her if I can't get to her. First things first, which is check out the next crossing east of here. I pull out of the parking lot and go down Beach Drive to the intersection of BC 99. Here, I can turn right and go to the border crossing, or turn left and head north back into Canada. As I make the left turn, I hear a police car burp its siren behind me. I look in the rearview mirror, and see that a Canadian Border Services Agency car is pulling me over. My heart comes to my throat.

Running would be futile. There are more law enforcement ground and air assets concentrated here at the border than in many big cities. I have no choice but to yield. Frantically, I try to recall any violations I may have committed. I'm in a hurry, so I may have been speeding, or I may have rolled through the stop sign at Beach Drive and BC 99. Regardless, my only option is to yield, pray that my identity holds up, and take my ticket.

I pull to the right and come to a stop. Both officers get out and approach my car, the driver coming to my window and the passenger going to the passenger side. These guys obviously know how to conduct a traffic stop.

The officer is acting relaxed and being polite and professional; however, to my seasoned eye, he is tense and alert. He says, "Good morning sir. Would you please turn off the engine? I'll need to see your license, vehicle registration, and certificate of motor insurance."

I switch off the ignition and began digging for the documents. "What'd I do, Officer?"

"Just show me the documents if you will, sir," he replies. The tone of his voice tells me this isn't just a traffic stop. I know they have biometrics and face-scanning cameras in use here, but to my knowledge, I haven't been near anything like that. If they knew, or even suspected, who I really was, there would be many cars, and they'd be doing a felony takedown, not a low-key traffic stop. They must be fishing, probably based on my looking through binoculars at the border. Someone sitting in an office watching CCTV monitors must have seen me sitting atop my van, scanning the US port of entry with binoculars. How stupid of me.

I immediately come up with an explanation and begin rehearsing the story in my mind, trying to anticipate every little detail they might ask me. I'm pretty good at making stuff up on the fly; it's what made me a good hostage negotiator and is how I escaped from my own negotiators and SWAT team. Testifying under cross-examination was always a breeze for me. You have to anticipate what they're going to ask and have your answers all ready in advance. The best way to do this is to know every potential hole in your case and have a pre-planned explanation.

I fight for conscious control of my breathing and heart rate, trying to absorb the sudden adrenaline dump and exert control over my shaking hands and tapping feet. That's exactly the kind of stuff these guys are trained to look for.

The officer takes my documents back to his car. Clearly, he's running my name. At this point, I'm pretty sure my run is coming to an end. Too well, I remember the words of the forger from whom I bought these documents. *They may look real, but the numbers are fake and they won't hold up to a computer check.*

After about three minutes, the officers converge and discuss something, then come back to my window.

"Mr. Scott, do you have any other forms of identification on you?"

"Sure. I have my Canadian Identification Card and my passport," I say. "Do you want me to get them out?"

"If you don't mind."

I begin rooting through my pockets. As I hand the documents over, I say, "Can you tell me what the problem is, sir?"

"Your driver's license comes back 'no record on file.' Probably just a glitch in the system. I'm just trying to figure out who you are, that's all."

"I don't know what to say to that, other than you have my ID, so you already know who I am." The officer doesn't reply; he just looks over the new documents. Another unit rolls up behind theirs.

This officer gets out and confers with the cop at the passenger side of my car. "Mr. Scott, do you mind stepping out of the van for a moment?" asks the officer at my window.

So far, I haven't been arrested, which is the only good thing about this encounter. I step out and face them.

"Sir, can you tell me what you were doing back there at the duty free shop?"

"Yeah," I say, glad that I had a chance to come up with a story. "I was heading down to Seattle to help my buddy out with a loan, but the port of entry looked pretty busy, so I stopped to check it out. Once I saw that traffic jam, I thought, 'the hell with this,' and decided he can wait 'til tomorrow. Why? Did I do something wrong?"

"No sir. Other than rolling through the stop sign at the turn-around. But you have to realize, we get a lot of people smuggling drugs or cash in and out of Canada here. Happens every day. You, uh, you're not trying to smuggle drugs or cash out of Canada, are you?"

I gave him an incredulous look. "You're accusing me of smuggling drugs? Are you serious?"

"I'm very serious."

"No, I am not."

"Are you hiding anything in your van you wouldn't want the police to see? Anything illegal?"

"Of course not."

"That's good. What I'd like to do in that case is have a quick look inside, then we can all be on our way. Is that okay with you?"

"Well, no, it isn't."

The officers exchange a look. "I thought you said you had nothing to hide."

"That's right, I don't. You asked me if I minded if you take a look. Well, yes I do mind. I have nothing to hide, it's just a matter of principal. Obviously, if you have a warrant, feel free to search with my blessing. Other than that though, I don't want a bunch of cops looking around in my vehicle. I don't mean to be rude, but I do have the right to say no, don't I?"

"Of course you do, sir. It's just that most people who aren't involved in criminal activity are eager to demonstrate that."

"Well I'm not. You pulled me over for running a stop sign, and now you're accusing me of smuggling dope? It pisses me off that you even said that."

"I'll tell you what," he says amiably. "My partner here, he wants to give you a ticket for running the stop sign. I told him I thought you were clean, and he said from the way you were acting, he thought you were dirty. To be honest, we bet a dollar on it. If you let me have a quick look in your van, I'll give you a warning about the stop sign. Now, I don't care if you have a little bit of bud, or even a hit of coke in there. I'm not interested in personal use amounts of anything, so I won't even confiscate anything like that. What I'm looking for is large, sellable quantities of narcotics, or cash in the amount of ten thousand dollars or more. My partner, he thinks there's something there, and I don't."

"I'm sorry, but this sounds terribly unprofessional of you guys. Really, you bet a dollar on whether I'm a criminal? I'm seriously offended."

Entirely unfazed by my righteous indignation, he says, "Come on, *you* know you're not smuggling dope over the border, and *I* know you're not smuggling dope over the border. Save yourself the money for the ticket, and the increased insurance rates, and everything else. Let me take a quick peek, okay?"

This is a pivotal moment. These guys are fishing, based solely on the fact that I'd been watching the border through binoculars. I've done what they're doing a million times. You think you might have something, so you try to bluster your way into a search. Usually, it turns out to be nothing, but the number of people who let you look who are actually in possession of something illegal, which of course you invariably find, never ceased to amaze me.

In this case, he's asked me if he can search for dope. Having worked the border, I'm sure he's seen every kind of hiding place. The stereo faceplate isn't fixed in the dash; it'll come out if pulled, and there is a loaded pistol behind it. One whose serial number is an easily-deciphered message that says 'Congratulations! You just found DJ Appleby, international fugitive!'

If I let him search, the chances are very good that he'll miss it. You wouldn't normally try to remove a stereo faceplate in an everyday search of a vehicle. There isn't any dope in the van, and I'll be on my way in three or four minutes with an apology. That's a hell of a lot better than them pressing the issue of my identification, which hasn't been mentioned again. On the other hand, if he bumps the stereo hard enough, it'll move, and then he'll find the gun.

If I say no to the search, they'll write me a ticket, which I don't care about, but then they might try to push the ID issue. They probably have all kinds of tools at their disposal. They can simply run my passport, which is on a different system than the driver's license. When it comes up without a record, they'll know all the ID is fake, and then I'll be done.

I have a quick decision to make. Take the chance on them finding the gun, or take the chance on them finding that my ID is fake.

"Fine," I say. "Take a quick look in the van. You're not going to find anything, and you know it."

"Thank you."

"Just please be quick. I'm not happy about being detained and accused."

"This won't take a minute," he says, nodding to the third officer, who returns to his car and comes out with a medium-sized brown mixed-breed dog.

"Hold on," I say, trying to reign in my panic. "I'm allergic to dogs. I won't have that animal in my van!"

"Oh, don't worry about him," he said dismissively. "He won't go in. He's new, and they're just trying to give him experience in the field. They'll just run him around the outside while I'm checking the inside."

I close my eyes and shake my head. "Just get it over with. I want to get out of here."

The officer climbs inside and begins rooting around. I can't see him from where I'm standing, but I can hear him concentrating his search in the back of the van. There's nothing there but my suitcase, a foam pad, and a sleeping bag.

Meanwhile, the other officer leads the dog around the back of the van, up the left side, and around the front, directing him to the wheel wells and engine compartment with his hand. The dog eagerly follows his handler's cues. I'm standing on the shoulder of the road behind the van. When the dog gets to the open passenger door, he stops suddenly, sticks his nose into the passenger compartment, and abruptly sits down, looking at his handler expectantly.

My heart begins racing, and I can feel myself paling. I've been around canines enough to know that he just alerted on the inside of the van. But how? There aren't any drugs in there at all.

The handler catches the eye of the cover officer and slowly brings his wrists together, which tells me I'm about to be arrested. I've done the same thing a million times. I've never realized until now how obvious this is to the bad guy.

There's nowhere to run. No way to fight them. I'm fucked and I know it.

Moving in unison, they step forward and grab my arms. The cover officer has a hold of my right hand and applies a textbook-perfect twisted wrist lock, then brings my right arm behind my back. Reflexively, I tense for just a moment, and he says, "Don't even think about it."

I relax, and they ratchet on the cuffs.

"What the hell?" I say. "Somebody want to tell me what's going on?"

By now, the first officer is emerging from the van. He's empty-handed and I breathe a sigh of relief. There aren't any drugs in the van; of that I am certain. Either the dog has made a mistake, or possibly he'd alerted on some marijuana or something a previous owner once had in it.

"Sir, the dog alerted on the interior of your van, and that gives me probable cause to put him inside. I don't need your consent to do that.

We're detaining you in handcuffs for our safety and yours. Is there anything you want to tell me about before I take him in?"

"There are no drugs in there, sir. I've only had that van for about two months. Maybe he's smelling some weed or something the previous owner had in it."

"Oh, he's not a drug-sniffing dog, sir. He's a firearms and explosives-sniffing dog. You don't have any guns or bombs in the there, do you?"

I just shake my head. That's it, I'm done. Just like that, I've lost Grace and I'm going back to prison.

The officer takes the dog into the van. Less than a minute later, he yells, "Gun!" and comes out holding the stolen Glock.

They unload the weapon and make it safe, then stuff me in the back of the cruiser. I know I'm taking the first of many steps that will lead me back to the Oregon State Penitentiary. It will probably take months due to the legal complexities of an international extradition, but in the end, I'm on my way back to Oregon to face charges of first-degree murder for killing Dr. McNab, and a host of other charges stemming from EK's attempted assassination of me in the hospital, which left a prison guard dead and led to my escape. There won't be any more deals to save me this time. Now I will die in prison, either by execution, old age, or at the hand of the European Kindred.

But none of that matters. What matters is that I have just lost my last opportunity to rescue Grace. If she's still alive, she's being raped to death by those filthy EK pigs. I can only hope she's already dead.

The most I can do for her now is beg these Canadian cops to contact the Portland Police Bureau and pass along the information about what's going on. However, the police have to play by the rules, which means they'll have to conduct an investigation and obtain a search warrant before going in to find her, which will do nothing other than tip EK's hand. They'll have plenty of time to either kill her or move her to a safer location.

Now she is truly gone.

Chapter 15

Grace Appleby, Clackamas, OR

I sleep away most of the day. When I finally drag myself out of bed, it's 4:00 PM. I pee a river, but I haven't been able to do anything else, not even once since Uncle Phil and I got back from Canada the night before last. I try, but as the limerick goes, there I sit, broken-hearted... The one thing Mrs. Goldberg doesn't have is a laxative.

I pack a bag with a couple of changes of clothes. The problem with Mrs. Goldberg's wardrobe is there's nothing like sweats and Ts; all she has is really nice stuff. She has nice shoes, but nothing useful, like sneakers or heavy boots.

I launder everything I've used, including her sheets and towels. When the load is dry, I re-make her bed and hang the towels. I'm not hungry, so I do the dishes. When they're dry, I put everything away, taking care to use a dishtowel and wipe away any fingerprints.

I'm feeling a lot better now physically. The swelling in my nose and lips isn't getting any worse. It may even be down a little, but I still look like a raccoon that got hit by a car. Thankfully, Mrs. Goldberg is one of those women of her generation who favor large-framed retro-looking sunglasses. Hers are Tori Burch, and they have oversized square lenses that are tinted darker at the top than on the bottom. They cover the bruises pretty well, especially from a distance. Up close, though, nothing can hide them.

I spend the hours until darkness watching TV and preparing for my journey. I take another nap in the evening, and wake around 11:30. Now I go through the apartment, carefully wiping away any traces that I've been there.

I'm itching to get started and need to be moving, so even though it's only 1:00 AM, an-hour-and-a-half before I want to go, I decide to leave now. If I get there early, I'll find a place to pull over and wait. I inventory everything I'll be taking, and do one last walk-through of the apartment. Obviously, Mrs. Goldberg will eventually know someone's been here, but the only things missing will be some clothes, some food, and some toiletries, none of which she may notice for some time. But I'm pretty sure she'll notice that her car's been stolen.

Her car is in her garage and the keys are hanging on a peg near the door. It's a brand-new blue Chrysler 300. It looks very expensive, with white leather seats and every available option. I make three trips to the garage, loading the duffel, Uncle Phil's money, and the bags of bloody clothing into the trunk. I've made sure to put several hundred dollars into my pocket for any incidental expenses that may come up along the way. Before I leave, I replace the key in the lockbox, and make one final sweep through the apartment. Once satisfied that I've left no trace of myself, it's time to go.

My thighs squeak against the leather seats as I get in, which makes me feel like a little girl. It's an elegant car for an elegant woman. Before starting the engine, I try to think of any detail I may have forgotten, but I can't think of a thing, and pronounce myself ready to go.

On my way out of the north driveway, I pass my building and can see a large X of crime scene tape across my front door. I can also see that my parking spot is now empty.

I get on I-205 and head north. I'm maybe five hours from the Canadian border, and I have no idea if I'll be able to make it across or not. If I am flagged in the computer, this will be a very short, one-way trip.

I don't know what will happen if they catch me. Can they detain me? Am I wanted by the police for anything? Officially, and quite literally, I'm a kidnap victim, but I've got a lot of explaining to do, like why I took evidence from the crime scene, why I broke into Mrs. Goldberg's place to hide from the cops, and why I'm trying to smuggle illegal weapons over the border in a stolen car. The biggest question is, why didn't I just call the police after escaping the van in the mall parking lot?

It won't take a criminologist to figure out that I've been helping my dad.

The drive is uneventful, and faster than I expected. I have time to kill, so I stop at a twenty-four hour Walmart somewhere north of Seattle, and put together an impromptu disguise. It consists of a short, spiky-haired black wig, some fake nose-rings that pinch closed around the septum or lip, a small Goth makeup kit, and another pair of sweats and a black hoodie. Hopefully, the dark look will camouflage my bruises.

Back in the car, I apply a light foundation, then layer on the black eye shadow. The makeup kit comes with a cheap eyeliner pencil, which I use to extend the outside corners of my eyes into long, Egyptian-looking wings. Next I apply heavy fake eyelashes, and round out the makeup with dark, blood-red lipstick. For the metalwork, I hang a thick silver ring with large steel globes from my nose, pinching it tight to both sides of my septum, and then add a fake tongue ring, and—*voilà!* Instant Goth. I can't bring myself to change out of the nice clothes, so I'm a Goth in a $500 outfit.

When I'm done, I drive around the back of the plaza and throw the garbage bag with the bloody clothes into a dumpster. It feels good to finally be rid of that filth.

Bellingham is the last major city south of the border, and I pass through it nearly two hours ahead of schedule, so I decide to pull over. I get off the freeway and find a dark corner of an empty strip-mall parking lot. I'm not really tired, but I manage to doze for a while.

It's light out when I get up, and I am able to get a decent look at myself for the first time. I look more like a cheap Halloween Elvira than a real Goth, but the disguise helps to cover my bruises and completely alters my appearance, and since that's the goal, I call it a win.

Finally, I swing through a Starbucks drive-through and drink a 20-ounce Nitro Cold Brew as I make my way toward the border. Just as Uncle Phil predicted, there are long lines at the Canadian checkpoint, and I settle in to wait. After only a few minutes, I'm having doubts. Are they on the lookout for me? Is my name flagged in their computer? What if they want to search my luggage? Suddenly nervous, I want to turn around, but how could I help my dad then? I have to at least try. Like the saying goes, go big or go home. Well, I'm not about to go home, so I set my jaw and stay the course.

The line slowly, but inexorably, moves forward. I'm now a bundle of nerves. The closer I get to the checkpoint, the more it's affecting my stomach. I squeeze my eyes shut and force myself to calm down. Looking at the line, I think maybe that Nitro Cold Brew wasn't such a great idea after all, but it's too late now. I have a strong bladder, but I've been in line for almost forty minutes.

As the cars ahead of me roll up to the stop line to await their turn, I go over in my mind exactly what I've got to do, step by step, just as Uncle Phil taught me. Be nice, be relaxed, be pleasant, and smile a lot. Be flirty if it will help. I try to anticipate the questions they'll ask, and how I'll answer them. Are you coming to Canada for business or pleasure? Pleasure. Where are you going? To Vancouver, to stay with my sister after my boyfriend beat me up. How long will you be staying? Three weeks. Whose car is this? It belongs to my aunt, Meg Goldberg.

When the car in front of me is next in line, I reach for my passport, only to realize that I've left it in the suitcase with the money, which is locked in the trunk. I can't believe I've made such a critical mistake! Now what? If I get out to get it, I'll only draw attention to myself, or even worse, they'll interpret it as a threat and detain me. I'm going to have to wait until I'm at the actual booth, and open my trunk there, exposing both the duffel bag and the suitcase to the officer.

The calm demeanor I've worked so hard to muster disappears like exhaled breath on a cold winter day. Nerves overtake me and I begin trembling. Suddenly, my guts are churning and I feel like I'm going to be sick.

The car ahead of me pulls forward to the inspector's booth, and I pull up to the stop line, facing a red light. When it turns green, it'll be my turn. There's a camera pointed right at me, and a sign stating that any amount of money over ten thousand dollars needs to be declared before entering Canada. Another sign warns that all firearms are prohibited.

Good to know, seeing that I'm about to show the border agent a trunkful of both.

Desperately, I try to think of a way out of this, but it's hopeless. Seconds later, the brake lights on the car in front me come on. The agent hands the driver his passport back, and they exchange a final word or two.

All I can think of is to flirt with the border agent. He's around thirty, black, and decent-looking. Maybe I can flash him. Frantically, I reach under my dress and wiggle out of my panties. As I bend over to stuff them under the seat, the camera flashes and my light turns green. Having no other choice, I pull forward.

The border agent leans out of his booth and says, "Good morning, ma'am. Would you please remove your sunglasses for me?"

Shaking, I pull them off my face. They clatter audibly as I set them on the dashboard. He scrutinizes me closely, and says, "Wow. Are you okay?"

"Yes. The bruises, right?"

"Yeah. The makeup doesn't exactly cover them."

"For what it's worth, I left him. That's why I'm here."

"Good for you. I'll need to see your passport please."

"Uh, yeah, well, I know how stupid this is, but I left it in the trunk. I'm sorry."

He sighs and says, "Would you please step out and get it?"

"Oh, yes, of course." My guts gurgle and cramp violently, and I have to clench hard to avoid farting. The problem is, I can feel that it's liquid hot, and there's no way I trust that it'll be just gas. With my hand on my stomach, I say, "Officer, I'm really sorry and I hate to ask, but is there a bathroom around here I can use first? It's sort of an emergency."

"No ma'am, there's not."

"I have my driver's license right here if that'll work instead," I say hopefully, pulling my wallet out of my pocket. "Will that do?" I flash him a nice smile and open my legs a little, pulling Mrs. Goldberg's skirt tight across the top of my thighs.

"No it won't. I'll need to see your passport. And please be quick about it. You're not the only car trying to get across this morning."

He opens the door of his little booth and steps out. I get out of the car, terrified, trying to think of a way out of this, but my mind is a blank. I'm starting to sweat, and now I've got his full attention, but in a bad way. "It's just in the trunk," I say pointlessly.

"Well, how about if you get it?" he says, approaching the end of his patience.

And then one of those crazy, really stupid ideas comes to mind, like breaking into my own car while a police officer was guarding it. Only this one is *really* off the charts. But I'm just about out of options.

When I open the trunk, the first thing I see is that the duffel bag has shifted. The barrel of the rifle is now protruding two inches from the top of the canvas, and a loaded 30-round banana clip has slid out and come to rest against the suitcase with the money and my passport.

Awkwardly, I bend over the duffel bag in a futile attempt to shield it from him, allowing Mrs. Goldberg's dress to hike up, exposing my ass to his view. As I unzip the suitcase, several banded bundles of $100 bills are exposed. The agent must still be looking at my ass, otherwise he'd be taking me into custody.

I could simply relax and allow it to flow naturally, but instead I push, and force out a violent and disgusting eruption of three days' worth of volcanic shit, ruining the dress and splattering off the ground beneath me. As if jolted by electricity, the border agent skips backwards, yelping, to avoid the flow. It's over in a second, leaving brown streaks dripping down my legs.

"Oh my *Lord*," he cries.

"*Oh God*," I squeak, turning around to face him, my hands going to my behind, where I accidentally/on purpose get poop on both the passport and my fingers.

Now crying with genuine humiliation, I wail, "Oh, I *told* you I needed a bathroom! Why couldn't you have just let me go? What's *wrong* with you?" I clean off the passport on Mrs. Goldberg's cream-colored dress, leaving a watery, brown smear, and hold it out to him.

"Oh my God, I am so sorry, ma'am," he says, looking horrified and warding off the proffered passport with outstretched hands. "Look, just put that away. I can see you have it, that's good enough. Just… Just take off, okay? You're free to go. There's a gas station three exits up where you can, you know, do whatever you need to. Oh, damn!" He slams the trunk, steps back into his little booth, and starts ripping paper towels off a rack. I get back in the car, this time sliding silently across the seat with no squeaking. The light in front of me turns green, and, humiliated, I pull away in genuine tears.

I am disgusted and appalled at my own actions, but as I leave the border behind me, it dawns on me what just happened. Somehow, I've managed to drive a stolen car containing illegal weapons and cash across an international border, and not only was I not checked, I wasn't even documented. No record of my name was created, and the picture probably won't even show my face, since I was looking down when the camera flashed. Even if it does, I'm wearing the Goth disguise.

The only record of my crossing is the license plate of Mrs. Goldberg's car, which won't be reported as stolen until she returns from Malaysia in three day's time. Not only did the poor border agent fail to check my passport, but he had actually closed the trunk on my contraband. Despite the humiliation and mess, the border crossing couldn't possibly have gone any better.

With the crossing now behind me, I start making my way north on BC 99 toward Vancouver. I lower all the windows, but am still nauseated, and have no idea how I am going to clean myself up.

I don't want my father to see me like this, although I know he'll at least get a laugh out of hearing how I crossed. Uncle Phil would no doubt have cackled in delight and beamed with pride over what happened.

There's a gas station at Ladner Trunk Road in Surrey, and I pull over, heading right to the outside bathroom in the back. Mrs. Goldberg's clothes are ruined, and her nice car is a mess.

I lock myself in the bathroom for half an hour while I feebly attempt to clean up and get dressed in the sweats I bought at Walmart. It's disgusting. I use the clean portions of Mrs. Goldberg's dress first, then every paper towel in the place, and even go into the men's room for more to clean the car. Fortunately, the leather seats aren't hard to clean. It would never come out of cloth. Again, I send my silent apologizes to Mrs. Goldberg. She's far too nice a woman to be put through what I'm putting her through.

Finally, when I am passably clean, I decide to take a motel room somewhere close by my dad's place before going to see him. I need to shower and thoroughly clean the car before seeing him.

I check into the Day's Inn on Kingsway, less than a mile from his place. Then, I go to a store and buy some disinfecting cleaner, several rolls of paper towels, and an air freshener for the car, as well as another set of clothes. When I get back to the motel, I thoroughly clean the car, then take a long, hot shower. I discard the last of Mrs. Goldberg's clothes, and dress in the clothes I just purchased.

Finally, just before 3:00 PM, I head over to my dad's place.

Chapter 16

DJ Appleby, Vancouver, BC

They search me, confiscate the five grand I brought, and take me to a holding facility. I am fingerprinted, photographed, and locked in a cell with steel bars and a concrete bunk. After maybe fifteen minutes, the arresting officer comes to interview me.

"So, Mr. Scott, would you care to tell my why you were trying to smuggle a loaded firearm out of Canada?"

I exert what I hope is my right to remain silent.

"Well, I can tell you this," he says. "It'll go a lot easier for you if you decide to talk to me. Where were you headed to in the States?"

"I'm not answering any questions," I say dully. It's only a matter of time until they figure out who I really am. The Canadian authorities already have my prints, and have been looking for Julian McNab ever since the escape from the hunting camp. If that isn't enough for them to find, once they run the serial number of the gun, it'll come right back as the one stolen from the correctional officer during my escape. No matter how, it's bound to happen now that I'm in custody.

"Okay then. We're still trying to get your driving record. Any idea why that hasn't come through yet?"

"Don't I get to talk to a lawyer or something?"

"Sure. There's a phone book there. Give one a call. I'd say you sure could afford one. Wanna chat about all that money you were carrying?"

I begin thumbing through the phone book. There are as many lawyers here as there are in a big city in the States.

"Of course, we'll provide you with duty counsel if you like. Save you the time and expense of hiring one of your own."

I close the book. It doesn't matter. I'm done talking anyway.

He asks me several more questions, then gets tired of talking to the wall and leaves. A few minutes later, the door opens up, and a nerdy young Asian man comes in.

"Hi Mr. Scott. My name's Anthony Ho. I'll be your duty counsel for your bail hearing if you don't already have a lawyer on the way. They tell me you have money of your own to hire an attorney, but you aren't talking to them about it. That's good. Best thing you can do is not answer any questions. But you'll be in court in an hour, and unless your own lawyer gets here before then, I'll be representing you at the hearing."

"You'll do," I say. "What's this hearing in an hour?"

"It's your bail hearing. The law says the police have to do one of two things with you in the first twenty-four hours after your arrest. They can either take you to court, or release you. With a charge like yours, the law says they have to take you to court 'without delay', which usually means the next available court session. That's in an hour from now."

"And the purpose of the hearing is to set bail, so I can get out of jail?"

"Exactly. You're being charged with Unauthorized Possession of a Firearm in violation of section ninety-one of the Canadian Criminal Code. That's a summary offense, with a maximum penalty of six months in jail and a five thousand dollar fine. Typically, that's not the kind of charge they can hold you on, so they set bail, which, I assume, you can pay."

"How much will it be?"

"Usually, it's the amount of the fine. In this case, five thousand dollars. When you come back for your trial, you'll get a portion of it back, less any fines the Crown imposes. Of course, if you abscond, you'll lose your bail, and will still be subject to a fine or imprisonment, after you're picked up on a warrant."

This tiny ray of hope is enough to turn my attitude completely around. Is it possible I'll get out of here before they find out who I really am, or that the gun was stolen from a dead correctional officer in Oregon?

"Yes," I say, "I'd like you to represent me."

"Good, fine. There shouldn't be any problem. The hearing won't last long."

"There was some problem with my driver's license," I volunteer. "They ran it, but I guess they couldn't find it in the system or something. I don't suppose that will change things, will it?"

"Oh, I doubt it. Did you provide them with other forms of ID?"

"Yes, my Canadian ID card and my passport."

"Then no, there shouldn't be any problem. I hate it when these guys hassle people for no reason. They take something like this and try to build it into something big. Fishing is what they're doing. My job is to get you out on bail as soon as I can, and that's exactly what we're going to do, eh?"

"I hope you're good at your job."

Ho smiles and says, "I like to think I am, Mr. Scott. And just so you know, I won't be able to represent you farther down the line in your case. For that, you'll have to hire your own counsel. I just do the bail hearings."

"Okay, thanks."

"So, tell me about your arrest. What happened?"

I proceed to tell him my story. I was headed to Seattle to loan some money to a friend, but I didn't want to take all day crossing the border. I stopped at the duty free shop because the US Port of Entry looked pretty crowded, and checked it out with my bird watching binoculars. There were way too many cars, so I decided to blow it off until later.

As far as the van goes, I just purchased it a month ago from a guy called Skip. I had found the add online. Craigslist, Autotrader, cars.com, one of sites, I don't recall which one. It was a good van at a good price. Everything worked but the radio, but I don't listen to the radio anyway, so I bought it. I've been driving it for a month with no problem, and then today, when I turned around at the border, the police stopped me.

I go on to describe the conversation I'd had with the border guy about searching the van, which ended up with me eventually granting them permission to search it. The dog hit on the interior, and the cop said he'd found a gun in the dashboard.

Ho asks if I knew about the gun, and I say no. Have I ever had the radio fixed? No. Do I own any guns? No. More questions, more answers. Blah blah blah.

Forty-five minutes later, we're standing in Provincial Court before judge Nickolas Harms. The Crown Counsel, as the prosecuting attorney is known here in Canada, is a very large and portly man with a gray beard and thick glasses named William Dubois. He is currently making an argument to the judge, asking him to deny me bail. Having been a cop, I can tell he suspects there's a lot more to my story than a measly gun charge and a computer glitch with my ID.

"Judge, the Crown requests that the subject in this case, Leonard Scott, be held without bail. Defendant was found attempting to smuggle a loaded firearm out of Canada into the United States hidden in a secret compartment in his vehicle."

Ho, also standing, says, "Anthony Ho, on behalf of the defendant. Your Honor, this is a summary offense, and there's no reason why my client can't be released on bail. It's done all the time."

Dubois says, "Actually, Your Honor, it's not done all the time. Not when there's a problem in making a proper identification of the arrestee. In cases like this, we routinely seek a continuance pending proper identification of the subject. The Crown wouldn't want to be responsible for allowing, say, a known child molester to slip back into the community."

Ho, feigning righteous indignation, says to Dubois, "If you please, sir!" He then turns to the judge and asks, "Your Honor, I ask that my esteemed colleague not be allowed to malign my client with baseless accusations. Mr. Scott has provided the arresting officers with his driver's license, Canadian citizenship card, and a passport. What more ID would the Crown like? His Whole Foods membership card?"

Judge Harms says, "Mr. Dubois, please refrain from hypothetical speculative references, sir. And, Mr. Ho has a point. Exactly what *is* the issue here?"

"There, uh, seems to be a problem with the defendant's identification, Your Honor."

"Well, please don't keep me in suspense, Mr. Dubois. What is the problem?"

"Uh, well, there doesn't appear to be any record of him on file, Your Honor."

The judge turns his gaze on Ho and raises his eyebrows. Ho scoffs and says, "Judge, I don't think my client can be held responsible for the Crown's computer glitch. If there's a problem with the computer system, it's hardly his fault. He has produced all the required documents. He's being charged with unlawful possession of an alleged weapon, not murder. And as far as that alleged weapon goes, it's one that was supposedly buried somewhere deep inside the dashboard, completely out of view, in a vehicle my client purchased only a month ago and had no knowledge of. The Crown has no way of proving my client even knew it was even there, and now they want to hold him accountable for their own inability to properly run a driver's license check? I hardly think that's fair, Your Honor. More importantly, what's the relevance of this computer glitch as far as bail goes?"

The judge looks at the prosecutor and says, "Mr. Dubois, I tend to agree with all of Mr. Ho's arguments. Now, do you have anything further that might sway my opinion?"

"Uh, well, Judge, as a matter of fact I do. The defendant was trying to leave the country, and was carrying a large sum of money. I believe there is a significant flight risk here."

"Flight risk?" counters Ho, throwing his hands up in the air in apparent disbelief. "Judge, Mr. Scott is a foreman on a construction crew! He *supervises* people. He maintains a household here in Vancouver. What would he be trying to flee from? A summary offense he didn't even know he was committing? As for attempting to leave the country, Mr. Scott had turned around at the border and was headed back *into* Canada. Your Honor, Mr. Scott has an exemplary record. He's never even had a speeding ticket. He's a good man; he was en-route to Seattle to help a friend with his finances, for crying out loud. There's not a reason in the world he shouldn't be granted bail."

The judge holds up his hands and says, "I've heard enough. I happen to be in agreement with you, Mr. Ho. Mr. Dubois, it's not incumbent on the defendant to prove his identification past providing the required documents, which he has already given you. Bail is set at five thousand dollars. Mr. Scott, can you pay that now, or would you like a surety?"

Anthony leans in toward me and says, "That's a person who will take financial responsibility for you in the event you fail to show at your trial."

"I'll pay that now, Judge," I say.

"Very well," bail is granted, and this case is set to be heard on September twenty-first at one o'clock. In the meantime, Mr. Scott, you are prohibited from owning or possessing any firearms or ammunition. If you own weapons, you are ordered to turn them over to your local police jurisdiction within twenty-four hours. You are also prohibited from leaving the country before trial, and are ordered to surrender your passport. Will any of that be a problem?"

"No, sir. I don't own any weapons. I've never even fired a gun, and now I can't afford to help my friend, so I have no reason to leave the country. No sir, it's not a problem."

"Very well. See the clerk on your way out. Next case!"

And with that, I am led out of the courtroom and back to the jail. I shake Anthony's hand, my head spinning as I realize that they're actually going to release me. I keep thinking that something will happen to stop it. Now it's a race to see which happens first, my being released, them tracing the serial number of the gun in the States, or my being properly identified.

Time drags as I'm being out-processed. I am given all my possessions back, including my cash and ID (sans passport). I am told that the police are holding onto both the gun and my van as evidence, and I'm given a receipt for both. The latter is probably just to piss me off. I sign a few documents, give them my money back in the form of bail, and am practically pushed out the door. It's 2:35 PM.

Miraculously, I find myself back out on the street in the middle of downtown Vancouver. I am penniless, but I am free. Now, it'll be a race for me to get home, pack a bag, and get my money out of storage before they discover who they just let go. The countdown has already begun.

From the way they had argued against bail, the authorities obviously suspect there is more to me than meets the eye. In fact, it's amazing that I got released before anything came back on the gun or my fingerprints. The one thing I can count on is that they will, without a doubt, soon figure out exactly who they just let go. And I suspect it will be within minutes, not hours.

I have no plans to be caught hanging around the police station. I know where I am, and how to get home. In fact, it's a straight shot down Main Street heading south. It's maybe a two-mile walk to my place.

The problem is, because it's such a straight shot, it will be easy for the police to find me if they start looking before I get home. And I don't think I'm being paranoid, either. I may not have time to make it home.

Instead of heading south on Main, I headed west on Cordova for several blocks, then south to Hastings, where I run into a crowd of what appears to be several hundred homeless people. It looks like someone is getting ready to feed them. I've seen a lot of homelessness in Portland, but not on a scale like this. The streets, like the people, are dirty and smelly, but I couldn't ask for better camouflage.

I hang out for several minutes and see no police, but the more I think about it, the more certain I am that I won't have time to make it home.

I approach a transient wearing a filthy blue knee-length pea coat and knit cap, and offer him my watch in exchange for the coat and hat. He seems delighted with the trade, and I take off once again, now headed south toward my place, trying not to gag from the smell of my new disguise.

As I approach the Science Museum, I see a patrol car cruising slowly by, the officer casually scanning the crowd. It's quite possible he's just checking out girls, but in my hyperaware state, I assume he's looking for me. I hide behind a group of Japanese tourists milling about waiting to get inside, until he drives out of sight.

Paranoia can be a good thing, because just as I am about to order an Uber on my burner, which I have yet to turn on, I remember that they can plot my position if they know my cell phone number. This is a new phone, and I've never even turned it on, but it was in police custody for a few hours, and now I don't trust it. If they cloned it, the moment I turn it on and the signal hits a tower, and that will give them a very good place to start looking for me. When it's triangulated with two towers, they can pinpoint me to within a few meters.

Time to lose the burner. I pull the battery and dump it in a nearby garbage can. Then I remove the SIM card, and drop it through a sewer grate. The phone itself goes into another trash can.

I wait for several minutes, and when no other police cars roll by, I set out again, constantly scanning ahead to look for places to go if I have to get off the street. The closer I get to my apartment complex, the more the hairs start standing up on the back of my neck.

Either I trust my instincts or I don't. They've served me well as a cop, and even better as a con. Two-and-a-half blocks from my place, I make a snap decision. I'm not going home.

It's Saskatoon all over again. Now I have nothing. No gun, no phone, and no money. If I try to use a credit or debit card, they'll know about it instantly, and they'll have me.

My only hope now is Guardian Storage. I need that money every bit as much as I did after the debacle at Banff. It won't take them two hours to discover that I've rented space at Guardian Storage, and when they do, I might as well walk into the nearest police station and turn myself in. Without the money, there's no possible way I can get to Oregon and rescue Grace.

The storage facility is only eight blocks away from here. I change course and head directly there. Five minutes later, I dump the coat in an alley and let myself into the building. I'll return for the coat once I have the money in hand. So far, so good.

I go to the locker, dial the combination, and raise the door.

No SWAT team is waiting for me inside. There's nothing here but my two suitcases. I open them and breathe a huge sigh of relief. All the money is there, along with my go-bag, which contains a change of clothes and personal toiletry items. I roll the suitcases out, re-lock the unit, and leave. Laying hands on my money is as anticlimactic as I could possibly hope for, but now I'm faced with nowhere to go.

I'm on foot, with two pull-along suitcases and no usable ID. Motels, car rentals, and airline tickets are all out at this point. I can't even use cash; my picture will soon be all over the news if it isn't already. I have nowhere to go but the street, and the street is the most dangerous place I can be right now. But somehow, more than anything else, I have to find a way to Portland and either rescue Grace or exact revenge on those responsible for killing her.

Why couldn't I have had the foresight to stash a car someplace near the money? I make a mental note to do that next time. But first things first. I have to get out of the immediate area. For all I know the street outside Guardian is swarming with police.

I'm going to head back to Hastings Street to hide among the homeless until I can think of something better. It's a long shot whether or not I can make it.

I wheel the cases outside, and seeing no cops, I collect my coat and head west, When I get away from the storage facility, I'll go back north on a side street or an alley. I stay off the main drag, sticking to the alley between W. 6th and W. 7th. The alley isn't that long, and there are only a few cars parked in it. It's way too public to steal a car. If I can make it till dark, I should be able to steal a car and get out of Vancouver.

Grace Appleby, Vancouver, BC

As I arrive at my dad's complex, the first thing I see are two Vancouver police cars parked just around the corner from my dad's apartment. There are a hundred reasons why they could be here and ninety-nine of them are insignificant, but instinctively, I know that they're here for the one that's not.

As his apartment comes into view, I see is a cop standing at his front door, cupping his hands around his eyes, peering in the window. Another one is looking into his bedroom window.

"No," I whimper, tears now streaming down my face. "Oh God, please, not now…"

A car behind me taps the horn, and I realize I'm stopped in the middle of the driveway. In my mirror I can see plain sedan with a young, fit driver. It looks like an undercover police car. I pull out of the complex and make a right turn onto the main street.

I don't know how they caught him, but it's no coincidence that it happened at the same time as I arrived in town. Somehow, this is my fault.

It's all been for nothing. Everything that's happened since I answered the knock at my apartment door has been for nothing. Worse, I know that somehow, *I* am to blame for it. I leave the complex and drive around aimlessly, wondering what to do now. They must be holding him somewhere in the city. I'll track him down, and at least visit him in jail.

I wander around for another few minutes, then pull into his apartment complex again. Why not just ask of the police where he is?

But now, to my surprise, all the police are gone. This makes no sense to me. One of the most wanted men in North America gets arrested, and that's it? No SWAT team, no command post, no crime scene tape? It doesn't make sense. They'd want to look into who's been helping him, what he's been doing, what crimes if any he's committed while on the run. They'd get warrants and spend days at his place collecting evidence, so where is everyone?

Suddenly, I recall how Uncle Phil and my dad taught me to be hyperaware, and I feel the need to do that right now. I begin scanning the cars in the lot, and immediately spot the car that had honked at me. It's now backed into a space almost directly across the parking lot from my dad's front door. The driver's still behind the wheel, pretending to look at his phone, but I see him glancing up and looking at my dad's place. As I drive farther down the lot, I find another occupied unmarked police car parked between my dad's apartment and the driveway.

Then it hits me. They *don't* have him. They want him, but they haven't caught him yet. They may not even be aware of who he is. That's what they were doing looking into his windows—trying to see if he was home.

If they actually knew he was on the FBI's ten most wanted list, they *would* have the SWAT team here, but they don't, so they don't know who he really is. But they're here, waiting to arrest him for whatever Leonard Scott did, not because he's Dean Appleby.

Hope surges through me.

I know the number for his burner phone. We agreed never to use them unless it was a matter of life and death, and I haven't tried calling him yet, even after what happened at my apartment. But if I don't warn him now, he will walk right into their trap. Without hesitation, I turn my phone on and dial his number.

I get a message saying the call cannot be completed.

I circle the streets around the apartments, and count four different marked police cars, one on each side of the compass surrounding the complex. It's a giant trap, just waiting for my dad to come home.

Dejected, I drive away, trying to think of some other way I might warn him. I park in a nearby drug store parking lot and start checking the internet on my phone. I find no local stories about my father. Then I check Portland's news sites, and discover that in addition to being a kidnap victim, I am now being sought as material witness in the disappearance of my father. I don't know exactly what this means, but it sure sounds as if I'll be detained if they find me.

Nothing I finds helps me with my immediate problem. I have to stop my father from walking into their trap. All I know is that he's going by the name of Leonard Scott, he drives a windowless white work van, and that he does siding for a guy named Dave. He's probably at work right now, but I don't know where that is. A search for siding companies run by Dave produces pages of results.

The only place he and I have in common is the coffee shop where Uncle Phil and I initially found him. He goes there in the mornings, so I won't be likely to find him there now, but it's all I can think of, so I head that way.

Ever since I hooked back up with him, I've been romanticizing about living a life on the run. Well, suddenly it's not so romantic anymore. I *am* a fugitive, and whereas it was fun doing it with my dad and uncle in the relative safety of his new life in Canada, things have changed.

If he goes back to prison, everything that's happened is for nothing. The rape, the murder of Uncle Phil, the horror of the van—everything. Things will never be the same. I've given up a legitimate life for nothing. If they catch him, then my life is no longer worth living. What will I even do? With a criminal record, I couldn't rent an apartment in my own complex, let alone manage the place.

Even if I find him and we're somehow able to get away from the police again, we'll always be one fender-bender, one emergency room visit, one wrong look at a cop from being discovered. We'll have to go somewhere new and start all over, once again living off the remaining money Uncle Phil gave us, only this time with no ID at all. How many times can we start again? My dad was right; living the life of an outlaw fugitive isn't as fun as it looks.

Wait a minute... Uncle Phil's money! That's it! That's the other link between my father and me. Even if the authorities have figured out that Leonard Scott is really Dean Appleby, and even if they know where he lives, do they know about his storage unit yet?

I'm betting they don't.

I race over to Guardian Storage, running through everything I need to do in my mind. I can't remember the entrance code to get in the gate, although I do remember that his locker is number one-seventy-four, and that the combination to the lock is a combination of our birthdays. I'll figure out how to get in the gate when I get there. If nothing else, I can just climb over the damn fence.

Even if I can't save my father, maybe I can at least prevent his money from falling into the hands of the police. And if they catch me, they catch me. At least then all the uncertainty will be over.

But when I get there, I see I'm too late. Two police cars are already there, and another is just arriving. With a feeling of dread, I turn into an alley to get away from the area.

DJ Appleby, Vancouver, BC

As I make my way through the alley, my cop radar starts going crazy. A car is approaching from behind. What's different about it is that it's accelerating. Cars don't accelerate in alleys.

There's no place to hide, so I whirl around to face it. It's not a marked unit, but it's angling directly toward me, and looks as if it's about to run me down.

Instinct kicks in, and I let go of the suitcases, abandoning over $100,000 in cash, and take off, still heading west. This being an alley, there's nowhere else to go. I'm about half a block from Cambie, a busy north/south street where I hope to disappear, but I can tell I'm not going to make it. Two seconds later, the car is abreast of me on my right.

Since it doesn't hit me, I turn to face the driver, expecting it to be the police. My eyes see and recognize her, but my mind refuses to accept it.

Grace? How is it even possible?

It *is* Grace! Leaning out the open window, she yells, "Dad! Quick, get in! The police are everywhere! Hurry!"

I still don't understand. She's was kidnapped by EK only two days before, and carried off naked and injured, in a van. Uncle Phil had been murdered in her apartment. Then they found the van in the mall parking lot with two dead EK thugs in it. That must mean that...

Thinking I must be dreaming, I come to a stop and just stand there, unmoving. My mind must be playing tricks on me.

"Dad, *move!*" she yells. "Get the goddamn suitcases in the trunk!"

Suddenly kicking into gear, I turn and run back to the suitcases. The car backs up to me and the trunk opens. I throw the suitcases and go-bag inside and jump in the passenger seat.

"How... When..." I stammer, bewildered, noting the bruises on her face. But she's alive! "Grace! Thank God!" My arms close around her and squeeze her as if she's just been raised from the dead. To me, she has.

"Not now, Dad, we have to go. The cops are everywhere! Your apartment is totally burned, and they're just arriving at Guardian now."

"Baby, I..."

"Just stay down" she commands, shoving my head down on the front seat. I comply immediately. There's something different about her now.

She's no longer the little girl she was, even after Uncle Phil got his hands on her. The change in her is significant. She just issued me an order with the authority of a military general, and I find myself obeying it like a buck-ass private.

"Do you have a place to go?" I ask, still not quite understanding that this is real.

"Yes, I've got a room at the—*Shit!* There's a cop coming up behind us, Dad. Stay down!"

I feel helpless, scrunching down on the floorboard like this.

"Shit, he's pulling us over... Okay, Dad, this is what's going to happen. I'm going to stop, but when he walks up to the car, I'm going to floor it. Just keep your head down and try to stay out of sight. Uncle Phil and I went over how to do this."

Blue and red lights flash off the headliner above me. Grace slowly pulls to the right and comes to a gentle stop. "Grace," I say. "Don't run. Don't put yourself in jeopardy for me. I'll give up. I can't stand the thought of anything bad happening to you."

"Shut up, Dad. Trust me, I know what I'm doing."

I believe her. I have nothing else to say. The patrol car's engine accelerates, and the noise and lights fade away as it passes us.

"Jesus, that was close," she says. "He's gone. But we have to get off the street. The cops are everywhere. There are six of them watching your apartment."

"Grace, please don't jeopardize yourself for me. I can take going back to prison. What I can't take is anything bad happening to you."

She turns and gives me a condescending smile. Somehow, we've gone through a bizarre role reversal, like she's the parent now and I'm the child. More appropriately, she's the instructor and I'm the pupil. Hell, I'm almost relieved she isn't mad at me.

"I'm not an innocent little girl any more, Dad," she says. "There's a material witness warrant out for my arrest. This is a stolen car, and I crossed the border with a trunkful of illegal cash and weapons."

"Jesus, Grace."

"And I've got blood on my hands. Times two."

"Honey, what happened?"

"I'll tell you once we're off the street. For now, I've got a room at Days Inn. Let's get there first."

She drives us to the hotel, where we park and walk without incident to the safety of her room, away from the sudden hostility of the street. Between us, we're carrying something like two hundred thousand dollars, and a canvas bag full of guns and ammo.

I'm not sure who the new Grace is, but one thing I know. The little girl she'd been the last time I saw her is gone forever.

Chapter 17

She tells me everything, sparing no detail. Even the parts no father wants to hear. How they beat her and questioned her about my whereabouts, then raped her. I'm proud of everything she and Uncle Phil did. She tells me about his philosophy of the hill worth dying over, and how first Gladys Knight, then Uncle Phil, and finally, she herself had all found themselves on the top of that hill, and what they'd each done about it.

She said her captors spoke of a guy named Ratt, who is the ranking EK guy on the outside, and how he ordered that she be taken back to the EK clubhouse for use as a sex slave as bait for me.

This brings to mind an oft-repeated story that I'd heard in prison. Several years ago, EK kept a craigslist hooker as a sex slave for two months, and raped her until she died. Supposedly, she's buried somewhere on the clubhouse property. I have no doubt this would have been Grace's fate had Uncle Phil not intervened.

She goes on to describe her ordeal in the van, giving Uncle Phil full credit for retroactively saving her life by gutting the one to whom she refers as Hairy, which sufficiently weakened him so that she could kill him in the van, and be able to get the drop on the one she calls Baldy.

Even I cannot decide if it the decisions she made after getting out of that van were wise or stupid, but I do know one thing. You can't argue with results, and she just saved me, both figuratively and literally. I'm just afraid it's going to take her years to recover emotionally from all this, if recovery is even possible.

By the time she gets to the part about her border crossing, we both need a little relief, and we end up laughing ourselves to tears. How Uncle Phil would have loved that part!

Despite the moment of levity, there is a murderous rage building up in me. The European Kindred did this to my daughter, and I will see to it that they are repaid in kind. I'm ready to leave now, and kill every last man with an EK shield tattoo.

I inspect Uncle Phil's AR-15 and find it to be in pristine condition, as is his pistol, a Sig Sauer 9-mm with a screw-on silencer. I'm glad Grace had the foresight to bring them. It wasn't necessarily smart of her, but they sure will come in handy. Those guns and I have a date at EK headquarters. There will be no mercy when I get there. Anyone unfortunate enough to be present will die. I intend to give Portland a new kind of active shooter—a cleansing version; one that will leave no traces of the European Kindred behind to further pollute the city.

I don't share these plans with Grace. Taking care of EK is something I will do on my own. Grace's job will be to carry on, because all fantasy aside, my visit to the EK clubhouse will probably be a one-way trip, and I have no intentions of taking Grace down with me. I pull her into a hug, and tell her that I'm going to go away for a few days, and when I get back, she's never going to have to worry about EK again.

Apparently, this is the wrong thing to say, because she pulls away from me and says, "You're kidding, right? Those guys killed Uncle Phil, Dad. They *raped* me. One of them is still out there. I'm not going to stop until I find him, and then I'm going to kill him."

"Grace, honey, don't you think you've been through enough? You're young enough to pick up your life again. *I'll* take care of the one that got away. I've been looking for a purpose in my life, and now I've found it. I'll take care of all the loose ends in a way that will make you and Uncle Phil proud."

"No Dad. Don't you understand, this is all about you? If you go back to jail or get killed, then *they* win, and that's not acceptable. Uncle Phil died so that you wouldn't have to go back to prison. Don't make his death be in vain. Don't make what happened to *me* be in vain. The whole point of all of this is that *you* make it. You have to live out your life in peace, on the outside, not in prison. That's why all this is happening."

"Hold on just a second, Grace. Do you really think that I'm going to stand by and let them get away with killing Uncle Phil? With… With doing what they did to you? And just go live someplace so I can go to work every day, like a schmuck? That's not who I am. I won't rest until I find that—"

"And you think me going back to my old life is who *I* am?" she asks, cutting me off. "Nobody's going to get away with anything. I'm going to find that Soul Patch guy and I'm going to finish what I started in that van!"

The look in her eye and the tone of her voice is downright scary. I seem to have forgotten my little Grace has been born again hard.

She drones on, but I am no longer listening. Something about her description of "Soul Patch" is niggling at me. She'd described him as having a long mustache hanging down from the corners of his mouth to the bottom of his chin, with a dark soul patch in between. It's a common enough look among prisoners. Not just EK, but anyone who wants to project himself as a badass, but still...

"Grace," I interrupt. "These three guys who did this thing, did they call each other by name?"

"No, they all had nicknames. The leader of the group, the one I call Hairy, his name was Skip, or Stitch, or Skid, something like that. He's the one Uncle Phil gutted and I killed first. Stinger, the guy I call Baldy, he's the one that actually killed Uncle Phil. He's the second guy I killed in the van. The one that got away, who I call Soul Patch, he's the one raped me. They called him Kickstand. He's the one I'm going after."

"Are you sure it wasn't Kickstart? Instead of Kickstand?"

"Yeah, that was it, Kickstart. Why? Do you know him?"

"I know him all right. His real name is Kevin Durst, and we did time together at Oregon State Prison. We had a... well, a disagreement. Why don't we do this, Grace? Let's take tomorrow to buy a vehicle and get our shit together, then tomorrow night, we'll take off and do this thing together. The streets will be a little quieter by then, and we can be in Portland by the morning, when they're at their most vulnerable. Then we'll finish what you and Uncle Phil started. Together."

She relaxes and smiles. "That's what I've had in mind all along, Dad."

Kevin Durst is the inmate who planned to murder a correctional officer when we were in the Oregon State Prison together. I ratted him out to a guard and foiled the hit, but the European Kindred figured out I was the informer, and tried to kill me. In fact, the last thing I remember about being locked up in the Oregon State Prison is Durst's boot coming down on my face as they beat and stomped me nearly to death. At the time, he was doing a ten-year stretch for armed robbery, and had less than two years to go. Apparently, he made it.

If I didn't have a mission in life before, I do now. Kickstart tried to kill me in the pen, and then kidnapped and raped my daughter once he got out. He's gotten away with it so far, and he's still out there now. But not for long. I will take my revenge from his flesh, and watch him suffer. When I am done, he will be begging me to kill him, and only then will I consider it.

But Grace will not be with me. I won't let her anywhere near EK or any of it's members. I won't even allow her to leave Canada. I love her too much. I love her enough even to betray her. I'll fix it so she can't ever be associated with what I'm going to do.

I have virtually no chance of making out of the EK clubhouse alive, and I'm not about to see Grace go down with me. Plus, the last thing she needs is to be immured into this outlaw lifestyle any more than she already is. Therefore, I've come up with a way to keep her out of it. She'll never understand it, and I know she'll hate me for it, but to me it's worth it. I think that even the new, hardcore Grace will eventually forgive me, but if she doesn't, then at least she'll be alive.

I'm going to turn her in to the police.

She'll see it as a betrayal of everything we've ever taught her, and she'll hate me for it. She may never even speak to me again, but in time, I believe she will recover, and if she does, there will be no more running. No more third-generation outlaw. Only Grace, alive and free to find some semblance of normalcy after what we've done to her.

I will give us one more day as outlaws together, and that's where our good memories will be rooted. Tomorrow night, I will leave without her knowledge, drop a dime to the RCMP, and then go directly to Portland to take care of Durst and EK. Without Grace. By the time the authorities work out the details of her extradition, I will be finished with my business, and Kevin Durst will no longer inhabit the land of the living. The same might hold true for me.

I imagine when all the dust settles, they'll probably drop the charges against Grace. No district attorney will want to be known as the guy who put a rape victim in jail for making poor choices in the hours after being kidnapped and raped. But it would be a completely different story if she were to go after Durst now. That would make whatever she did to him planned and calculated. The legal term is "premeditated," and premeditated comes with the death penalty.

They already have me on a death penalty case, so what's one more? What are they going to do, kill me twice? Grace doesn't need a death penalty conviction. Her job will be to survive the outlaw life, and become the first Appleby to return from it.

If I somehow make it out of that clubhouse, then I can always reevaluate my options. Maybe Grace and I could actually go to Morocco after all. Or, maybe I will simply turn myself in, and if Grace forgives me, then she can come visit me in prison. Either way, I have every confidence that if I live through it, she will eventually become my daughter once again.

Personally, I'm tired of life on the run. I have been for quite some time now. Though I am no longer incarcerated, I am anything but free. I'm tired of constantly looking over my shoulder, trying to figure out if everyone who happens to be glancing in my direction is either a cop or an EK hitman. And just for the record, of the two, I'd much prefer to be caught by the police.

My IDs are all blown, and I'm wanted in two countries. Morocco is nothing more than a pipe dream. It's like counting on the lottery ticket in your pocket to get you out of financial trouble. You can fantasize about it all you want, but everyone knows it's not really going to happen.

I've already done what I set out to do when I walked out of that hospital. I found Grace and reconnected with her. Now there's only one thing left for me to do—show EK and Kevin Durst exactly how big of a mistake they've made by involving Grace in business that was heretofore just between us. Once I am free of EK, I can be done with it all. Done with running, done with being a criminal, done with being Bad. Done with the whole fucking lifestyle.

Grace and I talk until dark, then, both exhausted, we fall into bed and sleep like the dead. In the morning, we wake to find my booking photo from yesterday's arrest plastered all over the internet. The local news outlets are pretty unforgiving to Vancouver PD for letting such a big fish go. It turns out the police never ran the gun's serial number through any data systems until thirty minutes *after* I was released. A multinational manhunt is now underway for me.

The car that Grace stole from her apartment is now a problem. If my cover hadn't been blown, I would simply take it back to Oregon and use it on my mission against EK. Grace said she left no trace that she'd been in that woman's apartment other than some missing clothes. Maybe I could even park it back where it belongs, and the owner will never know anyone was even there.

Now, however, they'll scrutinize the border crossing videotapes, trying to see when I crossed, and once they see what happened with Grace, that vehicle will be flagged. Police will no doubt be looking for it.

If Grace were actually coming with me to finish Durst and EK, we'd have to take care of the car in such a way that made it seem that she had nothing to do with stealing it. We'd have to make it look stolen, and the best way to do that is to make it look like EK stole it to come here to get me. But right now, it's still covered with our fingerprints and DNA, so it needs to be dealt with. I can no longer risk going outside, but Grace can still move about with relative ease, so it will fall to her to get rid of it and acquire new wheels.

She still thinks we're using today to make the preparations to hit EK's clubhouse tomorrow, so I assign her the task of getting rid of the Chrysler and acquiring a new set of wheels to use on our mission. I will need a good, reliable four-wheel-drive truck for tomorrow. I don't care what it looks like or how much it costs, it just has to be reliable.

Grace searches the internet, and comes up with three possible trucks for sale within a twenty-mile radius. She makes arrangements to go look at one, and I make sure she has enough money to pay for it. She dons her Goth costume and plants a little kiss on my cheek as she heads out the door. As much as I hate myself for what Uncle Phil and I have done to her, I have to admit that I'm proud as hell of her. She's twice the badass than most of the hardcore cons I've met. She won't hesitate to do whatever she needs in order to survive, and if I am ever in a jam, there's nobody I'd rather have fighting by my side than her. She's gone from little girl to supreme badass in less than two months. I only hope is that she can revert back to normal person mode just as quickly. And, that she'll eventually forgive me for what I'm about to do.

She returns three hours later carrying a Target bag and some fast food. "I got you a disguise, too," she says. "Sorry, it's kind of hokey, but it's the best I could do."

She pulls out a pair of blue jean overalls and a red John Deere baseball cap. The cap, which she must have picked up at a novelty shop or a costume store, has long, gray hair hanging down from it. There is also a pair of black-framed glasses that have clear lenses.

"Really?" I say, putting it on. It feels ridiculous.

"You look great, Farmer John," she laughs.

"I don't care if they send me back to prison, but I'm never going to wear this idiotic getup," I vow, taking it off. "Did you get the truck?"

She nods. "Blue '96 GMC Sierra. Four-wheel drive, extended cab, 187,000 miles, but lots of new parts and just tuned up. And don't worry, I didn't dump the Chrysler anywhere near where I bought the truck."

"Good girl. What'd you pay for the truck?" I asked.

"Five grand. Hand-to-hand cash deal; no paperwork, no record, and no questions. He signed over the title, and I signed it Jane Olson."

I smiled. "Good girl. Sounds like the perfect vehicle. You did well, honey."

"So, what's the plan?"

I hate lying to her, and I'm glad I won't be around when she realizes what I've done. Badass Outlaw Grace won't take my betrayal very well. "The plan is, we leave tonight around 10:00, and cross the border at this place I know of east of here, which is why we needed a four-wheel drive truck. We'll be at the clubhouse in Portland by 7:00 or 8:00 AM. Their normal routine is to party 'til 3:00 or 4:00, then crash and sleep till noon. So, they'll be at their most vulnerable in the early morning hours. We'll take them by surprise, bust in, and if Kevin Durst isn't there, whoever's in charge—this Ratt guy—will be begging to tell us where he is once we're done with him."

"Okay. You can have Ratt, but when we find Soul Patch, he's mine. Right?"

"Sure, honey. But before you make your final decision to go, I want you to consider something. There's a lot that can go wrong on a mission like this. We may not even make it to the clubhouse, let alone get inside, and if we do, our chances of making it out of there are pretty slim. And I don't have to tell you what will happen if they somehow get the drop on us. I don't even want to think about that."

A shadow crosses her face. "I don't understand what you mean by 'before I decide to go,' Dad, because that's not even in question. As to the rest of it, they're not going to get the drop on us, and even if they did, it won't matter. We'll be together, regardless how it ends. Either we get away together, we get caught together, or we die together. I'm good with any of those, as long as we're together."

Well I'm not. I'm not good with any of them, because in each scenario, Grace is present. If I were to allow her to come with me, she would no doubt die with me. Or worse, *not* die with me, and become their captive. Even if we successfully completed the mission, it would probably screw her up even worse than she already is. Doing what I intend to will probably fuck *me* up, and I have a lot more experience with evil than Grace does. I don't want that to happen to her, or to mess her life up with an arrest, and there's no way I will allow her undertake any endeavor that carries the risk of getting get caught by them again.

Shifting gears in my mind, I say, "Okay then. Where'd you dump the Chrysler?"

"It's about a mile from here. There's some kind of glassmaking plant in the industrial area behind the Esso station a few blocks south of here. It's in the back lot, right up against the building."

"Perfect. Is it clean?"

"What do you think I am, Dad, a rookie? Of course it's clean, there's not a fingerprint in it or on it."

"Good job, honey. We'll swing by it, make it look stolen, and plant some evidence in it to take the heat off you."

"What kind of evidence? What do you have in mind?"

The lies come easier now, because it's for her own good.

"Well, it's all based on the idea that you haven't done anything wrong. The spiky haired girl did it all. She's an EK hired gun. She stole the car and drove it up here to come after me. We're going to plant evidence that she pistol-whipped me, proving that it was *her*, not you, that drove that car across the border and shit on the guard. You had nothing to do with any of it. Then, after we're done at the EK clubhouse, we make it look like I just rescued you from there, and you'll be one hundred percent in the clear. All you have to remember is the spiky haired girl stole the car, crossed the border, and tried to kill me. You were being held at the clubhouse the whole time. Got it?"

"What about video from this hotel? It'll show me staying here, with you. And, I rented the room in my own name."

"No, it'll show the female Goth EK assassin, who used your stolen ID to rent the room. You haven't been out of the room in view of any cameras without the disguise on. We'll wipe the room down for prints before we leave, so we ought to be good on that. In fact, it'll just confirm that part of the story."

"Dad, you came in with me, without a disguise. They're going to know it was me, not some Goth assassin."

"I don't know, Grace. I'll make something up about going with her voluntarily, because I heard them torturing you over the phone or something, then I'll just say I got the drop on her later, and got away. They'll never find her, so I'll tell them I killed her or something. Trust me, I can handle that part of it."

"Oh my God, Dad, it might just work! What about you? What will you do after we kill Ratt and Durst?"

"I'll be gone long before the police get there. I know a place nearby where I can hang out until we figure out a way for me to get to Morocco. Once I'm there, I'll send for you. You'll be legit and you have a passport. You'll simply fly down there and never come back, and we live happily ever after. What do you say?"

"Are there contingency plans if things don't go smoothly?"

"Not yet. Like I said, it's a work in progress. Don't forget, we're the Applebys. We're good at shit like this. If things go south, you take off. Turn yourself in somewhere nearby, and stick with the story that you were being held the whole time, and you escaped when I started shooting the place up, and we'll just wing it from there. Just remember, we'll be back on Uncle Phil's hill, which means we won't stop until the mission is over. One way or the other.

She nods to herself and says, "I can live with that. Let's do it!"

She's placated for now because she has faith in me. Ten hours from now, she will hate my guts, but I have faith in her that she'll come back to me. The important thing is, no matter what happens after I leave, she'll come out of this in one piece.

We take showers and go to bed at five. She has an alarm on her burner set for 11:00 PM, at which point we'll just leave. The truck's gassed up and everything is in place.

Grace falls asleep immediately. Her trust in me is complete. I have no doubt she'll sleep well. It's almost scares me that she sleeps so well, considering the emotional damage she must have from everything she's been through and done. Everything I'm doing now is about fixing as much of that damage as I can.

I lay next to her for an hour listening to her rhythmic breathing, then sneak out of bed and get to work. First, I put a thousand dollars in her jeans pocket with a note that says, 'I leave all my money and everything I own to Grace Appleby. Signed: Philip Appleby," and date it one week ago. Then, I load the duffel bag containing the guns into the truck. Finally, I don the ridiculous Farmer John outfit, kiss her lightly on the cheek, and slip out the door.

She picked the perfect vehicle. It's solid, it runs well, it's a four-wheel drive, and its nondescript. I have no problem following her directions to where she dumped the Chrysler. There are no security cameras anywhere visible. The location is good and I can work here without worrying about being discovered.

First I rip out the panel under the steering column, find the ignition wires, strip them, and get the engine started. It's got enough gas to idle until it is discovered. Next, I prepare the pistol she took from the guy she calls Hairy. I wipe it down thoroughly. Grace has told me that she never field-stripped it or touched the ammo, so the inside and all the rounds in the magazine will have Hairy's fingerprints all over them, but no part of the gun will have our prints on it.

Once the gun is ready, I clean the blade of the knife with spit, and wipe it against my pants, then make a small incision on the tip of my left little finger. I spread the blood along one corner of the magazine butt-plate, allowing it to run through the crevices along the grip. Finally, I yank out several hairs from the roots and strategically place them in the blood on the weapon, then carefully place the gun on the ground next to the open driver's door.

Then I head back to our motel. I've only been gone about fifteen minutes. Half a block down the street from the motel is a phone booth. I've already scoped it out and know there aren't any cameras around. Using a paper towel, I pick up the receiver and dial 911.

"Emergency Services, what's the nature of your emergency?"

"That guy you arrested yesterday, who's the escaped prisoner from the United States? You know, the former cop? Well, his daughter is staying right here at the Days Inn on Kingsway. Room 21. I know it's her. And there's a guy staying there too. I think it might be, you know, *him*."

"Sir, can I have your name? How do you know—"

I drop the phone without hanging up, hating myself for what I am doing. Silently praying for her forgiveness, I get in the truck and hit the road.

Three hours later, I'm cruising down Canadian Route 3, also known as the Crow's Nest Highway, taking care to keep my speed at 45 km/hr, five under the posted speed limit. I'm heading to a spot where the highway angles south and comes within a hundred yards of the US border in Central Washington. I haven't seen another car in over two hours.

I'm trying to imagine every possible scenario for the confrontation at the clubhouse when I am suddenly rammed from behind by a vehicle I had no idea was following me.

"Shit!" My heart comes to the back of my throat and my foot mashes the gas while I look in the rearview mirror. A few car lengths behind me is a blacked-out car matching my speed. As I watch, it's headlights come on. I grab the Glock from the glove box, wondering what the hell is going on. It's a quarter to two in the morning, and this is an extremely remote section of highway. There hasn't been any traffic here for hours.

Clearly, it isn't the police, and it's obviously not EK either, or I'd already be dead. But it's no accident they're here.

I slow down and pull to the right shoulder, and so does the other car. After I stop, it creeps up and stops behind me with its parking lights on. The door opens and a figure steps out. I step out as well.

There's only one person it can be, and now I'm the one who is afraid.

"You left me, you fucking son of a bitch! I woke up and you were fucking *gone*! And you called the fucking *police* on me? I should shoot you myself and save EK the trouble! What the actual fuck, Dad? *Why?*"

Thirty minutes later, after sanitizing and leaving the stolen Subaru she was driving, Grace is finally starting to calm down. She tells me she woke up when I left. She thought she heard a door closing, and came out to investigate. When I wasn't there, she figured I went to go plant the evidence at the Chrysler, but then, she had the feeling something wasn't right and got dressed. Apparently Grace has developed that "sixth sense" that has served the Applebys so well over the years.

That's when she discovered the money and the note, and realized that I had betrayed her.

She went to the rear parking lot and hot-wired the first car she came to, then loaded up the suitcases with the money and took off. She was on her way out of the lot when police cars came pouring in the front, and she simply drove away.

She knew I was heading to the place where the highway dipped down to the border, and mapped the route out on her phone. If she couldn't find me, she'd chance crossing no-man's land in her stolen car. She kept it floored the whole way, risking a stop by the police, and by some miracle, caught up to me without wrecking or getting pulled over.

She's still infuriated at me for leaving her, and won't even talk to me. I'm as pissed as she is, because all I want is for her to be safe, and now she's here with me. But on the other hand, she's hell-bent on going to the EK clubhouse and so am I, and I could actually use the help. Like it or not, she's with me, and will stay with me. I may be the legendary Bad, but I'm not bad enough to dump her again. I'd have to break one of her legs or something.

So now, it appears that she'll get her wish, that whatever happens at the clubhouse, we'll do it together. I don't know. Maybe it's better this way.

We drive on in silence, and about an hour later, we come out of the wilderness and into an area that's being developed. The speed limit drops and houses appear. Some are occupied, and others are in various stages of construction. Then we come to an intersection with a stop sign. I turn right, heading south on a street divided into housing plots. Here, they're just digging sewer lines and putting in other utilities. The street goes south for a few blocks, then, at the point closest to the US border, it curves back to the north. I stop at the southernmost point, and shut the engine off.

"We're here," I say solemnly. "The United States is only a hundred or so yards that way. Grace, honey, I don't suppose I can talk you out of this, can I? It really isn't too late. I can get you across the border, even back to Portland, and you can still turn yourself in. You've got Uncle Phil's money and his house. You can pick up your life and move on. You can *live*. Please, will you do that for me? Will you make my life worthwhile by living?"

She turns to me, her face burning with anger and disappointment. "I am so fucking pissed at you right now. I cannot believe you just said that. We *talked* about all this last night. Remember, the hill worth dying over?

How together as father and daughter, we're going give them a fight they won't soon forget? Well, you lied to me and you ditched me, and you snitched me off to the police. All I have to say about that is fuck you."

"Grace, I—"

"No, fuck you, Dad! I will never forgive you for leaving me up there. But now I'm here. Now you're stuck with me, and you know what? You're not in charge any more. If it *really* is the hill worth dying over, then you're with me, and we will do it together. Remember, Durst raped *me* while his friends laughed and waited for their turn, not you. *I* watched Uncle Phil die, not you, and he didn't die for you, he died for *me*. *I* got myself out of that van, and now *I'm* going to find the one that got away. This is *my* hill, not yours. If all that stuff pisses you off and makes it your hill too, then come fight with me, and we'll do it together. If it's not, then *you* get out and I'll fucking do it alone. Now I'm warning you, do not fucking suggest that again. Ever."

Her words are so hard they bring tears to my eyes. Hers, however, are as cold as steel. What in God's name have we created in her? I'm no longer afraid for her, I'm afraid *of* her. With a resigned sigh, I reach out and take her hand. Thankfully, she doesn't slap me away. "Okay, honey. We will do it together, I promise. Please forgive me for trying to leave you, but know that I don't regret it. I was only trying to take care of you. You're the only person I love, Grace. But I feel goddamn honored to have you fight by my side. I promise, there will be no more deception, or talk of leaving you out. Let's go do it."

For the first time since last night, she smiles at me, and we're together again. "Then why are we sitting here? The sooner we get there, the sooner we can leave."

I start the engine and shift into four-wheel drive. As we bump over a curb and head south across open land, she very quietly says, "Just know if you try it again, Dad, I'll kill you myself."

We bounce and jounce southward, down a slight embankment and into a little gully. It's rough, and the truck bottoms out, but a moment later we pop out onto a smooth gravel road and I bring the truck to a stop.

"That's it, Grace. We're here. Welcome to the United States. Now we just follow the roads south, and eventually we'll end up on Highway 97, which will take us down to Yakima, and I know how to get back to Portland from there."

"How long to Portland?"

"I'm not really sure. Maybe six or seven hours."

She asks, "How do you feel about being back?"

"I don't know. I thought it would feel good, but it doesn't. I guess there's no difference between Canada and the US for me now. I'm wanted in both countries, and both now have my fingerprints and picture. I have no more good aliases. I'm actually worse off than I was the day Uncle Phil dropped me off at the border. At least then I had a whole country to hide in."

"Okay then. So, after EK, we'll figure out how to get to Morocco. We'll learn Arabic, I'll get a job and a hot stud and make you a bunch of brown grandbabies. You can find yourself a nice little Moroccan honey to keep you warm at night, and—"

"Grace! Jesus, I know you're a full-on badass now, but I'm not ready to discuss my love life with you!"

She laughs, and it's a good sound to hear. It means we're good again. I desperately hope I'll get to hear that laughter after whatever happens later today.

Four hours later, we stop for gas in Wenatchee, Washington. We cross back into Oregon and it's a straight shot down I-84 to Portland. We're maybe four hours away.

The drive is uneventful. At a go-nowhere exit just outside of Portland with a spectacular view of the Columbia River, we retrieve the weapons from behind the seats. The suitcases containing every penny of Uncle Phil's money are still back there.

I screw the silencer onto the barrel of Uncle Phil's Sig, rack a round into the chamber, top off the mag, and place the gun in my waistband at the small of my back. I give the AR-15 to Grace and show her to load a magazine into it. I demonstrate how to charge the weapon, and of course, she grasps the concept immediately. Then I have her load and charge it. After making sure the safety is on, she stashes it within easy reach under the front seat, and we hit the road for the final leg.

Scattered among the boulders on the south bank of the Columbia River is a spiky black wig, a couple of fake nose rings, and a red ball cap with ridiculous long gray hair.

We are idling on the side of Foster Road half a block away from the driveway to the EK clubhouse. Uncle Phil's silenced Sig is in my hand, and Grace is cradling the AR in her lap. Before we launch, we have a come to Jesus moment.

"You know, Grace, my biggest regret is not getting to know you when you were young. I think of all the years we could have been this close, and I wish I could go back and do it all over again. I promise you, things would be a lot different."

"I'm not so sure I'd want it any different, Dad. I kind of like the way things are now. I'm not talking about our *circumstances* per se, but you know, how we are. I mean, look at us. We're together. We're close. Hell, Dad, we're a couple of badasses, and we're going to go in there and do a good thing. We're going to make things right. We're going to avenge Uncle Phil, and before they die, those assholes will wish they'd never met any of us. Think how happy Uncle Phil is, looking down on us right now. I feel him with us, don't you, Dad?"

"Grace, you do understand that we're as likely to die in there as we are to succeed, don't you? That's why I didn't want you to come. I don't want to lose you."

She smiles a shy, little girl smile; full of faith that good will triumph over evil and the sun will rise tomorrow. "Dad, *we're* not the ones who are going to die in there. And it doesn't matter if we do, because either way, we win. Walking out of there is better than not walking out of there, but it really doesn't matter that much. They did what they did to Uncle Phil and me, but they still didn't beat us. I came back. They thought they had me, but I walked out of that van, and those two shitbags didn't. Now it's time to go back and get the one that got away. After that, I really don't care that much. I'd rather go to Morocco together, but I can live with going to prison, and I'm okay with it if this is the end. This really, truly is the hill worth dying over, for both of us, and I believe that with all my heart."

I squeeze her hand, and say, "You're right baby. It's been my hill since those guys came to your apartment. I just want you to know that it'll be an honor to fight side-by-side with you. I really mean that."

She leans over and hugs me so tight it squeezes the breath out of me. "I'm ready. Are you?"

I check the silenced pistol to ensure there's a round in it for maybe the fourth time. "Hell yes. Let's go take that hill!"

Chapter 18

The EK clubhouse is a nondescript building in a commercial district in the middle of Portland on a half-acre plot in an industrial area near SE 103rd and Foster. It is completely hidden from street view, tucked away among towing companies, transmission shops, and HVAC businesses. There is a metal gate across the driveway, which is closed and chained.

Before I just drive the truck through the gate, I decide to check it first, and find that the chain is merely draped across the gate and is not locked. It's the first indication of the lax security that I hope will be their downfall.

I actually feel it now—victory. Seeing Grace kneeling beside the truck's open passenger door with the AR leveled at the house while I quietly remove the chain and drop it into the dirt, I am infused with a feeling of invincibility. When I swing the gate open, it squeals in protest, but as we've experienced so many times, nobody hears us, and nobody cares. There's no movement from the clubhouse, and we get back in the truck. Slowly, we idle into the lot, the gravel crunching quietly under the tires, and come to a stop near the building.

"Cameras everywhere," says Grace, pointing them out as we approach the door. She's right, but again, I feel it doesn't matter. Finally, we're standing on the porch, directly beneath a camera. There is no response whatsoever from inside.

"These fucks would have already had us if they were watching," I say. "Now remember Grace, Kevin Durst, AKA Kickstart, AKA Soul Patch, is our highest-value target. Ratt, who ordered the rape, is next. All roads will lead to them. We'll deal with any other loose ends as they arise. You ready?"

She nods and says, "I'll see you on the other side."

"Okay, baby girl. Let's roll."

I stand back on my left foot, cock my right leg, and give it everything I have with the heel of my boot, right over the deadbolt. The jamb splinters and gives way, and the door swings inward, bouncing off the wall behind it with a loud bang. I follow its swing into the room with Grace hot on my heels, meeting no resistance whatsoever.

There's a single occupant in the room, a long-haired, bearded con sitting on the couch watching TV. He's obviously been caught entirely unawares by our entry. Startled, he jumps to his feet, but freezes as he looks down the business end of Grace's rifle. He just stands there looking stupid with his hands held out to his sides.

"I won't give you any problems, man. Just stay cool, okay?" he says quietly.

From somewhere in the back, a voice calls out, "Jesus Christ, Mitch, what the fuck are you doing out there? Keep it down, man! I *still* got a hellacious fucking hangover!"

"Say one word and you're dead," I say, locking my eyes on his over the front sight of my pistol. I've never seen this man before. He nods, and I say to Grace, "Cover him. If he moves, kill him." Not needing an acknowledgement from her, I do a quick, cursory search of the room and see that no one else is here.

The room is basically a large living room, with a flat-screen TV, a wet bar, a pool table, and a couple of couches and chairs scattered about. There's a small kitchen off to the left, with a closed door at the end of it.

On the right side of the room is a bathroom with an open door, and two other doors, both of which are closed. On a desk in the corner is a computer with two screens showing all the cameras covering the grounds. Had this guy been sitting there, we'd be dead now.

"Who else is here?" I ask quietly. "Lie to me even once, and I will kill you. Understand?"

"Completely. It's just Ratt, Kickstart, and me. I swear to God, man."

"If you're wrong, you'll be the first to die here today."

I open one of the doors on the right, and find a small room, like a den. There's a man passed out in an easy chair. He doesn't move, and I recognize him instantly. It's Kickstart. I give a thumbs-up to Grace, who can cover him along with the hippy guy from where she's at.

"Don't wake him up until I get everyone else, and then we'll all have us a little chat."

She nods. Her kinetic energy reminds me of a police dog slavering over a bad guy, nothing but barely-restrained enthusiasm waiting to be set loose. I check the other door, and it's just a large closet. Lastly, I go the closed door off the kitchen and find that it too, is unlocked. Inside is another man facedown on a bed. This one is semi-awake. When I come in, he sits up, blinking.

"Who the fuck are you?" he asks.

I don't recognize him. Keeping the pistol at the low ready, I pull up my right pant leg and show him the shield tatted to the back of my calf. "I'm EK. And you are?"

"I'm Ratt. I'm the ranking guy on the outside. If you're EK, you should know that. What the fuck are you doing here, barging in with a fucking gun like you own the place?"

"Well, Ratt, my name is DJ. Pleased to meet you. Of course, you may know me by my prison name, which is Bad."

He blinks a few more times, then a synapse fires somewhere in his brain. "You're Bad? Snake River Bad?"

"In the flesh."

His eyes flick to a chest of drawers next to the bed.

"Don't even think about it, Ratt. You make any quick moves, and you'll be shitting out of a new hole. Tell me you understand me."

"You're not EK. I heard all about you. You got yours coming, Bad. You're a fucking rat is what you are."

"Well, that's confusing," I say. "I thought *you* were Ratt."

"You should get out of here while you still can, smartass. You're gonna wish you never came back here."

"We'll see who wishes they weren't here in a few minutes. Now get your ass into the living room. We're going to have us a little church session. Move it."

He gets up and I hand him off to Grace. Oh, how his eyes widen when he sees her standing there with an AR-15. It's a Kodak moment if there ever was one. Ratt takes a seat on the couch next to the first guy while I go back to Kickstart's room.

He's still asleep, and I slap him across the face. He yelps and jumps up, but freezes when he sees me. I can see that he recognizes me instantly. "Mornin', Kevin. Ever hear that old saying, what goes around comes around? Well, guess what? It just came around. Move your ass into the living room."

He looks at me, then glances out into the living room and sees Grace. A look of resignation comes across his face, and he sighs. "Shit. Well, I guess this is your big fuckin' moment, isn't it? If you're gonna kill me, then kill me, asshole. Or better yet, have her do it. Wouldn't that be more fitting, based on our history? Or don't you have the balls for it?"

"'Funny that you mentioned balls, Durst, seeing that you aren't going to have yours much longer. As for killing you, well, you're gonna be begging me to do that soon enough. You aren't getting off that eas—"

He lunges at me, but I'm ready for it. I redirect my aim to his knee and pull the trigger. The suppressed report is about as loud as a firecracker; perhaps half the volume of a normal gunshot. He crashes to the floor, screaming and holding his shattered right knee. Oddly, enough, the most distinctive sound is the musical tinkle of the shell casing bouncing off the floor.

Grace yells, "Dad! Are you okay?"

"I'm fine, honey. Can't say the same for Kickstart though. Better bring the others in here."

As they grimly march in at the business end of her AR, Durst, who'd been moaning and holding his bloody knee, looks up and says, "You fucking *shot* me! What the *fuck*!"

"You still have another knee and two elbows left, Durst. You'll keep your mouth shut if you want to keep them."

Ratt says, "Okay, Bad, you made your point. Obviously, you got some kind of agenda in mind, or you would have already killed us. You got our attention. What is it you want?"

I point the gun at his knee and tell him to shut up. He shuts up.

Shifting my aim to the third guy, I say, "What's your story, Slick?"

"Stay chill, dude. I'm Mitch. I got out last month, and got nowhere to go, so I came here. I know why you're here man. I'd be here too, if I were you."

"Yeah? Why don't you enlighten me then."

"I seen all this shit go down. It started just after I got paroled and came here. Ratt here wants to make a name for himself, and he thought he could do that by getting you. I told him it wasn't the best idea, man; that they called you Bad for a reason, but he's trying to gain status, you know? He—"

Ratt interjects, "I knew you were a snitchy little pussy, Mitch. Go ahead and flap your jaw. Write your own fuckin' death warrant. You're gonna die here, just like Bad. EK is a lot bigger than me. You're both fucking *done*."

I redirect the gun back to his knee and say, "I'm not going to tell you again. Utter one more word. I dare you."

He doesn't, and I turn back to Mitch and say, "Keep talking."

"He wouldn't let it go, man. At first I thought he was just trying to impress the guys at the top, but then he sent Skid, Stinger, and Kicky to your daughter's place, figuring if they followed her long enough, she might lead them to you. You know? But she wasn't there. They kept going back, like for a couple weeks, but every time they went there, she was gone.

"It really pissed Ratt off that he couldn't grab her, so the last time, he told them if they ever did get their hands on her, they were to, uh, sorry dude, but his words were 'gang rape the shit out of her, then bring her back here for the rest of us.' He said if we had her, *you* would come to *us* instead of us having to hunt you down. I wasn't cool with it then, and I'm not cool with it now, but I'm not gonna lie to you, man. That's how it went down."

I look at Ratt and say, "Well? What do you have to say to that?"

"Jesus Christ, Bad, you're shitting me, right? You seen guys like him before. They'll say anything to keep their tit out of the ringer. He's flat-out fucking lying to you. He's as dirty as the rest of us!"

I say, "Interesting choice of words, Ratt. 'As dirty as the rest of us.' You're wrong. I believe him, and you know why? Because I was EK for two solid years. I know the kind of shit you guys are capable of. And, it makes sense. You're trying to make a name for yourself; keep your position as the ranking guy outside. You ordered her raped, and you ordered her kidnapped, both of which were grave mistakes on your part. Take a look at her now. Not exactly what you had in mind when you pictured her here, is it?"

He doesn't say anything, but I can see he's really pissed. One thing he isn't, I note, is a coward. Pushing him a little farther, I say, "I got some more news for you, fucky. *I'm* the new ranking guy on the outside. You ain't shit. Your new street name is Mouse, not Ratt. Mitch, you're a witness to this. Got anything to say to that, Mouse?"

He jabs an index finger at me, accentuating his anger with every word. "Hey man, *fuck* you, and fuck your slut daughter. If not for that scabby old fuck, we *all* would have, Mitch, too! Is that good enough for you, you miserable piece of shit? So go ahead, shoot me in the fucking knee!"

I shoot him in the knee, and he screams as loud as Durst did.

Mitch pales and says, "Holy shit, man!" He puts his hand up as if to ward me off, and says, "Just so you know, Bad, I got a daughter, too. I haven't seen her in five years, and her mom tells me she's on the needle now, but she still means the world to me. If anyone ever did to her what they did to your little girl, I'd do exactly what you're doing. I joined EK to survive in prison without getting butt-fucked, man, not to be a part of shit like this. What Ratt ordered, and what Kickstart, Skid, and Stinger did was fucked up. I don't know what I'd have done if they brought her back here. I mean, I'm not the kind of guy who could stop them from doing bad shit to her, but I swear to God, dude, I'd have never touched her. I'd would have probably, like, let her escape or something. I wish I could tell you I'd have never let them bring her here, but they own me. You know how it is, man."

"Yeah, I know how it is, and I believe you. But if I even think you're lying to me, your knees are going to look like theirs."

"I'm cool with that, because I'm being straight up with you. Just tell me what you want me to do, man. I'm on your side here."

"Right now, your job is to bear witness. I'll decide what to do with you later."

Grace finally speaks up. "Dad, I'm sick of looking at these guys alive. Let's finish them, and him too," Grace says, pointing at the hapless Mitch. "Then we need to do like the good shepherd said, and get the flock out of here. We've been here too long as it is."

She's right. It's definitely time to go. It's hard to believe we've been so fortunate. I hadn't really thought we'd be able to find Durst, let alone get the drop on both him and Ratt. It's funny; I had planned this as a one-man, one-way operation. I hadn't considered the possibility of the mission being successful, let alone getting out alive. And I sure as hell didn't plan on Grace being here. I don't have an exit plan other than getting in the truck and driving away. Now I'll actually have to think about how to get us to Morocco.

But first things first. I tell Grace, "I think Durst should be neutered first. What do you think?"

"I couldn't agree more."

"Do you want me to do it?"

"No. Like I said, he's mine."

"Okay. Gun, or knife?"

She contemplates for a moment, during which I see all kinds of emotion cross Durst's face. Mostly, it's fear. "Gun. I've had enough of knives after the van."

She slings the rifle and I hand her the pistol butt-first. She points it at Durst's crotch and she says, "Say goodbye to that premature ejaculation problem."

"Come on, man! Point taken, okay? I'm *sorry!* Your old man ratted us out, okay? Revenge is just the way things are—"

She fires a shot into to his groin. This time, the screaming is too loud to hear the shell casing bouncing off the floor. His hands immediately go to his crotch, and blood starts dripping through his jeans between his fingers. She shoots him two more times in quick succession. Both shots are spot on, and the first goes through the fingers of his right hand. Durst screams until his eyes roll up in his head, then he passes out.

Grace lowers the gun and stares at him.

Mitch looks at her with horror and awe. "Oh holy Jesus!"

I give it a few seconds, then ask "Do you want me to finish him?"

She doesn't answer. She just stares at him, the gun pointed at his head. "Grace?"

Finally, she shakes her head. "No, I don't think so. I think I'd like him to remember me every time he squats to pee. If he doesn't die, I want him to wish I'd finished him off. Every moment of his miserable fucking life."

She's right. It's a fate worse than death, and he deserves it more than being put out of his misery.

Grace turns her gaze to Ratt, and points the gun at his crotch. His eyes are wild, and he's cringing. "No! I'm *sorry!* My knee is enough! Come on, Grace, I never touched you! *Please!*"

She thinks for a moment, then lowers the pistol and says, "No. You didn't."

She turns to face me, about to say something, and pauses. Then, she turns back to Ratt, raises the pistol and fires a round into his crotch. "But you ordered it," she says calmly.

"Oh, fuck, I think I'm gonna puke," says Mitch, now several shades paler than he was a moment ago.

This seems to remind Grace that he's here. She turns and points the gun at him. Before she can fire, I redirect it upwards and gently take it away from her.

"He's a witness, Dad. He's seen everything."

She's right of course. Without him, I can still tell the police I did the shooting, not her. With him, there's no claiming that Grace was a helpless victim. And he *is* EK. But a strange thing is starting to happen to me. Somehow, I'm losing my stomach for this. It's as if I've reached my capacity for violence and killing. I've been doing it for four solid years, and I don't want to do it any more.

I remember planning to go from EK hangout to EK hangout, killing everyone I found, but that murderous rage is now gone. The great Bad Apple can no longer live up to his own reputation. All I want to do now is lie down and go to sleep.

The concept of escaping and trying to make our way to Morocco is too daunting to even think about. I don't feel like I have the energy to drive away from here, let alone flee the country. At this point I'm actually glad to have Grace here. I don't know if I'd have the strength to get us away and plan our next moves without her.

We've done what we came to do. We got both the major players, and Mitch isn't one of them. The problem is, if we *don't* kill him, his testimony about what happened here could put Grace in prison for decades.

Mitch can probably read what's going on in my mind. To his credit, he doesn't plead or beg. He says, "Look, I know I'm a liability, man, but I just want to say, I think what you guys did here today was righteous. I got no problem with it. I wasn't lying when I told you that I—"

A booming voice, originating just outside the front door, cuts him off. "THIS IS THE PORTLAND POLICE BUREAU! TO THE OCCUPANTS OF 10525 SE FOSTER ROAD, YOU ARE SURROUNDED. YOU ARE ORDERED TO LAY YOUR WEAPONS DOWN AND COME TO THE DOOR WITH YOUR HANDS UP. DO IT NOW!"

Chapter 19

I'd recognize that voice anywhere. I brought Leon Williams onto the hostage negotiating team six years ago, back when I was the lead negotiator. We called him Darth Vader because of his deep, authoritative voice. He and I were once good friends. This will be the third time he's called me out of a barricaded or hostage situation, though he probably doesn't know that yet. Won't he be surprised.

Remembering the video monitors, I lean into the living room to have a look at them. Whereas they used to show the grounds, driveway, and front door, they now show nothing but static. Mitch, who went to the floor with the announcement, looks at me, his eyes wide with fright. Grace, now at my side, has a look of grim determination on her face. The AR-15 is still in her ams, her finger extended along the rifle's body outside the trigger guard. I'm so proud of her I could cry.

The old Grace is gone. No more innocent little girl, and certainly no longer a victim, she is now a fighter, armed and ready for combat. Mentally, she is prepared to fight, and she is no stranger to combat. Her hands are as bloody as my own. If I wanted to fight my way out of here, she'd be willing to fight by my side to the death, and with that realization, my pride turns to shame. What happened to my innocent daughter? What have we done to her?

"Fuck," she yells in frustration. "What's the plan, Dad?" There's a hint of desperation in her voice now, the first I've ever heard. Though we planned for this, she clearly didn't think it was a real possibility. I think she was okay with us dying in here together, but I don't think she seriously considered us getting arrested.

I, on the other hand, have. I could take prison if I were to go back to the Intensive Management Unit at Snake River, but that's not very likely at this point. My plans for the endgame never included ending my days on death row. They included either getting away, or going out on my own terms, which is the main reason I didn't want her here in the first place.

"Grace," I say calmly, "Hand me the rifle, honey." She hesitates, probably thinking of my betrayal of her in Vancouver last night. Finally, with tears welling in her eyes, she pulls the sling over her head and hands me the weapon. Even after last night, she still trusts me.

If we do this right, Grace can still come out in decent shape. Probably not without criminal charges, but nothing that will make her do hard time. Mitch has now become my most valuable bargaining chip. Maybe I can even work out a two-part deal—life without parole at Snake River for me, and immunity for Grace. In exchange, I will surrender without harming Mitch or putting a bullet into the brains of the other two.

I can think of numerous reasons, however, why they probably won't go for it. First, I've already made that deal once, the last time I was arrested. I traded the death penalty for life in prison after the Killer Burger incident. That's the kind of deal you only get once in a lifetime. Another reason is, now I'm facing yet another capital murder charge for killing a fellow inmate at Snake River. It doesn't matter that he was the man who molested me as a child. I killed him in cold blood after planning it for weeks. That's all that matters. Then there's the whole escape and international flight to avoid prosecution thing, not to mention taking hostages again and putting six bullets into two of them. When Durst dies, which he will, I will chalk up yet another capital offense with yet another death penalty.

Since my numerous offenses include crossing an international border, I'm pretty sure they'll charge me federally, which means that upon my conviction, I will have to do my time in a federal super-max prison.

I can't do that. The police have me surrounded. My former SERT team and hostage negotiators are just outside my door. There's no escape from here. My daughter is by my side, ready and willing to die for me. The reality of it all descends upon me with an unbearable weight, and I realize that I'm done. I don't have any more fight left in me. I no longer have the stomach for it. Just the thought of going back to prison and living that life is overwhelming. I can't be Bad any longer. All I want to do right now is eat my gun. It wouldn't even be hard for me to pull the trigger.

If Grace wasn't here, then I would have killed Ratt and Durst the moment I found them, and I'd either be heading back up to Canada now, or, if the police arrived before I got away, then I'd be dead, too. In either case, this SERT callout would be over before it ever got off the ground. But Grace is here, so, before I shoot myself, she has to leave.

Why couldn't she have been arrested in Vancouver like I planned?

Darth Vader repeats his announcement.

"Dad?"

I turn to her and hold her at arm's length. "Grace, we knew this was a possibility from the beginning. There is a plan for this. You're going to walk out that door with your hands and your chin held high. *I* shot Durst and Ratt, not you. You didn't do anything. You were being held here since they kidnapped you, and I came here today and rescued you."

Mitch says, "That's how I saw it, and I been here the whole time. You got my support on that."

Ignoring Mitch, Grace says, "Dad, you can't trust this guy. He'll say anything to save himself right now. And don't even mention me walking out of here without you again. We *talked* about this. I'm not giving myself up without you. Remember our agreement? Whatever was going to happen would to happen to both of us. We either escape together, get arrested together, or die together. I said I was fine with that, and so did you. You can't go back on me now. There's no way I'm walking out of here unless it's with you, and that's a promise. So, we've got to come up with something else."

"No Grace, there *is* nothing else. Listen to me. I've got a plan, and it'll work. I'll give them all of these guys, and Mitch unharmed, and they'll agree to give you immunity and send me back to Snake River. You'll come out of this free and clear. But you are going to have to walk out first."

"No. I won't do it. If I walk out of here, I'll never see you again. Because I know you. I know what you'll do once I'm gone, and you can't do that, Dad. I won't let you."

"Yes you will, Grace. You have to go out first, otherwise, they'll know you're cooperating with me. You have to look innocent, and that's the only way. I'm not going to do anything bad to myself. Listen, it'll work. We've covered our tracks well enough. They'll buy it. If they don't, the most you could get would be a little minimum security federal time for helping me in Canada. When you get out, you'll have Uncle Phil's money, and a note from him leaving it all to you. Things will be different then.

You'll be able to come and see me whenever you want. We can still be father and daugh—"

"No, Dad. Even if you don't shoot yourself, everything you're saying depends on *him*, and he's one of them! He'll say anything to stay out of trouble. Why would even think he would lie for us?"

Mitch says, "Grace, I've been a fuckup for most of my life. That's how I ended up in prison in the first place. I been looking for a chance to do something right for a long time. I heard all about Bad here when I was in the joint. I mean, your dad's a fuckin' legend, man. I know what these assholes here did to you. This is the opportunity I've been looking for to turn my life around. Listen to your father. He's right. He's got this shit dialed in. I'm going to tell them they've been holding you here ever since Kickstart brought you back from your apartment. We'll both say that Kickstart killed Skidmark and Stinger in that van 'cause they were fighting over you, and that him and Ratt's been passing you back and forth like a two-dollar whore ever since. Then this morning your old man comes busting in like hell itself, shoots them in the balls, and saves you. *That's* our story, and it'll work. I got nothing but respect for him."

"'I got nothing but respect for him,'" she mimics in a mocking tone. "Like we're supposed to just trust you. You're one of *them*. Do you really expect us to put our lives in your hands?"

"Yeah, I do. Sometimes you can't do everything alone. Sometimes you need a little help from a friend, man. There's nothing wrong with that."

She turns to me and says, "I think we should shoot him. He'll say anything to get out of here alive. There's too much evidence that says we did it. Not just here, but everywhere in Canada, too. If he talks, we'll both go to prison, and when I'm out, they'll never let me see you. We can't let them win, Dad, not after everything that's happened. I couldn't handle that. I can handle us going out together, in here. I could even do it if you couldn't. I could shoot you and then shoot myself. If you want to let him go, fine, but let's you and me just end it here for us both, on our own terms. Okay Dad? That way, they can't say they beat us. They'll never be able to say they locked us up. I'm really, honestly okay with that."

I'm horrified, because she means it. This new Grace, this machine that Uncle Phil and I turned her into, is capable of doing this. Oh my God.

"Well *I'm* not! EK caused all of this. If not for them, we'd be living in Vancouver with Uncle Phil right now. Grace, if you die, that means EK wins. It doesn't matter how they achieve it. They'll win, and there's no fucking way I'm going to allow that. Not now, and not ever. The one thing that I absolutely must have, is you alive."

My mind is trying to process our chances with the story that Grace was being held here. Mitch's testimony could go a long way toward making that fly, but I can't make up my mind about him. He seems sincere, and he's saying all the right things, but I know that survival instinct. A man will say anything to save his own skin. I've seen it many times over the years. If I can get Grace out of here, none of it will matter. I won't hesitate. As unpleasant as it will be, I'll put a bullet in his brain along with the other two, right before I put one in my own. Even Grace will come to understand it had to be done.

Mitch is smart enough to see what I'm thinking. He looks me right in the eye and says, "I got no reason to lie to you, Bad. That'll be my sworn testimony. You can trust me. Like I said, I got nothing but respect for you."

Before I can say anything else, Ratt's phone begins to ring. I fish it out of his pocket, surprised that it's still intact, and wipe the blood off on his shirt. The screen says No Caller ID. It's them.

Grace looks at me and says, "Dad, don't answer it. We need to finish this without—"

Ignoring her, I slide the bar across the bottom of the screen. "Hello?"

"Hello? Hey, thanks for picking up," says a voice as familiar as my own. "My name is Beth Quinlan, and I'm a police officer with the Portland Police Bureau. Is this William McHenry?"

Beth was my partner when I was the lead negotiator for SERT. We had worked together for years before I went bad. Since then, we've negotiated together on two separate occasions with me as the bad guy for real. The first time, I humiliated both her and the entire Portland Police Bureau when I fooled them all into letting me go and I escaped. The second time, after they'd cornered me in a house in southeast Portland three days later, I ended up surrendering in shame on live television and went to prison. Now, once again here we are.

I say, "Hello, Beth."

There's a very pregnant pause, then, "Who is this?"

"You know who it is."

"Oh my God. DJ!"

"Welcome to round three, Beth. Long time, no negotiate."

"God *damn* it! I told them I didn't want to be primary on this one, because I had a feeling it was going to be you."

"Yet, here you are."

"Yeah, here I am. But I don't want to be. I don't want to negotiate with you, DJ. When this call came in, we were fully aware that it was the headquarters of the European Kindred. We're also aware of what's been going on between them and you, and I knew this just had to be you, so I assigned Malaka to be primary, but Marc overruled me and ordered me to do it, just in case it *was* you."

"Marc Shrake? Is he the lieutenant now?"

"He has been for the past two years."

"Well, good for him. Tell him I said congratulations on the promotion."

"This isn't a social call, DJ, and you're not a cop any more."

"Yeah, well, Marc, I know you're listening in at the command post, so congrats. Look, Beth, I get that you don't like talking to me, but I'm actually glad it's you. I've missed you."

"Well I'm not gonna lie to you, DJ. I can't say the same thing. Christ, I can't believe we're doing this again. Why do you have to keep haunting me? Why can't you just stay in fucking prison?"

"Why do you hate me so much, Beth? We were once partners, and very good friends."

"The DJ I was friends with is gone. Friends don't fuck over their friends. I'll never forget what you did to me at Killer Burger. You made me look like an idiot and I got suspended over it."

"I don't see what you're so bent out of shape about. I seem to remember being at the end of my rope on our second go-around, and you telling me where to shoot myself to minimize the mess. I seem to remember coming out of that house in tears on live television."

"Don't put that on me. You're the author of your own troubles, DJ. You have been since the day you first went bad. You should have taken my advice about shooting yourself in Shawn's bathtub. Then we wouldn't be here. It still isn't too late, you know."

"Christ, Beth, this is a recorded line. You can't say things like that!"

"Why not? I'm not about to treat you like you're some unlucky hostage taker that got caught in a mistake. You know every negotiation strategy ever written, and you've got more experience doing this from both sides than anyone else on earth. I don't have to play negotiator games with you. They can fire my ass. I don't care."

"Well, at least we don't have to waste time building a rapport."

"They'll never be a rapport between us, again DJ. But since we *are* on the phone again, why don't we skip the preliminaries, and you just tell me what's going on in there? Who are you holding, and how badly have you hurt them? Does anyone need medical attention, or are they all dead?"

"I like that about you, Beth. Straight to the point. Since you asked, I'm holding four hostages. Two of them, a guy named Ratt and a guy named Kevin Durst, are in pretty bad shape, and the other two, some ass-clown named Mitch and another guy they call Hiccup, are what we'll call as-of-yet unpainted canvases."

"Unpainted canvasses. How utterly you, DJ. Okay, well, let's talk about these guys Ratt and Kevin Durst. I know from our intel-gathering who they are. They're both EK, and we all know what EK did to your daughter and uncle. And by the way, I'm sorry for that, DJ. I really am. I also know that you and Durst have a history from your days at OSP. So, why don't you just start by telling me how bad you've hurt them?"

"It's refreshing to be able to speak frankly, isn't it? Since you asked me straight up, I'll answer you straight up. I shot Ratt twice, once in the balls and once in his left knee. Durst, I shot four times; three in the balls and once in his left knee. There are reasons for that. Both are still alive, though neither of them deserve to be."

"My God, DJ, what's happened to you? You should listen to yourself. You're not even human any more."

"Don't give me that self-righteous bullshit, Beth. These men raped my daughter. You'd have done the same thing."

"No, I wouldn't. You turned animal in prison."

"Wrong again. I always *was* an animal. I just covered it well when I was a cop. But don't kid yourself, Beth. We're all animals deep inside. You have it in you, too, you just choose to deny it."

"You're so off the charts it isn't even funny. People like you end up one of three ways; in prison, in the mental hospital, or on their way to one of the above. But now we have to talk about what it's going to take to get those wounded guys out, and I mean now. Because if we don't, they're coming in to rescue them in one minute. Talk now, or... Well, you know what to expect."

"I haven't decided if I want to let them out. There are options available to me that don't include going back to prison, you know. Remember my HNT motto."

"I remember. 'Suicide is always an option.'"

"It is. Even you can understand that not everyone who's hurt deserves to be saved."

"It doesn't take an animal to understand that. Thirty seconds, DJ."

"I guess I'll see you on the other side, then."

"DJ, in your last moments, I want you to consider something. After what those guys did, they deserve a fate worse than death. So, why not give it to them? Why would you put them out of their misery when that's what they want? Wouldn't that be the humane thing to do? You'd do it for a dog. But making them live after getting their dicks shot off? That's *got* to be a fate worse than death. They won't even be able to pee standing up. They'll spend the rest of their lives *wishing* you killed them. So, prolong their misery. Give them a fate worse than death, by sending them out."

"See, Beth? I told you that you have that animal nature in you, and you do. You had to tap into your inner animal to come up with that so quickly. Are you afraid of what's inside you, Beth?"

She falls silent for a moment, and I know she just got handed a note from her partner. One of Beth's weaknesses as a negotiator is she can't read and talk at the same time. Finally, she says, "This ends here and now, DJ. They're getting the green light. Last chance. Put the phone down and walk out that door, or suffer the consequences."

"I'm not coming out, Beth, but leash the dogs. I'll give you both of the wounded guys, free gratis for nothing. How's that sound? One of my other hostages will drag them out onto the porch, and you can claim a huge victory for round one. I'm all finished with them anyway."

There follows a very brief moment of silence, then she says, "Sure, DJ, we'll take that. Thanks for the offer. But make it now."

"See what a good negotiator you are? On the phone for ten minutes, and you've already got two hostages. I'm hanging up now, and someone will drag them out. But nobody grabs my boy, or the remaining hostage will pay a very stiff fine. If you get my drift."

"Agreed."

"Do I have your word on that? Check with Marc first if you have to."

"He's giving me the thumbs-up as we speak. Nobody will mess with your man. But they both wounded guys have to be on the porch in one minute."

"Done. Call me back five minutes after you pick them up."

"Okay. Talk to you then."

We both hang up, and Grace immediately says, "What the hell was that, Dad? I mean, I get the made-up guy named Hiccup, but what's up with the rest of it? You were telling her you were going to kill yourself! But you're telling me you're not."

"I'm just trying to get us out of here, Grace. I'm going to see to it that—"

"No you're not! Dad, I know you too well. You're going to try to make me leave next. But I already told you, I'm not going anywhere without you."

"Yes, you are, Grace. Open your eyes. There's only one way out of here when this thing ends, and that's for you to walk out free, and me to go back to prison. The absolute best outcome is to give them Mitch in exchange for sending me back to Snake River. If they won't do that, then I'll have to explore my other option. There's no other outcome to this."

"No, Dad. I know what that means."

"Grace..."

For the first time in all of this, she breaks down in tears. "This isn't the way it was supposed to go, Dad. You have to be strong enough to live."

But I'm not. I don't have any more fight in me. The prospect of doing prison again is beyond me. Not when I've had a taste of life like I have. Not after I shared a world with Grace and Uncle Phil, living free on the outside. Memories of those weeks are the only thing keeping me going at this point.

"Oh Grace," I say, bringing her in to me. "They'll make the deal. You don't have to worry. Right now I'm here, and we're together. They'll make the deal, I know they will."

She fights for just a moment, and then she relaxes and lets me hold her.

"Do you promise, Dad? Because I can't lose you. Not now."

"I promise, sweetie. I promise."

Mitch pipes up. "Hey man, I know you guys are like, busy right now, but if I'm gonna drag these two pieces of shit out there in time, I gotta do it now."

I say, "He's right. Grace, stay away from the door. Mitch, drag them out. Dump them on the porch, and if you're sincere about helping us, you'll come directly back inside. If you're blowing smoke up my ass, you'll give yourself up."

"I told you I'm with you, dude, and I am. Besides," he says, shaking his head, "I seen what you do to people who cross you."

Grace and I move to the kitchen. Mitch grabs the still-unconscious Durst by the ankles and without ceremony, drags him toward the door, leaving a wide streak of blood in his wake. I'm pretty sure he's already dead. He doesn't even moan. It's a wonder his legs are still connected, seeing that he's got three bullets in the crotch and one in the knee. Mitch gets him out onto the porch, then comes back in for Ratt.

Ratt is still conscious and moaning, but his moans turn to screams of anguish and pain as Mitch starts dragging him toward the door. The pain must be excruciating, because he begins twisting and fighting Mitch, kicking at him with his good leg. Mitch is having trouble dragging him out the door because of it.

Suddenly, I see an opportunity. If I can get Grace to help him, I can close the door on all three of them while they're still on the porch.

"Grace, give him a hand."

She grabs Ratt by his good leg while Mitch takes the injured leg, and together they start dragging him toward the door. Grace holds it open and starts moving out onto the porch, but then looks at me. I must be telegraphing my moves, because she drops the ankle and scurries inside. She still holds the door for Mitch, but now she's standing behind it in a manner that makes it impossible for me to close her outside.

Mitch unceremoniously drops Ratt's legs, eliciting another scream of anguish, then jumps back inside. Grace closes and locks the door.

There's the scuffling of many boots on the porch, and more screaming from Ratt. I hear the team leader's muffled command of, "Move," and the sounds retreat the way the team came. A moment after they go back around the corner, everything gets quiet again.

Either they will deal with me, or they won't. I spend the time between the phone calls planning my next strategy. If I can talk them into offering me Snake River, I will take the deal, but first, they're going to have to agree not to charge Grace. I know I'm asking for the moon, but this is an either all-in or all-out situation.

If they don't go for it, I'm going to have to find a way to force Grace out of here, because all-out means all the way out, not just for me, but for Mitch, too.

Exactly five minutes later, the phone rings.

Chapter 20

"Your timing is impeccable, Beth."

But it's not Beth. A different female voice answers. "Hey DJ. It's me, Malaka. Beth's, uh, not available right now. Sorry. But it's good to hear your voice!"

I literally hold the phone away from my ear and stare at it. They switched negotiators on me? I can't figure out what tactic they have in mind, but whatever it is, it's not going to fly. I remember Malaka very well. I'd been one of her coaches when she got out of the academy, and I had actually encouraged her to try out for HNT before I got arrested. I'm genuinely happy to see her make the team. But she's far too nice and too inexperienced to be caught in the middle of all this. If their strategy is to get me talking about old times with a good friend, it's not going to work. I have no interest in playing musical negotiators, not even with Malaka. My life is at stake here, and so is Grace's. If they knew how close they were to losing me, they wouldn't pull this Micky Mouse shit.

"Beth's not available? Bullshit. Make her available, Malaka. Get her back on the line. Now."

"DJ, she just stormed out of here saying—"

"I don't care Malaka! I don't want to hear it. Whoever came up with this lame-brained idea to switch up on me is going to get people killed. Now I've always liked you, Malaka, and I always will. Come visit me in prison when this is over if you want to chat, but in the meantime, get me Beth! And tell Marc no more bullshit. Tell him I fucking mean it!"

I hang up, wishing for the old days, where you could slam the handset so hard onto the cradle it would ring the little bell inside. If they were trying to get me frazzled, they succeeded.

The phone rings almost immediately. I slide the button and say, "This better be Beth."

It isn't. It's Malaka again, and she says, "DJ, don't hang up! Listen, she's not coming back, okay? This isn't some kind of HNT ploy to switch negotiators on you to piss you off. Beth's refusing to to talk to you, DJ. When Shrake ordered her to get back on the phone, she stormed out of the van saying she quit the team. I'm sorry, DJ. She's already gone."

"Jesus fucking Christ, Malaka, do you guys not take me seriously? Do you think I'm joking around here?"

"DJ, please talk to me. You know what Beth can be like. Of course we're taking you seriously. Remember that DV guy we had at Motel 6, the one who peed all over his wife when she was sleeping? Beth got there and—"

"Fuck the good old times, Malaka. You may not have noticed, but they're gone forever. Now if you're really taking me seriously, then listen up, because this is what's going to happen next. I'm going to hang up, and then, in exactly five minutes, my phone is going to ring. Not one second before and not one second after. If it's Beth, we'll keep talking, and eventually get this resolved. If it's you, or anyone other than Beth, I'll send out Mitch's left hand. Now, is that serious enough for you?"

"Come on, DJ, don't say things like that. We can—"

"I'm not done. If I have to give you his hand, I'm still going to expect my phone to ring five minutes later. Every five minutes, you'll get a different body part, until Beth decides to talk to me. And don't bother reminding me about standard operating procedures. SOPs say that if the hostage taker makes demands on a timeline and threatens harm to the hostages, then you send in the hostage rescue team. I already know that, and if Marc wants to go that route, I can't stop him. But he needs to know that I have a fully-auto AR-15 and .40 caliber Glock in here. Every one of those guys lined up outside my door has seen me shoot. They all know I was the best shot on the team. I've already killed one police officer, Malaka. Tell Marc if he sends them in, they're going to take losses. Probably more than one, because I'm a determined man."

"DJ, please don't say that. They're calling Beth now, and—"

I hang up on her.

I have the beginnings of the mother of all headaches. The stress of this is getting to me. Now, even Grace is keeping her distance from me. I think she's afraid I might throw her out. Mitch, who heard my threats, won't even look at me. He's not sure whether or not I'll carry them out.

Neither am I.

Exactly five minutes later, the phone rings.

"Hello?"

"You're a fucking asshole, DJ."

"Hi Beth. Nice to have you back. You're going to have to work on your phone greeting, though."

"Cut the shit, DJ. I can talk to you any goddamn way I want, and you know why? Because I'm not a negotiator any more. I quit the team. I'm only talking to you now because apparently you're threatening to carve up your hostage like a Thanksgiving turkey and I was ordered to do it. Therefore, I don't have to play by the rules any more. So, let's just get down to it, shall we? Now that you've coerced me back onto the phone, feel free to put on your little dog and pony show. We're all listening."

"Don't sell yourself short, Beth. You're not just here because you were ordered, you're here because that's the kind of person you are. You're doing it because you know it'll make all the difference in the world how this turns out. You're doing it because you couldn't live with yourself if you didn't."

"DJ, you may think you're in a good position in there, but you and I both know you're not. We both know how this is going to end. Remember the last time we negotiated? Which one of us went home, and which one came crawling out of Shawn's house on the evening news with tears on his face? Nothing's changed since then but the time and place. It's still you and me, and you know that later tonight, when all this fucked-up shit is over, I'm going home to drink my ass silly, and you're going to jail to spread your's open while someone takes a good long look inside. So why don't we just get started?"

"I don't know what kind of new strategy you're trying to pull, Beth, but take care not to go too far, because now you're starting to piss me off. I didn't ask for you to come back so you could treat me like shit."

"Then why *did* you ask for me? Because I sure as hell don't want to be here."

"Because... Because you know me better than anyone else. Because we were such a good team. You were my favorite cop on the force, Beth. I want you on the phone because you, of all people, understand me. I haven't changed. I've just allowed the dark side to become prevalent. You know the kind of man I am at heart. If anyone can make them see me for who I am, you can. I need you to advocate for me. I believe you care, Beth. I *need* you to care."

She's silent, and I don't even think anyone's passing her a note. I think maybe I'm breaking her down, but when she comes back, she's doubled down on her resolve.

"Get off it, DJ. I don't buy that bullshit for a second. A psych 101 student could see why you wanted me back. You're compensating for the last time we negotiated, when you were weak. You surrendered in tears on television, and you never got over it. But not this time, no sir. Now you have another chance to show us who the real DJ is. Or should I say who the real Bad is? You're not weak any more, are you? Now, you're strong. You shot the dicks off the men who raped your daughter. That took strength, and you're throwing that strength in our faces—in *my* face. Now, you've set yourself up as God, with the power to decide who lives and who doesn't. And you know what? You actually have that power, and I recognize it, so I have to bow down to it. *That's* why you wanted me. I can't make you cry any more, and you want me to know it. Plus, you realize you're in a hopeless situation, so it's time to put your money where your mouth is with your HNT motto. And since I'm the one who bested you before, you want it to be me on the line when you cap yourself. Well, I could see all of this coming, DJ, and that's why I walked away."

"Maybe I was wrong about you, Beth. Maybe you really don't care."

"Hey, I'm still here, aren't I? And care enough to tell you the truth, which is that I don't see anything left of the man who allowed that final shred of humanity to make him cry last time. I think that guy's already dead. You think it'll show strength if you eat your gun, but let me tell you how the rest of the world will view it. They will see it as the ultimate act of weakness. It makes crying on TV look like amateur hour in the weakness department. If you want to show *real* strength, DJ, let Mitch live. *That's* ending this in a position of power. The ability to grant clemency is the greatest power a man can wield. Anyone can pull a trigger, but it takes real constitution to walk out of there and face your shit like a man."

"That's quite a spiel for someone who doesn't want to negotiate."

"I *don't* want to negotiate. And, I'm sick of talking, so why don't *you* start talking so we can end this? Who is this mysterious Mitch?"

"Well, I guess you got me there. I don't know his name. He's just some EK poser who's been living here since he got paroled. Hang on a sec. Mitch! They want your name and birthdate."

Mitch says, "It's Mitchell Frances Wood II. September 13th, 1986."

"I heard him," she says. "And he's still a... what'd you call him? An unpainted canvas?"

"Mitch, tell her that you're okay."

"I'm okay, man, but get me away from this psycho before he shoots my nuts off too!" This last part was said with a wink. I'm starting to think he really is on my side.

"Okay. How about this Hiccup character you mentioned. Who is he?"

"You tell me, Beth."

"We all know he doesn't exist. You made him up so we wouldn't snatch Mitch when he was dragging out the other two."

"Well, that one was obvious."

"You're not as smart as you think you are, DJ. Since we're introducing everyone, why don't you tell me who the girl is."

"You already know who she is, too."

"Your daughter Grace, who's been missing since she was kidnapped from her apartment in Clackamas four days ago."

"That's right. She's why we're all here today."

"Okay. So Mitch is still an unpainted canvas, and it's probably safe to say that Grace isn't a hostage, so why don't we talk about how to bring the curtain down on your little play? I'm tired, and want to go home."

"All right, fine. I actually do have a resolution in mind."

"Good. But before we start dickering over the death penalty again, let's do Grace a favor, and get her out of there."

"Now we're on the same page, Beth. But Grace is a grown woman, and I can't make her do anything. I've tried to send her out, but she won't go. I don't think she trusts you. She says we're going to walk out of here together."

"Why don't you put her on the line? Let me see if I can talk some sense into her."

"Sure. Good luck."

I hold the phone out to her, and she takes it. I can only hear one end of the conversation, but I can tell Beth is trying to get her to come out. Grace keeps saying she's afraid they'll come in shooting if she's not here. Then she starts answering questions about the van, how Durst killed the other two and brought her back here. She's sticking to the Mitch story, and even cries when she says she was repeatedly raped here at the EK clubhouse by Ratt and Durst. She maintains that Mitch has been sympathetic to her the whole time, and wraps it up by describing how I showed up and got the drop on them, and here we are. She handles herself like a champ.

Grace is quiet for a moment, listening to something Beth is telling her. During her silence, I try to hear what she's told Beth from an HNT intelligence-gathering perspective. If I were Beth Quinlan, the main thing I would extrapolate from what Grace told me is that she is utterly devoted to me. I'd conclude that, apart from the fact that I'm not holding her against her will, what's going on is no different than an extreme case of The Stockholm Syndrome. It would be clear to me that if Grace refuses to come out, no matter what the reason, she should be considered hostile to those who come in to get me. If I were in charge of HNT, I would advise the entry team that Grace not only is sympathetic toward me, but with access to my weapons, she, too, should be considered a hostile, and not treated as a victim.

How stupid of me to put her on the phone! When they come in here, they're not going be in rescue mode, they're going to be in stop the threat mode, and Grace will be one of the threats. All I did by putting her on the phone was make things worse. Now I have to get her out, no matter what it costs me.

Grace finishes up her conversation and hands me back the phone. Beth says, "DJ, this is gone on too long. That EK clubhouse is not the place your daughter needs to be. She's not safe in there with you. It's up to you now to ensure her safety. If she won't come out without you, then you need to come out with her. This isn't a negotiation tactic, it's common fucking sense. Bad shit could happen in there at any moment, and she doesn't need to be there when it does. You need to do this for her."

"Nice try, Beth, but I'm not coming out. Grace is her own woman now. I can't tell her what to do. Believe me, I want her out of here. I've tried to get her to leave, but she's strong-willed, and she won't go."

"And neither will you. DJ, you know what this looks like to us. You don't want the entry team coming in there and treating her like a hostile, do you? You can prevent that by coming out. You need to do that. For her."

"Don't tell me what I need to do for my daughter, Beth. Instead, try looking at what I've already done for her. She's no longer being held captive by those animals. They'll never be able to rape another girl for the rest of their lives thanks to me. So quit trying to tell me what to do with her. If you don't want to put her in danger, don't send in the fucking entry team!"

"Open your eyes, DJ, and see this from our perspective. I'm gonna let you in in on a little confidential information, here. We think you and Grace are working together. Detectives think she somehow managed to get the drop on those two pigs who kidnapped her. They think *she* killed them, and got away before Durst even went to the mall to pick them up."

"She's a rape victim, Beth, not a superhero."

"I believe that, but it looks like she's a pretty tough rape victim. We know she stole a car that was parked next to that van, and went back to her apartment complex and hid out at a neighbor's place until they were done with the crime scene. The woman who lives there had notified Grace in her capacity as assistant manager that she'd be overseas for a month. That woman's car was stolen the day of the kidnapping, and was later recovered less than a mile from the motel in Canada where you were staying."

"And you think that Grace did that?"

"Me? I don't get paid enough to think, but no, it's pretty hard for me to imagine a rape victim being able to do all that. But detectives and CSI? Their job is to read the evidence, and the evidence says she did it. And if she did, then it will make a *world* of difference. In your version, Grace is a victim, but if she was a real victim, she'd come out now, wouldn't she? If this other version is true, that would make Grace your accomplice, which is how she's acting by *not* coming out. And that would make her guilty of a whole lot more than just aiding and abetting.

"The one thing I can tell you, DJ, is this. Nothing will help her more than walking out that door right now. It'll be even better if you two do it together. Because if they have to come in there to get you, they'll have to get her, too. You don't need me to spell it out for you, DJ. You're not stupid."

"No, Beth, I'm not stupid, but you sure are. This theory that Grace is some kind of Wonder Woman is pure bullshit. She was raped, beaten to within an inch of her life, and handcuffed. How do you suppose she killed two hardcore EK enforcers? And what do you suppose Kevin Durst was doing while Grace was killing his buddies? Trying to talk her out of it? Jesus Christ, Beth!"

"I don't have all the answers, DJ, but clearly, it's not that cut and dried. Remember one of the most basic tenets of criminal investigations; the evidence always tells the story."

Beth is right. There's no way our cover story will hold up against a thorough investigation. We were bound to have been captured on some surveillance video somewhere. I can't have Grace charged criminally, not for what's taken place here. Aiding and abetting me in Canada is one thing; she won't get any real time for that. But they're going to prove she came down here with me with the intent to do what we did here, and when they do, she'll go away for twenty-plus years. Gunshot residue in her clothing and on her person will show who shot these guys in the balls, and when Durst dies, they could charge her with a capital crime.

The pain in my head is getting worse by the second. I bite my lip to ground myself, then say, "It sounds like you're trying to build a case against a young girl who was brutally raped and beaten, had her dog tortured and killed in front of her, watched her uncle get murdered, and was kidnapped. Hasn't she been through enough, Beth? For chrissakes, why can't you just let her be?"

"Why can't she just come out? Even if all that proves to be true, maybe it still isn't too late. If she surrendered now, that would go a long way in the eyes of the DA. If she showed remorse, it could make all the difference in the world. Nobody's going to want to see a true victim like her go to prison after what she went through. Hell, when her story comes out, she'll be a hailed as a hero by women all around the globe. They DA will offer her a sweetheart deal to make it go away. She might not even have to go to prison. But they won't make that deal if they have to come in and get her. That changes the entire game, which is why she has to come out."

She's got me backed into a corner. The story that Grace was held captive the whole time, and that the spiky-haired girl took her neighbor's car up to Canada to kill me simply isn't going to fly.

In fact, nothing is going to fly. This time, I think I've finally done it. I've painted us both into a corner from which there is no escape. I have only one dull little tool left in my bag, and if that doesn't work, I'll eat my gun whether Grace is still here or not, and just hope they take pity on her.

"You know what, Beth? I'm okay with the world coming after me. I'm a bad guy, and I deserve to go to prison. But after what you just said, I can see the writing on the wall. I know where this is headed. You all have turned your back on Grace, too. So now, I'm going to give you the bottom line. Listen up and sharpen your pencil, 'cause I'm only going to say it once."

"I'm listening."

"Okay then. If you want to get Mitch back without being parted out like a used car, here are my demands. One. I get notarized letters from the DA guaranteeing that I won't be sentenced to death. Two. I get a notarized promise from the state of Oregon that I will serve the rest of my time at Snake River, back where I was when all this got started. Three. I get a notarized document from the DA that grants Grace full immunity from any prosecution for anything she may have done up to this very moment. That's it. For all three, you get an end to this standoff, Mitch in one piece, and my full cooperation in your investigation. I won't even lawyer up. You take that offer up the chain and get back to me in thirty minutes."

"I'll forward your demands, but I can't make you any promises."

"I understand that. But you better understand this. This is a one-time offer, and it's based on all three criteria. Two of them will get you nothing. Three gets the whole shebang. And I'm going to negotiate any more. Turn me down, and what happens next is on you."

"There's a lot of moving parts to this, DJ. It'll probably take longer than thirty minutes. Give me at least an hour."

"Thirty minutes, Beth. If you can't get it done by then, Mitch'll give you a hand. That'll buy you another thirty minutes."

"DJ—"

I hang up. I'm tired of playing games. I know they won't go for all three conditions, but the first two are basically just a smokescreen. If they offer full immunity for Grace, I'll take it, even if it means death row. I'm certain that given twenty-three hours a day, I can find a way to take myself out, even there. Where there's a will, there's a way.

Chapter 21

Thirty minutes later the phone rings.

"Tell me something good, Beth."

"I can't. You're not going to like this, DJ, but the DA said no."

"No? Just like that? No to what part?"

"No to everything. They're denying all of your demands. They're not going to give Grace immunity because they don't believe your bullshit story. And they say they're not in the business of letting defendants dictate the terms of their prosecution, or where they may be incarcerated. I'm sorry."

I don't say anything. In the interlude that follows, my mind works at lightning speed. I can't say it wasn't unexpected, but I really thought they might cave on the Grace thing. Like any hostage taker, I'm only in charge up to a certain point. In the end, regardless of what happens to the hostages, the ultimate power over *me* lay with those on the outside. The only power I have with regard to my own fate is to take myself out of the game. Suicide really is an option.

Beth says, "DJ, say something."

"I'll call you back in fifteen minutes."

"Make it five, DJ. They want to wrap this thing up."

"Fine." I hang up, turn to Grace and say, "They're calling my bluff. They've denied all of my demands, probably because they know me well enough to know that I'm not going to start chopping off hands. If I miss the call, they're coming in. You have to leave, right now, Grace."

"No."

"Grace, you're strong, and amazing, and I love you to death, but now I'm in charge again. I'm your father, and I say you're walking out that door right fucking now. Now go do it!"

She sits down on the couch and crosses her arms.

The clock is ticking. I have maybe two minutes. If I don't call them on time, they'll make entry. The noise in my head is killing me.

I lash out and grab her right arm, yanking her off the couch and throwing her over my shoulder like a sack of potatoes. I carry her to the door, with her kicking and punching me the whole way. I manage to get the door open, but then she lands a ball shot on me like I've never had before, and I go to my knees, dropping her half-in and half-out the door. She scrambles to get inside, but I grab a leg and yank her back her out onto the porch.

Suddenly realizing that this whole scene is within full range of the side-one sniper who is no doubt telling entry to move, I hazard a glance at the corner of the building to see if they're on their way yet. Grace takes advantage of this momentary inattention, and lands a devastating throat punch with bladed knuckles, leaving me choking and gasping for air. She leaps for the door, but somehow I get my fist closed around a handful of hair as she dives back inside, and drag her back toward me. I get a foot planted on her chest, then kick her down the stairs.

She tumbles down right into the point man of the oncoming entry team as he rounds the corner, almost knocking him over. The others run into him and get jammed up.

I'm easily within beanbag or Taser range, but I manage to get inside before anything happens. Tufts of Grace's hair swirl in my wake. As I slam the door, a flashbang detonates, driving me to the floor. I expect the team to burst inside, but Grace is fighting them as hard as she fought me. A taser pops and sizzles. Grace screams, and then the sounds of their struggle fade off into the distance. The only sound left in their wake is the earsplitting noise inside my head.

Somehow, she has managed to save me yet again.

I scramble to my feet and go for the gun in my waistband, wanting to get it done before I lose my nerve, but the gun is no longer there. I look up to find Mitch standing in the kitchen, pointing the silenced Sig directly at my face. He's also got the AR slung around his neck. He's holding the rifle's clip in his free hand, and is flicking the bullets into the trash can, which is about half-full. The empty clip goes in as well.

"Your gun fell out while you were fighting. I'm sorry to do you like this, Bad, but you seem pretty frazzled right now and I don't want to risk you taking me out with you. I don't know Grace very well, but I'm pretty sure she'll do the right thing and stick with our story. I know I will. She'll be pissed, but she'll get over it."

He pulls the magazine from the pistol and and empties it as well, then tosses the empty mag into the trash can.

"Here, man," he says, tossing me the now-empty weapons. "You can hold me hostage again now. Maybe they'll still change their minds. But I got to be straight with you. If you go for those bullets in the trash, I'm gonna be outta here." He then walks into the living room and sits down.

I don't even know what to do any more. The only important thing is Grace is gone now.

The phone rings. At first I ignore it, but it persists. Fucking Beth. With a sigh, I pick it up and slide the button.

"Jesus, DJ, you just beat up your own kid! What the fuck was that?"

"What do you want me to say? I'm sorry I fucked up your entry?"

"You definitely did that. They got the go order when you were fighting. You kicked Grace right into the arms of the point man in the stick. He was holding an unpinned flashbang, and she she knocked it right out of his hands. He'll take some shit over that."

"I hope you guys have a good laugh over it. Goodbye, Beth. I... I love you."

"No, I won't let you make a tearful goodbye scene, DJ! Don't—"

I disconnect the call and toss the phone on the couch. With a supreme effort, I get up and go into the kitchen. "Go ahead and take off, Mitch. I hope you do what you said. Thanks for being cool."

"I got your back, brother. I'll see you on the other side." With that, he gets up and walks out, leaving the door wide open.

I fish a .40 caliber round out of the trash and load the pistol. As I put it in my mouth, I turn to look out the door, knowing that the side-one sniper has me in his sights. I hope they're still under a shot of opportunity. That would make things easy. The phone is ringing, but I don't answer it. The barrel tastes smoky and dirty.

The sniper shot never comes. In that brief moment before I pull the trigger, Darth Vader's voice comes booming through the house.

"DJ! The DA relented! They're agreeing to the deal. Don't do it, DJ! Pick up the phone!"

I freeze. My head is ringing, or maybe it's just the phone. I don't know, and I don't care. I'm standing here like an idiot, holding a gun in my mouth, facing a sniper who has orders to kill me, and neither one of us is doing the job. How fucking bizarre is that?

"The DA has relented, DJ! Pick up the phone," yells Darth Vader's amplified voice.

The noise in my head almost drowns out his words. Slowly, I lower the pistol and answer the phone. I can't even bring myself to say hello.

"The deal is on, DJ! They've relented. You won! They changed their minds, and agreed to all three conditions."

"I don't believe you," I whisper.

""Believe it, DJ. They've agreed to everything. No death penalty, Snake River, and blanket immunity for Grace. Blanket immunity! You got it DJ, you got it all."

"I want in writing."

"They're preparing the document now."

"How do I know it's any good? How do I know they won't go back on it?"

"The DA told me that in light of your record, they'll honor it. They're not taking the Benton County deputy's killing into consideration because you've already been convicted of that. As for the rest of it, they're considering *who* you killed in prison—the man who molested you. Plus the fact that you didn't harm Mitch, just the men who went after your daughter. But the biggest thing is the correctional officer whose life you saved back in the state pen. You almost gave your life to save a prison guard's life, and they haven't forgotten that. The DA says that's what made the difference. There won't be any going back on this deal, DJ. You're getting what you asked for. Grace won't even be investigated. You hear that? They're closing the file on her. She'll be free to visit you at Snake River whenever she wants."

I close my eyes, and the noise in my head finally begins to abate.

Chapter 22

I am dissociated from myself. As if from the outside, I watch myself put the phone down and walk to the door. It's no different from the last time I gave myself up to SERT.

So much had happened since then. I lost Grace, and then I found her. Then I lost her again, and during that time, she suffered things no human being should ever have to suffer. But she's a third-generation Appleby outlaw, and her relatives taught her well. Working together, we all managed to make things right. Together, we defeated the bad guys, and meted out justice. Street justice. Relative justice.

The cost has been high. Uncle Phil is dead. Grace has been broken and violated. But, she will heal. Doing what she did to those who harmed her has gone a long way toward recovering her mental health, although I fear what we've turned her into. I hope she can recover from that, too.

I'm going back to prison, but that's where I deserve to be. At least I'm going back where I was, where I can actually do some good.

It is my hope that Grace will eventually find peace, and learn to get past the terrible things she's had to see and do. I am comforted by the knowledge that Uncle Phil and I prepared her mentally to survive the coming hell. Knowing that I helped her is my saving grace.

Saving Grace. That's actually a good name for her. She saved me from a life alone, without purpose, just by being there with me when I needed her. Saving Grace is also what I've been doing since she was a little girl; saving her from a mother who never cared for her, and then from a mundane life spent uselessly doing nothing. It's what Uncle Phil and I were doing when we trained her up in our ways. We were teaching her how to save herself. In effect, saving her.

That's what the whole bloody affair was all about. Saving Grace.

I come back to myself as I step outside the door. The arrest team is arrayed in front of me. The red dot from the sniper's scope briefly crosses my field of vision as it wavers around under my nose.

"Get on the ground, DJ!" shouts the hands-on guy. I don't recognize him in his SERT getup, but I decide not to follow his commands. I know what he's going to do in response, and I look forward to it. I deserve to get knocked down. I deserve a hell of a lot more than that.

"I said get on the fucking ground, DJ. I'm not going to tell you again."

I close my eyes and interlock my fingers on the back of my head. A moment later, I am shot in the solar plexus with a 12-gauge beanbag round. I go down gasping, the air driven from my lungs, and then two big guys pin me to the ground with their knees while others roughly handcuff me. The pain feels good. I am yanked to my feet and taken to the back of the Bearcat. Roughly, they throw me inside.

The entry team swarms into the clubhouse. It's a relatively small structure and doesn't take long to clear. A smaller team of three clears our truck. In a moment, they start drifting out the door, shedding gear and gathering in small clusters to talk. The clinking of equipment being shed and weapons being cleared brings back fond memories. One guy laughs at something. For them, it is over. For me, it's just beginning.

I'm given a copy of the district attorney's agreement. It is quite satisfactory. It gives Grace blanket immunity from prosecution, which is the only really important part. It also guarantees I will be given a life sentence without the possibility of parole in exchange for my continued cooperation, and ensures that I am to be incarcerated in protective custody in the Intensive Management Unit at Snake River for the duration of my sentence. A codicil from the Department of Corrections confirms this. It's where I belong. I was the top of the food chain there, and now I'm going home.

I do everything they ask me to do. I decline a lawyer, answer all their questions, and give them a full statement. I'm brutally honest and truthful about everything. They already know Grace was in Canada with me. We're on video in the motel lobby, and probably a dozen other places. It doesn't matter, the agreement covers her, no matter what. The only lie I tell is about who neutered Ratt and Durst. I just don't want them thinking Grace is capable of something like that. *I* don't like thinking Grace is capable of something like that.

I am not surprised when they tell me that Durst was DOA at the hospital. The only surprising thing is that they made the agreement knowing that.

I feel bad for poor Mitch. He wanted to help me so much. I really like the guy. I hope they don't violate his parole for being at the clubhouse, or for lying. I make a mental note to look him up when I get settled in Snake River.

The detective who is interrogating me was a colleague of mine back in the day. When we're finished, I ask him to to pass along a message to Mitch for me. He's to tell him, verbatim, "I got nothing but respect for you, man."

To Beth, our negotiating score now is now a tie. I won round one, she won round two, and round three is a draw. I score it differently. Two to one in her favor. After all, I'm going to county jail tonight to open my ass for inspection, while she goes home to get drunk on hers. But whatever the score is, it's final. There will be no further negotiations between us. I told them to tell her whenever she thinks about it, just look who's in prison and who's not.

When they ask me about the money, I tell them the truth. I know there will be a fight over it, and I don't want it to end up in the general coffers of the city of Portland. It's family money. Now, it's Grace's money.

Much later, we discover that Uncle Phil left a thoroughly detailed paper trail of how it all came to be. He also left a will, leaving everything to me, and for a couple hundred dollars, I have papers drawn up to legally transfer it all to Grace. She has his house to live in and enough money to give her a very good start in life.

Eventually, the questioning ends, and I am taken to Multnomah County Jail, where I am held until my hearing. When I am finally arraigned on a host of new charges, I plead guilty to every one of them. The honorable Suzanne Payne is the sentencing judge. She is a strong advocate of capital punishment, and is clearly not happy with the deal I've engineered. As if to illustrate her opposition, she stares me hard in the eye and says, "Mr. Appleby, I am cooperating with the district attorney and the other parties to this agreement only out of my deep respect for them, but I do not like doing so. I think you should be put to death for your crimes. However, in accordance with the pre-sentencing agreement,

I now sentence you to three life sentences without the possibility of parole."

"Thank you, Your Honor," I say.

Wanting to further drive home her displeasure at not being able to stick the needle in my arm herself, she leans over the bench and proclaims with all possible gravity, "To be served consecutively."

Unable to resist, I say, "All due respect, Your Honor, but I'm only planning to serve the first." This elicits muted laughter among the standing room-only crowd. I'm told it was picked up by the TV cameras and played on the evening news. Sometimes, it's the small things.

I'm then driven six hours back to Snake River, where I resume my former place as shot-caller among the sex offenders, child molesters, and other prison vermin. Top dog on the Island of Misfit Toys.

Every day, I walk past the cell in which I killed Douglas McNab, and it feels like the world is once again spinning on an even keel.

Epilogue

February, 2020

Just like the last time, I run a nice, tight ship here in IMU. Once again, the COs love having me as the boss. Most know me from my last stint. I make their job easy. Here, I'm still known as Bad, which, I guess, is even more appropriate now than before.

My reputation has preceded me. I'm looked upon as a bit of a rock star and a legend here. Cons still ask me for my autograph, which, I'm told, sell well on the outside.

Several months after I arrived, I got a message from a CO at the Oregon State Pen, a guy named Porter who's life I once saved. He wanted me to know that William James McHenry, aka Ratt, aka Mouse was found dead in his cell at lights-out on Halloween. He'd developed gynecomastia, a condition in which he'd grown breasts as a result of the hormonal imbalance he suffered after Grace's shot destroyed his testicles. The remains of his penis had to be surgically removed and a urinary stint put in place, giving him a decidedly female appearance when naked.

Ratt had been prostituting himself for cigarettes and commissary. Most of his clients wanted to feel his crotch and fondle his tits while buggering him. Many cons simply took what they wanted from him without his permission, but I'm told he didn't care. He never lacked for cigarettes. For trick-or-treat, he twisted a sheet around his neck, secured it to the top bunk, then did a backflip and went as a corpse.

Grace is the only one who comes to visit me. It took her a long time, but she finally forgave me for throwing her out of the EK clubhouse, and we now enjoy the same kind of relationship we had when we were on the lam. She, too, seems to have retired from the outlaw life. Both the Multnomah County District Attorney's Office and the United States

Attorney's Office have kept their promise of blanket immunity. Nobody ever investigated her for anything, and nobody ever will.

I've been hoping Beth Quinlan would come by, but so far, she hasn't. If the tables were turned, I'd go visit her. It hurts a little that she doesn't come around.

Yesterday, I got a visit from an author; one I've actually read. He writes true crime with a focus on bad cops. I was fascinated by a book he wrote about a San Diego PD officer who was a serial rapist during his off-duty hours. He's published several other books in that same genre, and now he wants to do one about me. He says he already has a publisher and a very lucrative deal lined up.

He guarantees me the option to co-write it, and offers to give me final approval over the manuscript before publication. I can even write the forward and give the book its title. For this, he will pay me fifty percent of the profits. It didn't take long to decide to do it. The proceeds will go directly to the title character.

I'm going to call it Saving Grace.

The End

About the Author

Barry W. Ozeroff was a police officer for 28 years. During his career, Barry was a patrol officer, SWAT sniper, hostage negotiator, and traffic motorcycle officer. He is the recipient of numerous awards, including the Oregon Peace Officer's Lifesaving Award, and the Gresham Police Department Medal of Valor. He currently works as the Lead Court Security Officer at the United States Court of Appeals for the 9th Circuit in Portland, OR.

Barry is the author of *Sniper Shot* (2005), *Return Fire* (2012), *The Dying of Mortimer Post* (2010), and *Bad Apple* (2017). *Bad Apple II: Relative Justice*, is the second of the *Bad Apple* series, featuring cop-turned-con DJ "Bad" Appleby. Look for the third in the series, *Bad Apple III: Judicial Notice*, coming soon from iBooks.

Please feel free to sign in and leave a review at
https://www.amazon.com/review/create-review/?channel=glance-detail&asin=B071F42C59&ie=UTF8&

For sales, editorial information, subsidiary rights information
or a catalog, please write or phone or e-mail
iBooks
Manhanset House
Shelter Island Hts., New York 11965-0342, US
Tel: 212-427-7139
www.ibooksinc.com
bricktower@aol.com
www.IngramContent.com

For sales in the UK and Europe please contact our distributor,
Gazelle Book Services
White Cross Mills
Lancaster, LA1 4XS, UK
Tel: (01524) 68765 Fax: (01524) 63232
email: jacky@gazellebooks.co.uk

Milton Keynes UK
Ingram Content Group UK Ltd.
UKHW020714090624
443590UK00012BB/115/J